Bea Paige

Symphony

FINDING THEIR MUSE

CONTENTS

Symphony

Finding Their Muse – book four

#1 Steps https://books2read.com/Steps
#2 Strokes https://books2read.com/Strokes
#3 Strings https://books2read.com/StringsFTM
#4 Symphony https://books2read.com/FTM4
#5 Finding Their Muse boxset https://
books2read.com/FTMBoxset

The Brothers Freed Series (contemporary romance / reverse harem)
#1 Avalanche of Desire https://
books2read.com/AvalancheOfDesire
#2 Storm of Seduction https://books2read.com/StormSeduction
#3 Dawn of Love https://books2read.com/DawnOfLove
#4 Brothers Freed Boxset https://
books2read.com/BrothersFreed

Contemporary Standalones
RH Fairy tale retelling
Cabin of Axes https://books2read.com/CabinOfAxes
Age gap romance
Beyond the Horizon https://books2read.com/Beyond-the-horizon

The Sisters of Hex series (paranormal romance / reverse harem)

Sisters of Hex: Accacia
#1 Accacia's Curse https://books2read.com/AccaciasCurse
#2 Accacia's Blood https://books2read.com/AccaciasBlood
#3 Accacia's Bite https://books2read.com/AccaciasBite
#4 Accacia's Trilogy https://books2read.com/AccaciasTrilogy
Sisters of Hex: Fern

#1 Fern's Decision https://books2read.com/FernsDecision
#2 Fern's Wings https://books2read.com/FernsWings
#3 Fern's Flight https://books2read.com/FernsFlight
#4 Fern's Trilogy https://books2read.com/FernsTrilogy

The Infernal Descent trilogy (co-written with Skye MacKinnon)
#1 Hell's Calling https://books2read.com/HellsCalling
#2 Hell's Weeping https://books2read.com/HellsWeeping
#3 Hell's Burning https://books2read.com/HellsBurning
#4 Infernal Descent boxset https://books2read.com/InfernalDescent

ABOUT BEA PAIGE

Bea Paige lives a very secretive life in London… she likes red wine and Haribo sweets (preferably together) and occasionally swings around poles when the mood takes her.

Bea loves to write about love and all the different facets of such a powerful emotion. When she's not writing about love and passion, you'll find her reading about it and ugly crying.

Bea is always writing, and new ideas seem to appear at the most unlikely time, like in the shower or on driving her car.

She has lots more books planned, so be sure to subscribe to her newsletter:

beapaige.co.uk/newsletter-sign-up

Facebook: https://www.facebook.com/BeaPaigeAuthor/
Instagram: https://www.instagram.com/beapaigeauthor/
Bookbub: https://www.bookbub.com/authors/bea-paige
Pinterest: https://www.pinterest.co.uk/beapaigeauthor/

This book is dedicated to my readers,

Thank you for falling in love with Rose and the men of Browlace Manor.
Thank you for believing in their story. Symphony is for you all.
Bea xx

PROLOGUE

EMMIE

In my hand I hold onto the letter I wrote to Erik some twenty-one years ago. Wrote but never posted. The paper is discoloured, the words faded. It's been ten years since I last read it and as I unfold it now, the paper barely holding together at the centre, the memory of the night I wrote it comes flooding back to me, filling my senses alongside the musty smell of old paper.

My hand trembles as I hold the letter delicately between my fingers and thumb, my eyes tearing up at the apology scrawled across its surface and the secrets kept hidden under lock and key for all this time. Within the envelope sits a faded photograph and another document that holds secrets hidden away for years. Secrets I've selfishly held onto.

My eyes glance over my words. I'd been so young and foolish back then. A whimsical girl who had been full of hormones, lust and naivety. If I could go back in time and shake myself I would. My actions that summer destroyed two people I cared about, and like ripples on a pond, my decision to listen to a twisted, embittered woman expanded and grew, still having an effect all these years later.

But with age comes clarity and if there's one thing I do understand, Ms Hadley is just as responsible for Layton's condition as Erik is. As *I* am. But more than that, she's responsible for her own son's ill health.

A glass cage…

I can't even begin to fathom how destroyed Erik must have felt to lock himself inside one. I don't know anything about the man he is now, or his experiences since that fateful night. I only remember the boy he once was… and my God, he was gifted, smart, funny, *loyal*. I'd hoped over the years that he'd grown into a man that could live up to the memories I treasured, but the truth of who he is came out alongside the lengths his mother had gone to keep him hers.

For the most part this might be an island of decent people, but it still comes with a small village mentality. Everyone talks, even the police officers it would seem. It has become apparent that Erik suffered over the years. He didn't walk into his future without a backward glance like I had thought. That night broke him just as much as it destroyed Layton, and all because of *her*; his wicked mother and, of course, me.

"*Love*, are you coming?" Tim calls from downstairs.

My heart squeezes in my chest at the thought that I could very well destroy our marriage with what I'm about to do. I never told Tim about Erik and Layton, or what happened during that long hot summer. Tim's my heart, my *own* love. He is who I adore above all else, but I have to make amends to the boy I'd betrayed and the man he almost killed. I can't sit back and stay silent anymore. Neither Erik nor I can change what happened, but he at least deserves to know the full truth, no matter the consequences to me.

"Coming, just grabbing a jacket," I lie, folding up the letter, returning it to the box and placing it back into my wardrobe.

Standing, I take a look at my reflection in the mirror; there's only the slightest whispers of the girl I once was in the colour of my hair and the shade of my eyes. Otherwise, she no longer exists. Her easy smile long since hidden beneath years of regret and guilt.

"You should've posted the letter," I whisper to my reflection, to the ghost of the girl staring back at me.

"*Love*, we're going to be late!" Tim reminds me, his deep voice sending a familiar warmth flooding beneath my skin.

Drawing in a deep breath, I straighten my spine and slide a stray strand of hair behind my ear. If only I'd been brave enough to send Erik the letter. Better still, if only I'd been brave enough to say no to Ms Hadley in the first place, then perhaps none of this would've happened. But I was a child who had secrets of her own. Secrets Ms Hadley had used against me. Secrets that had the power to destroy, that *still* do.

Standing here now, about to go out for our anniversary dinner, I know what I must do. I have to make things right because that woman cannot be allowed back into Erik's life to cause more pain, more damage, and there's a chance that might happen if I don't do something. She has the assistance of Viktor Sachov and I know the power he has. He got Erik out of a prison sentence after all, and together he and Ms Hadley blackmailed me into silence.

Tim appears at the door to our bedroom, an exasperated

look on his face but with a hint of a smile that he reserves only for me.

"You couldn't look more beautiful," he says, misunderstanding the look I'm giving myself in the mirror. He takes a step towards me and grabs my hand as I let out a shaky breath. "Are you still thinking about that awful woman?"

"No," I lie, following him out of our bedroom, down the stairs and out into the cold night air.

"You need to let it go. You might have told..." he screws his face up trying to remember her name.

"Rose," I say.

"Yes, that's it, Rose. You might have told her how to find Ms Hadley, but you can't hold yourself responsible for what happened there. No one could've predicted what that old witch would do."

"She's in hospital right now, Tim. Ms Hadley *shot* her..."

Tim stops abruptly and turns to face me. "No. Stop that. You had nothing to do with that. Nothing at all. You weren't to know Rose lied about who she was. They all lied, telling us she was a relative of Ms Hadley's. I don't know what the hell is going on between them all, but this is *not* your fault. Do you hear me?! This mess isn't yours, so don't you dare take it on, Love."

He wraps his arm around my shoulders and pulls me into his side, pressing a kiss against my forehead. I allow myself a moment to melt into his warmth. He's my rock, the man I love with every single part of me, but he's wrong. It is my fault. The actions of a stupid girl have helped lead to this point.

"This is so messed up," I respond heavily.

Like Tim, the majority of the islanders have been shocked by Ms Hadley's actions, but not me. I've been a victim to her wickedness. I *know* what she's capable of. I've known all along, and in a few weeks when Tim goes away to start a new build on the mainland, I'll be leaving for Cornwall and taking that letter with me, because this time I won't let Ms Hadley destroy Erik's chance at a happy future. He deserves the truth. They all do.

And I'm going to be the one to give it to them.

CHAPTER 1

ROSE

You're going to get through this...
I've been saying that same phrase to myself every day since I was shot and that's what I remind myself as I'm wheeled into the operating theatre room for the second time in as many weeks. Machines bleep, the harsh light of the theatre is bright and blinding. I turn my head away, looking to the side at the anesthesiologist who smiles at me as dark spots dance in front of my eyes.

"Back so soon? We're going to start thinking that you enjoy being operated on," she winks.

"Didn't they tell you? I have a fetish for needles," I quip back, trying to lighten the dark mood I've been in these past couple of days since Ivan and Erik left for Browlace. Returning home wasn't easy for either of them, but it was a necessity. At least Anton remains.

"How are you doing?" she asks, checking her equipment.

Scared shitless, that's how I'm doing.

"Oh, you know, just peachy," I respond, then wince at the sarcasm. It's not her fault I got shot and have a dodgy knee. She laughs, shaking her head as my surgeon pats my arm, drawing my attention away from her.

"Afternoon, Rose. Are you ready to get this knee fixed up?" he asks, raising his bushy grey eyebrows. Beneath them, his brown eyes are sharp with intelligence and as warm as coffee on a winter morning. Dr Smithton was a good choice. Following my operation to fix my shoulder, Ivan and I discussed the options available, and he'd promised me that Dr Smithton was the best orthopaedic surgeon in the business. He came with an endless list of recommendations, but it was his manner that sold me; kind and to the point. He'd promised me that once I was over the operation and weeks of recovery, my titanium knee would give me a new lease of life. Dr Smithton has even suggested that if I got my rheumatoid arthritis under control, I could take up ballet again. Not professionally of course, but as a hobby. That promise alone, and the fact that Ivan had made me a special promise of his own, had me sold. The thought of dancing with Ivan is something that I hold onto, even though I'm terrified this could all go wrong, and I'll end up in a wheelchair permanently.

So here I am. Terrified. Hopeful. Feeling sick with worry.

"It's the best artificial joint money can buy, and without blowing my own trumpet, I'm the best in the business, so things are looking up, Rose..."

I laugh at his confidence and his arrogance. Normally that combination would piss me off, but in this situation, it's comforting.

"Thank goodness," I say honestly, wincing as I shift on the gurney.

"Shoulder still hurts?" he asks.

"Yep, but I'm getting there."

"Well, rest assured we'll make sure you're taken care of after this is op is over. Are you ready to proceed, Rose?" He flashes me another genuine warm smile.

I dread to think how much this operation has cost Ivan but both he insisted that I get the best possible care that money can buy. I'm still recovering from the gunshot injury and the resulting operation to fix my damaged shoulder. It still bloody hurts and I still have flashbacks of Ms Hadley holding the gun and taking aim, but right now I need to concentrate on getting through this ordeal. Flinching at the memory, I push aside the anger that still boils inside and give Dr Smithton an honest answer.

"I'm ready, but that doesn't make me any less terrified. The last time I was operated on it was a necessity. I'm not fond of hospitals, frankly, or needles…" my false laughter trails off as Dr Smithton regards me.

"You need a new knee, Rose. This operation is a necessity and whilst it might put you in a wheelchair for a few weeks, you'll be in one permanently if you don't go through with this."

I sigh heavily. "I know you're right," I respond. My previous career as a ballet dancer combined with my medical condition have worked against me, leaving me practically crippled at thirty. That and the fact Ms Hadley tried to kill me a few weeks back meant that my condition has flared up with the stress. Everywhere fucking hurts; I feel like shit. That feeling goes way deeper than my obvious injuries, but right at this moment no one but me is aware of that fact. There's no point in telling them all how much pain I'm really in. They'd make me wait and I'm done waiting to feel better.

Besides, I *need* this operation. I have three men counting on me. One of whom is waiting in my private room for me to return whilst the other two have returned to Cornwall.

I smile, remembering how Anton had pressed his lips against mine not more than ten minutes ago, his tongue sweeping into my mouth possessively. He stayed behind to keep me company whilst Ivan and Erik flew home to Browlace, an unfortunate necessity after Erik had a minor relapse at the hotel they've been staying at whilst I've been at the hospital.

My heart aches for Erik. He's come so far, but he still has a long way to go. I so want him to get better. We *all* want to undo the damage done by his past, by Ms Hadley. Going back to Browlace was the right decision, no matter how hollow I feel from their absence. Besides, it won't be long until I'll see them again. Dr Smithton has promised I'll be able to return to Browlace just as soon as he thinks I'm fit enough to travel in Ivan's private jet.

"Mr Sachov and Mr Hadley are putting in place the best possible care for you back home. Once I'm certain you're fit enough to travel, we can get you back to a more familiar environment to recover from your operations," Dr Smithton says, confirming his promise from a few days before.

"I miss them…" I mumble, the words releasing from my lips before I can stop them. A couple of months ago I would never have acknowledged those feelings, let alone voice them, but things have changed. *I've* changed. I'm still getting used to this new me; the one who doesn't run from her feelings, doesn't push them away.

"I understand," he responds.

Ivan and Erik left two days ago. Even with Erik's episode at the hotel, I don't think either would have gone had it not been for the phone call from Ivan's lawyer giving him news about Ms Hadley's case. Whatever discussion they'd had sealed the deal, and Ivan and Erik returned home. Up until that point, they'd purposely kept any news about her arrest and upcoming court case from me, trying to protect me whilst I get through these operations. Whilst I appreciate their thoughtfulness, I want to know what's happening with Ms Hadley. I need to know she's going to be locked away for good for what she tried to do to me, to *us*.

That fucking bitch.

Rage spikes in my blood, and for a moment I forget I'm in the hospital about to have an operation. Sensing my change in mood, Dr Smithton squeezes my arm.

"They're good men. They care about you," he responds, and even though he doesn't say anything to the contrary I know he has his own personal thoughts about our assumed relationship. The fact is, right now, even I'm not sure how to label *us*. There's been no time to discuss what we are, if we're anything at all frankly.

It's complicated, that much I *do* know.

"Fix me, Doc," I say, meeting his gaze with a wobbly smile.

If I'm completely honest with myself, I'm not in the least bit ready to face the next eight to twelve weeks of recovery. Knowing I'm going to have to rely on Ivan, Anton and Erik to care for me has plagued my thoughts and fuelled my insecurities. Feeling weak and vulnerable isn't an easy pill for me to swallow. I've looked after myself, protected my heart for so long that feeling beholden to others is difficult, to say the least. Even now, even after everything that happened in that glass cage with Erik, I still struggle. But this time, I'm not running. This time, I intend to see this through. Whatever we are together, I want to explore it.

Yet, despite everything that's happened, I still worry that once we get back to Cornwall and the harsh reality of day to day life, their promises to look after me will be replaced with annoyance and disappointment. I should have more faith in them, in *us* and our budding relationship, but Ms Hadley's attempt at taking my life has shocked us all to the core and rocked the foundations of our relationship. The bullet might have ripped through skin and muscle almost destroying my ability to lift my arm ever again, but it has done something far worse than just injuring me, it's somehow managed to upset the delicate equilibrium between us all. I sense it.

Ivan is preoccupied with thoughts that he's unable or unwilling to share right now. Erik is reeling from the betrayal and Anton hasn't picked up his sketch pad and pencil in days.

It's no surprise then that I whilst I'm fucking terrified, I want to get this over and done with. I want to get fixed and I want to heal, because they need me, and I need them. It's as simple as that.

"Just doing some last minute checks. Okay, Rose?" Dr Smithton says.

"Sure," I mumble distractedly, my thoughts returning to Erik and that damn prison.

When I'd walked out of that glass cage with Erik and those new scary emotions that I hadn't felt for a very, very long time, I'd been filled with hope for a future with these men. I'd believed that perhaps, finally, I could heal. I could live the life I've always wanted but had never thought I'd deserved. Then Ms Hadley had fired the gun...

Pressing my fingers against my eyelids, I try and regain control of my fear.

The sound of the gunshot still haunts me now. I can hear it in every door that slams shut, in the crash of a dropped tray, the sound of a car backfiring far below on the street, any loud noise really. I'm living with the constant reminder of that split second decision, and what could've happened if her aim had been any better. I'm pretty sure it's the same for my men… *my men.*

Yes, they are. They're *mine*, and I am theirs. A flood of warmth fills my chest, surprising me in the moment.

"Rose, are you okay?" the anaesthetist asks me.

"I will be soon," I answer, opening my eyes and drawing in a deep shuddering breath. I remind myself of what I'm made of as I push away all thoughts of Ms Hadley. Her time will come, but not now.

"You can do this," she reassures me.

"I can."

I always knew I was strong, but until those few days in that glass cage with Erik, I hadn't known quite how much. He'd pulled me apart, then put me back together again all whilst Ivan and Anton had watched, supporting us both as we unravelled. I'm still raw, still reeling. But I'm not destroyed by the experience. In fact, I'm so much stronger for it.

I'm Ivan's Domina.

I'm Anton's muse.

I'm Erik's saviour.

I'm the one.

And I won't let that bitch destroy the healing that's started to take place for all of us.

"You ready?" Dr Smithton asks me.

"I'm ready," I respond, drawing on the strength I need to get through this operation and the unwritten future on the other side of the darkness. It's murky, unclear, but there are shards of light penetrating the inky blackness. I concentrate on the possibilities of a happier future and nothing else, as Dr Smithton motions for the anaesthetist to start.

"Like before, you'll get a warm feeling in the back of your

throat. Count back from ten for me, Rose," the anaesthetist says, her fingers running gently over the skin on my hand.

I nod, ignoring the scratch of the needle and the almost immediate sensation of warmth in the back of my throat.

"Ten... nine... eight... sev..." my voice trails off as darkness swallows me for the second time in a few short weeks.

CHAPTER 2

ROSE – TWO WEEKS LATER

It's been almost a month since Ms Hadley shot me. For three weeks I was confined to a room in a small private hospital in Edinburgh, mainland Scotland. Now, back at Browlace, I look out of the window of y newly appointed bedroom and watch as Ivan greets my knee surgeon, Dr Smithton. He's here to give me one last once-over before he returns home to his family in London.

Despite lots of rest and physio, I'm still crippled by my injury. If Ms Hadley's aim had been any better, I would most definitely be six feet under. That coupled with the fact that I'm slowly recovering from knee replacement surgery, has made healing a long and drawn out process. On a more positive note, I've found out that there's nothing quite like a near death experience to put everything into perspective. Life is too damn short to do anything other than live. Erik has showed me that, and I'm going to start properly living just as soon as I'm fully healed from my injuries and out of this damn wheelchair.

Today, hopefully, is the beginning of a new start for us all.

Dr Smithton gives Ivan, and now Anton- who has joined them both- his signature warm smile before following them inside. I'm not surprised he's so happy given the amount of money Ivan must have paid him to take care of me. I dread to think how much in total he spent getting me fixed up and back to Browlace. As soon as I'd been given the go ahead to fly, Ivan had chartered a private flight back from Edinburgh to Newquay Airport, complete with two nurses and Dr Smithton as company. The nurses left yesterday, and Dr Smithton will get to return home to his family this afternoon, several hundred thousand pounds better off no doubt.

A light knock at the door draws my attention back inside the room. My pulse suddenly thumps in my neck at the thought that it might be Erik, but instead Fran enters holding a tray with a steaming mug of Earl Gray and a plate filled with toast and scrambled egg. I quickly hide my disappointment with a smile. It's not her fault she isn't the person I want to see. It's been almost three days since Erik and I have talked and even then, it was brief, our conversation stifled. He's hurting and being here confined to this damn wheelchair and this room is preventing me from helping him heal. Ivan and Anton have been a little absent too, only staying for a few minutes at a time causing my insecurities to sky rocket.

This new me, the one who allows herself to feel is refreshing on the one hand, but a nightmare on the other. I'm not used to juggling all these damn emotions.

I grit my teeth in frustration. The second Dr Smithton leaves I'm calling a meeting. I need to know what's going on in Erik's head, in all their heads, because I'm more than certain this withdrawal has everything to do with Ms Hadley's court hearing.

"Morning, Rose. How are you feeling today?" she asks me, a kind smile lifting her lips and showing off a dazzling set of white teeth. I'm pretty sure they're false, given the occasional movement when she talks.

I turn the wheelchair so that I don't have to twist my head awkwardly. It still hurts to use my arm, but every day I feel the strength returning, that in itself should give me something to smile about this morning. Not to mention the fact that Dr Smithton will hopefully sign me over to the team of physios and the local consultant from today onwards, but more importantly that I might be able to get my life back just a little.

"Better, actually. The swelling on my knee is finally beginning to subside, and I'm not so stiff today, thank God. Although the bruising is pretty horrific. Still, hopefully soon I'll be able to put more weight on this leg for longer periods."

"Well that is good news, Rose. I'm pleased, and I know the boys will be happy to hear the same," she responds, placing the tray on the foldaway table before bringing both over and placing them within reach. It's sweet that she calls them boys, because they are so very far from being boys. They're men; complicated, troubled, deep, and very much mine. At least I hope so.

"I feel like a burden," I mutter, not meaning to say that out loud. It isn't like me to show vulnerability, but ever since my time in Erik's glass cage, that vulnerability is just below the surface. One slight scratch and it bleeds through the cracks for everyone to see.

Fran rests a hand on my arm. "You are no more a burden than I am, Rose. Those boys think the world of you. We all do.

Concentrate on getting better, everything else can wait," she says knowingly.

I give her a half-hearted smile. "Then why are they avoiding me? I've been back almost a week and I've barely seen them bar a few minutes here and there between the nurses, Dr Smithton and the physio's visits. If they wanted to spend time with me, they would've made it happen."

An ugly feeling of self-doubt creeps into my head at the thought that, just like my mother, they don't want me. The sensible part of me knows that isn't true. We've been through too much together for them to abandon me now but when Erik carved open my heart and drew out all the emotion I'd kept locked away, it unleashed all my insecurities too. I'm still trying to manage them now. When you begin to care for people, there's so much more to lose when they turn their back on you. I know that from experience, and I'm hoping that Ivan, Anton and Erik understand that too, because their absence hurts.

She sighs, perching her bottom on the window ledge, worry creasing her eyes. "You know as much as I do, that not one of those boys wishes for you to feel this way. Seeing you like this, believing that somehow, they're responsible. It's hard on them, Rose."

"But they aren't responsible, Fran. *She* aimed the gun. *She* pulled the trigger. *She* tried to kill me. None of this is their fault."

I can't even bring myself to say her name out loud. It's as though, that just by uttering it I will somehow conjure her up like some wicked witch in a fairy tale. She's the old hag with the poisoned apple, and we've all taken a bite. I know why she wanted me dead. She hates me, that much is abundantly clear. I've spent hours mulling over what happened, trying to figure out why she would choose to hurt her son that way. Why she would try to take away Erik's chance at happiness… that is what I can't, won't *ever*, understand.

"No, you're right, it isn't their fault. But that doesn't stop them from feeling guilty, feeling responsible for her actions. That woman," she spits, as angry as I am in the moment, "was their mother figure. Ivan brought her into his home because he trusted her. Erik loved her like only a son would, and Anton, though the wariest, still cared for her. She's been in their lives for a very long time. It's hard to know that you've been betrayed by someone you've put your trust in. I should know, I feel the same way."

"And yet, here you are telling me this instead of them. I thought they trusted me enough to tell me how they feel. I might be physically weakened, Fran, but I'm *not* weak. I can take it."

"They're just protecting you. I don't pretend to understand what this relationship is between you all, but I do know one thing; those boys would rather die than see you hurt again."

"Protecting me from what?"

"It isn't my place to say, Rose. Ms Hadley…" her voice trails off as she chews on her bottom lip.

My back goes ramrod straight, and my fingers tighten over the armrests. "Ms Hadley, *what?*" I snap. She flinches, and I feel guilty. She's been nothing but kind to me.

"I'm so sorry, Rose, for what she did to you, but…"

"But *what*, Fran? Please, I need to know. I have to know what's going on. I can't help them if I don't."

"What she did to Erik, it's beyond cruel…"

She stutters, unable to bring herself to say it.

I grab her hand pulling it into my lap, squeezing tightly. "Fran, please… I'm not beyond begging. I'd walk through fire to help save these men." That truth spurs me on, filling me with determination. I will not let Ms Hadley destroy us. I refuse. "I need to know," I insist.

Silence spreads out between us whilst Fran decides whether she should open up or keep quiet.

"Please," I beg.

"They think she killed his mother," she says in one long, stuttering breath.

What?!

For a fraction of a second all I hear is a weird kind of whirring in my ears as Fran's revelation carves a deep gash in my heart, ripping the tender organ open. My fingers uncurl from her hand and I cover my mouth.

"*No...*" I manage to utter, looking at Fran with wide eyes.

She speaks rapidly now, but I don't hear any of it... I can't hear a damn thing but the terrible sound of my own rage beating inside my skull in time with my bleeding heart.

She killed his mother...?

Fran stands suddenly, that action forcing me back to the present. Her hand lifts to her chest as her gaze rises to a point behind me. I shift in my seat, ignoring the pain in my knee and shoulder to see what's surprised her. Standing in the open doorway is Erik, his face as white as Fran's is now.

"Please leave, Fran," he whispers, a quiet kind of pain filtering into his words.

"I'm sorry, Erik," she mutters, resting her hand on my shoulder and squeezing gently. "Rose has a right to know what's happening. She cares about you."

"I know," he mutters, clenching his jaw. He flicks his gaze at Fran as sadness leaks into his amber orbs, before returning his gaze to me. "Please, could you give us a moment?" he says to her.

"Of course."

He sidesteps out of the way as she passes him, not for one second taking his eyes off me. The moment she's out of the door, he closes it, the tenseness in his shoulders evaporating even though he still holds it in the tightness of his jaw.

"Erik…" my words fail me in the moment as the realisation of Ms Hadley's evil spreads between us. Even when she's not here, she still has the power to hurt us.

"Rose…" he responds, my name a broken note on his lips.

I hold out my arms, wanting nothing more than to feel him within them. In ten strides he's on his knees before me, his arms circling my waist, his head pressed against my lap. In the moment, there's nothing I can say to make him feel better. All I can do is hold him and hope it's enough.

CHAPTER 3

ERIK

Rose's fingers slide through my hair as I press my cheek against her thigh. There are so many things I need to tell her, need to say, but the words are caught in my throat. It's all I can do to breathe, let alone voice them. But like always, Rose just waits for me to gather myself. She gives me the time to reel my thoughts into something coherent, and school my anxiety into something more manageable.

I've begun to rely on her, a lot. That both comforts and scares the shit out of me, because caring for someone this much comes with huge responsibilities.

"Fuck," I murmur, angry at myself for not being there for Rose when she's the one who's needed me. "I wanted to come back sooner…"

"Shh, it's okay," she soothes.

"No, it really isn't."

For the past three days I've been oscillating between blind fury and suffocating sadness. Too many emotions for my already rattled brain to deal with. The flashbacks have returned and with it my need to return to the glass cage in my room. It's taken everything I have not to walk into it and lock the door. The sooner I get that damn thing removed the better, because I refuse to return to that prison when the one person who holds the key to our healing is sitting in a wheelchair needing *my* support, *my* care, *my* attention.

"I missed you. I've missed all of you," she murmurs, and I flinch at the undeniable anguish I hear in her voice.

Pulling back, I squat on my haunches and drink in her face. Even like this, confined to a wheelchair, she exudes strength despite the vulnerability she's now able to express. My fingers curl into her thigh as I hold onto her, anchoring myself in the moment.

"Ivan, Anton?"

She heaves out a sigh. "They've visited a handful of times, but they've both been distracted…"

Fuck.

"I'm sorry, Rose. We've been arseholes. None of us really know what the fuck to do with ourselves… We're just trying to process."

"I'm here. I *can* help."

"We know…"

"Do you, *really*?"

I shake my head, trying to find the words to explain. Guilt lacerates my chest, breaking me apart. I feel guilty about what Ms Hadley did, guilty that I didn't see it coming, guilty that I've left Rose to her own thoughts after everything she's done for me, for us. Breathing slowly out through my mouth, I slide my hands up Rose's thighs and grasp her hips, holding on for dear life.

"We're all trying to figure out what went wrong. We're grown men, *smart* men, and yet none of us saw this coming. Trust isn't given lightly by any of us, but we trusted her.

Ivan and Anton both watched over her when we were together, and whilst they felt her anger, neither suspected she'd go so far. That's fucking hard to let go. They feel culpable and I feel responsible."

"It wasn't their fault. But barely saying more than a few words to me over the past few days, that is."

"I'm so sorry, Rose. I couldn't come, not when I was so…"

"What, Erik?" she questions me, her fingers gliding over my shoulders, easing out the tension. Her need to touch me, to make a connection despite her frustration, sends a spike of happiness to my heart. This woman… *Only* this woman can touch me like this and not draw out the violence that still lurks within me. It might have lessened, but it's still there. The monster within only ever a moment of madness away.

"You've had more episodes, haven't you?" she questions, her voice soft, a little hurt.

"Yes," I admit, clasping her hand and drawing her fingers to my lips. I whisper a kiss against her knuckles, and her cheeks flush a pale shade of pink. "I haven't lost consciousness the same way I have before. I don't black out and forget. That's a huge step forward, Rose."

A fucking giant leap, all because of this woman.

"And now *I* haven't been there for *you*," she says, echoing my own guilt.

We both want so much to heal the other completely, and yet, right now, we're both prevented from doing so. Rose, because she's weakened physically, and me because I'm too wrapped up with guilt and remorse because of what Ms Hadley did to her, triggering those fucking flashbacks.

"Being here in this house with us is enough," I lie. I need her touch to remind me that I can be the man I so desperately want to be.

"It isn't, and you know it," she scolds me gently, seeing through me.

I bite her knuckles hard, the urge to dominate, to distract her, suddenly rushing up my spine and overtaking the moment. God, I want to fuck her.

"Erik," she groans, not in the least bit disturbed by the act.

Running my tongue over the small indents on her skin, I remind us both of our unique connection. I know Rose will submit to both the pain and the pleasure, giving me what I need both physically *and* emotionally. Only a few weeks ago I tore open her chest and held her beating heart in my hand, and she let me. She fucking let me.

"When you're fixed, the things I'm going to do to you, Rose," I blurt out.

Her nostrils flare as she presses her thighs together at the rush of endorphins and the energy crackling between us. Always this energy, so overwhelming but utterly right. I wonder if it's the same with Anton and Ivan, then I remember how they are together and know without a doubt it is.

"The things I'll submit to..." she responds, before a dark cloud passes behind her eyes drawing her thoughts in another direction.

"Talk," I demand. "Don't hold it in, we're beyond that now."

"You do realise that you're being a hypocrite. Refusing to tell me what's going on. Two can play at that game, Erik."

"Rose," I warn.

She sighs heavily, but she doesn't withdraw from me. Instead, she squeezes my fingers tightly, then opens up. Giving me a gift with every word she utters; her vulnerability is like precious gems twinkling in the autumn sunlight. I want to gather them all and lock them away inside my own blackened heart.

"I feel as though I'm losing grasp of you all. I'm not good at sitting around and waiting for shit to fall apart. I'm in too deep, Erik. I need you all to anchor me. I've never needed anyone, not really. I could only rely on myself." She draws in a long shuddering breath before continuing. I sense what she isn't able to say, this is huge for Rose. Huge, and the three of us are fucking blowing it.

"Fran told me about Ms Hadley, about what you all think she did to your…"

Her words trail off as I stiffen.

"Say it," I demand.

"You think Ms Hadley killed your real mother, don't you?"

Despite the subject matter and the betrayal I feel at the hands of the woman I once called mother, I reward Rose for being open with me. She winces as I push between her parted legs, my side pressing against her sore knee. She doesn't ask me to move away, so I don't. Clasping her face in my hands I draw her face towards mine.

"Erik, don't try and distract me," she persists, even though I know she wants my kiss just as much as the answer to her question. Conflict brews beneath her pretty meadow-green eyes.

"Right now, it's just supposition. We don't know anything for certain." I grit my jaw, a restless energy snaking around my heart. Fuck, that's a lie. Back in the outhouse, I saw the truth in Ms Hadley's eyes just beneath the depths of evil lurking there. She had the same look as the woman who tortured me. Unhinged, passionate, obsessed, *crazed*.

My own fucking mother.

"Erik, the truth…" She frowns, her perfectly arched eyebrows drawing together.

My hands drop away from her face, my shoulders slumping. "Yes, I think she killed my real mother."

"That *bitch*," she spits, rage and fury lighting an inferno within her. The power of it takes my breath away. "She's going to wish she fucking killed me because there's no way I'm going to sit back and let her get away with this. What's happening with the case?" She breathes heavily through her mouth, her chest rising and falling with anger. I'm pretty certain that if she could walk right now, she'd leave us in search for Ms Hadley and fucking kill her. Something I should've done that day.

"I don't want to discuss it right now, Rose. Soon, but not now."

"Erik, we *need* to talk about this. I don't want any of you protecting me from the truth. I may be stuck in this damn metal seat with wheels, but I'm strong enough to deal with whatever's going on. Haven't I proved as much to you all?"

"Wheelchair," I point out, evading her question.

Of course she's strong. She's stronger than all three of us put together. This woman is the only reason I see a future that isn't filled with endless years of torment. Ivan and Anton are besotted with her as much as I am. She's a perfect fit for our kind of fucked up. No one else would ever work.

"Shut up," she responds, crossing her arms over her chest. "I know very well this is a damn wheelchair, though it feels more like a prison of its own."

I lean in closer, my tongue sliding out to wet my lips. "Kiss me, woman," I growl, loving how her attitude makes me want to punish her just the way she craves.

"Erik!" Her sharp tone makes me smile despite everything.

"I'm going to kiss you, whether you want me to or not, Rose. So, I can make this easy or hard, what's it to be?" I glare at her, not willing to back down. Loving the distraction, craving her kiss, her touch.

"Hard," she purrs, her nostrils flaring as she turns her face away from me and looks out of the window. My fucking cock twitches at her rebelliousness. She knows exactly what's she's doing, seeking out the punishment she desires.

"There will come a time I will give you all that you crave, Rose. But I must trust myself with you first. I don't need Anton and Ivan watching every time we fuck."

"*I* trust you," she bites out, still refusing to look at me. "You broke me and pieced me back together, Erik. What does that tell you?"

"Soon," is all I can manage to say in response.

I'd promised her in the glass cage that the time would come when we could explore her submission and my dominance. I'm trying to get to the point freely, and I *am* getting there. I'm on the verge of becoming the man she wants, the man I need to be, but I'm not there yet. Not with Ms Hadley and her wickedness still hanging over us all.

"The hard way," she repeats, calling my bluff and pushing the point. Testing the boundaries and my resolve.

My fingers seek out her jaw as I crowd her body with my own. Sliding my free hand behind her back I force her forward to the edge of the seat whilst my fingers grip her chin tightly. Rose draws in a sharp breath, desire, anger and the edge of pain snapping in her eyes. She might be angry with me in the moment, but she's sure as fuck turned on too. I see it in the parting of her lips and the heaving of her chest.

"The next time you deny me what I need, there'll be consequences, Rose. Today, you have a free pass."

"I don't *want* a free pass. You withhold the truth from me, I withhold what you want in return. Tell me what's going on!"

"Rose…" I grind out. The sound of her name on my lips comes out as a shattered prayer. My desire, unmistakable. I need this kiss. Fucking need it, and I'm going to take it any way I can. Perhaps then, I can tell her what she wants to know. Her touch anchors me in the present, keeps me sane when insanity is calling my name.

Ignoring her struggle to pull her body away from mine, I press my lips hard against hers. She whimpers, her fingers digging into my shoulders as her body relaxes despite her anger. Our teeth clash with force as my tongue darts into her mouth, my fingers seeking out her long hair, tangling in its length. She groans into my mouth, her own hands finding the back of my head and pulling me closer.

I'm not gentle.

This kiss is intense, filled with regret, an apology and a burning desire that lights me up and singes my skin. Like a tinderbox that has a match struck against it, we go up in flames as I scold her plump lips with the fire of my kiss. I absorb every pant, every moan, every fucking sound, telling me how much she wants this, wants me, and fuck the consequences. Now that I've cracked Rose open, she's so expressive in her feelings. She kisses me back with abandon, with relief and hope, and in response I give her the side of me that I've been holding back these past couple of weeks. She got a glimpse of it in the glass cage that first time I took her. That was the unfettered version, and whilst it was nearer the truth of who I am, it's not as simple as that. I am both the man and the monster. Two sides of the same coin at war with one another, always. With Rose, somehow, I've managed to find a happy medium, a place where I can be both. I want to explore that more, but not until she's healed fully.

For now, this kiss will have to do. *It must.*

CHAPTER 4

ROSE

E rik stands abruptly when the door to my room opens and Anton, Ivan and Dr Smithton walk in. He turns his back to them, adjusting his crotch.

"Are we interrupting?" Ivan asks, his gaze moving between us.

"Not at all," Erik responds, turning back to face them all, his face deadpan.

Anton raises an eyebrow and Dr Smithton pins his gaze on me, avoiding all eye contact with Erik and the very obvious bulge in his trousers.

"Dr Smithton is here to check Rose over. You okay with that, Erik?" Anton asks, noticing the way Erik frowns as Dr Smithton moves towards me.

"Am I okay with another man other than you two touching my woman? Not particularly, so you'd better be quick," he retorts, glaring at Dr Smithton unkindly who raises an eyebrow in response, then moves towards me despite the threat.

"This is my job, Erik. I'm not in the business of making a pass at my patients, no matter how lovely," Dr Smithton retorts, winking at me.

Oh, God. Nothing like pouring gasoline on a flame.

"Good, because I *am* in the business of knocking out anyone who tries it on with Rose, doctor or not," Erik snarls, bringing forth a snicker from Anton and a grin from Ivan. Despite the awkwardness, I'm glad to see them both smiling. It's been a while. Then I remember I'm pissed at them both for avoiding me, so I close my smile down just as quickly.

"Alright, alright," I interrupt, heat warming my cheeks and the sweet spot between my legs. It's more than a turn on that Erik has gone all alpha male on me, and that kiss, well... I push all thoughts away of what I'd like to do now that I've finally got all three men in my bedroom. Even when I'm pissed off, I still want them, *need* them. I can admit that now. But thoughts of their naked skin and the pleasure of their touch is better left for moments when my doctor isn't about to take my blood pressure.

"Guys, Dr Smithton doesn't need you three in the room whilst he checks me over, especially if you're going to be rude," I say, giving Erik a look and trying and failing to cool my own sudden desire.

He crosses his arms, and bares his teeth, making us all laugh, except Dr Smithton, who is busy sliding my trouser leg up and gently pressing his fingertips against my still bruised knee. Thank goodness I decided to wear loose trousers, I'm not sure any of them would appreciate it if I sat in just my knickers before him. As it is, the smiles fall from Anton and Ivan's face as he examines me. Erik just scowls even more. I guess I've got to manage three jealous males then. Though, honestly, I think I'd react much the same if some attractive female doctor was touching them the same way.

Dr Smithton cups my knee, drawing a sharp breath from me. Fuck, that hurts. Such a simple act reminding me that I'm still very human and still very breakable.

"Careful," Erik warns, taking a step forward, the tension rising. Thankfully Dr Smithton is completely oblivious. Or if he is aware of how close he is to getting manhandled out of the room, he's doing a great job at hiding it.

"Please, leave. Let Dr Smithton do his job," I say quickly.

"Rose, we're staying," Ivan pipes up, crossing his arms over his chest. Today, he's dressed casually in dark jeans and a button down shirt. I wonder briefly how he's coping with the business side of things. Then I remember he was managing fine before I came along.

I shake my head. "No, you're *not*."

My tone changes as Domina appears. It's been a while, and Ivan's reaction is immediate. He lowers his gaze, and I see the tip of his tongue run over his bottom lip. I've missed him, and his submission. Clearly from the sudden rush of colour to his cheeks, he's missed it too. Knowing that I still have that kind of power over him, even now like this, makes me feel a hell of a lot better. I didn't realise quite how much I needed to know that he still wants me like that.

"Rose, keep still, please," Dr Smithton reprimands gently as I squirm in my seat.

Drawing in a deep breath as the pressure of his fingers over my knee joint increases, I press my eyes shut. When I open them again, I look back up.

"Let Dr Smithton do his job. Then we can *all* talk, okay?" I say, making sure I look at each of them in turn. They're not hiding from me this time. If I have to drag my sorry arse out of this wheelchair and hop around the manor to find them, I will.

"You've got it," Anton says, grabbing hold of Ivan and gesturing for Erik to move. He gives me a wide smile and this time I don't worry about whether it's covering up something more sinister beneath. I've already fallen into Anton's darkness and survived it.

Truth be known, of the three men, he's fast becoming the person I can rely on to rally the other two when stubbornness and pride takes them over. In some ways, he surprises me most of all. In those few days alone together after my operation, he was attentive, funny, charming and most of all, kind. There had been no sign of the man who'd stop at nothing in his pursuit to see colour, and whilst I'm happy he appears to have accepted who he is, I know from the lack of colour covering the skin on his hands that he's not been painting of late.

That troubles me. That needs to change.

"Fine!" Erik stabs out. "Look after *our* girl."

Dr Smithton nods, doing a good job at remaining professional. "I wouldn't dream of doing anything else," he responds with a genuine smile.

Erik grits his jaw, then strides past Ivan and Anton, heading out the door.

"How long, Doc?" Anton asks.

"Should be done in about half an hour."

"Be back then, Rose," he confirms, swiping a hand through his long hair. Today he's wearing it down, tucked behind his ears; I have the sudden urge to tug on it. "Want me to get anything for you?"

"No, I'm good," I respond, eyeing the still uneaten plate of food Fran had brought me.

"You sure you don't need one of us to stay?" Ivan presses,

concern filling his eyes as his gaze rests on my bruised knee. It's not a pretty sight. Two large bruises bleed black and blue into one another, the edges tinged a crimson red. It's hideous.

"I'm sure. See you in a bit," I say, dragging my gaze from my discoloured skin and watching them both leave the room, the door closing gently behind them.

Dr Smithton examines my knee for a good ten minutes, then after some gentle manipulation he withdraws his hands and pulls up a seat.

"I'm glad you've been following my instructions, Rose. It might look unsightly, but you're healing beautifully." He tilts his head at me, then smiles.

"What?"

"There's a long way to go before you're back to any ballet… let alone anything else as *vigorous*." He lets that statement hang in the air between us for a bit, before chuckling. We both know what he's talking about and the ease with which he accepts my relationship with Ivan, Anton and Erik give me a strange sense of relief.

"You don't disapprove?" I blurt out.

"My professional side is only concerned about your healing. My personal side is glad you have people who care about you. Who am I to judge how you choose to live your life?" He pats my hand in an almost fatherly gesture. My chest squeezes as I'm reminded of the man who tried to be a father to me but failed. I didn't know I needed someone like that in my life, until right this second.

"Thank you. I appreciate everything you've done for me."

"You're going to be okay, Rose. Once you've gotten over this surgery and your shoulder injury, there will be no stopping you. I have every faith that you'll be able to dance again.

Though, of course, how soon hinges on your rheumatoid arthritis."

"It's under control. My bloodwork came back okay. As you know, this new medication I'm on seems to be doing the trick keeping it at bay, for now at least. I don't feel the same kind of dull ache everywhere that I usually do. It's refreshing."

"That's good news. Now then," he says, standing. "I'm signing you over to another private consultant and a team of local physios. They'll start working with you in the next couple of days."

"How long before I can get out of this damn wheelchair?"

"Ah, well, you'll be pleased to know I've brought some crutches with me today." Dr Smithton points to the other side of the room where a pair of crutches are leaning against the wall. Ivan or Anton must've brought them up.

"Bloody perfect," I groan, giving him a rueful smile when he gives me his "stern doctor look". I realise I'm not an easy patient but seriously, fucking crutches now? I'm not sure what I was thinking really, I guess I was avoiding the next stage after the wheelchair. A huge part of me was hoping I'd go miraculously from sitting in a wheelchair to walking. *Stupid*.

"You might want to get up and go right this second, but if you do, you're going to cause more harm than good," he says, already knowing me better than most.

"So now I've got to hobble about on those."

"Yes."

"Perfect," I retort ungratefully, which he graciously ignores.

"The good news is, I would expect you to be able to put your full weight on your knee in about a week or so. A couple of weeks after you should be able to walk with just a cane. You're four weeks into your recovery now, in another month's time you'll be walking without assistance. Providing, that is, you maintain the exercises to keep the joint and surrounding ligaments supple."

"Okay, I can cope with that, *just*." I smile, despite myself. I can do this. What's a few more weeks? "What about ballet?" I ask tentatively.

"You can practice simple stretches as soon as you can walk without a cane. On pointe, it's likely to be three to six months, give or take. Even then, I'd be very, very cautious. Don't push yourself before you're ready."

I nod, gritting my teeth. That will be the longest time I've gone without dancing. I miss it as much as anything else. The freedom to move, to stretch my body, pushing it to its limits. I'll never get back to the intensity that I was used to in the Royal Ballet, but there's something so freeing about working your body until it can't do anymore. I guess that's partly why I'm in such a mess now. I need to be better about taking care of myself.

Dr Smithton regards me, waiting for me to speak. When I don't, he fills the silence.

"You have three men who will do just about anything for you, it would seem. Might as well make use of them, no?"

"Make use of who?" Ivan asks, walking into the room. I'm pretty sure we haven't got to the half an hour point yet. Dr Smithton smiles and holds his hand out for me to shake.

"Looks like my time is up. Take care of yourself, Rose. If you can't do that, then make sure these men do," he says.

I take his hand and give him a warm smile of my own. "Thanks again, Dr Smithton."

He nods, releasing my hand and grabbing his case. After a brief conversation with Ivan, he leaves the room.

Ivan pushes the door shut, leaning on it. A crackle of sexual energy fills the space between us. "So, Rose. Looks like you've got a new toy?" He says with a wicked grin as he grabs the crutches and brings them over to me. "Want to give them a try?"

"There are other toys I'd rather play with," I mutter, pulling a face.

"Me too, Rose. Me fucking too."

I laugh, then remembering how much he's been avoiding me, glare at him. "Where have you been these past few days?" I ask, locking the brake on my wheelchair then push upwards, ignoring the slice of pain in my knee. Fuck. So much for looking after myself.

Ivan rushes forward. "What are you doing? Hold on to me," he urges, holding both crutches in one hand, and snaking his arm around my back.

The second his arm slides around my waist, I feel a warm rush of heat. I haven't been physical with him since that time with Anton in the hotel on Kirkwall. I've missed the contact, so fucking much.

"Are you going to answer me?" I press, trying not to succumb to the intense feeling of rightness between us. I'm pissed off and will remain that way until he explains himself. "Well?" I insist when he doesn't answer right away.

"Too much shit going on in my head, Rose. Every time I look at you, I'm reminded of what she did, what she tried to do. It's driving me fucking insane. If we'd lost you..." his voice trails off as he tries to school his emotions.

"See, that's the point. You *haven't*. I'm here... I've missed you," I admit, quietly.

"Fuck, Rose. I'm sorry."

Ivan drops the crutches, wraps me in his arms and pulls me against his chest. "Is this okay?" he mumbles, the warmth of his lips pressing against the curve of my neck. He knows that between us, Domina makes all the demands. She initiates physical contact. But in the moment, I don't have the will or the heart to tell him to back off. Right now, I need his comfort. Funny how things can change.

There's a tenseness he holds in his body as we hug, and I know what he really, truly needs. He needs Domina. But right this second that isn't an option, because I need the truth before we try and figure out a way to make this work for us all.

"Lift me up, Ivan. Take me to the bed. Then fetch Erik and Anton. We need to talk."

Ivan doesn't hesitate, swooping me up into his arms, he strides over to the bed and lays me down gently.

Within five minutes all three men are in the room once more.

CHAPTER 5

IVAN

Rose regards us all from her spot on the bed. She has her legs stretched out in front of her as she leans up against the headboard.

"Maybe you should all sit. This might take a while," she says, motioning with her good arm.

Her good arm… fuck.

A slice of shame runs over my skin as I fight to maintain control of my guilt. It eats away at me like acid on skin. I should've known fucking better. I should've seen it coming.

Anton catches my grimace and a flicker of regret passes behind his eyes as he perches on the end of the bed drawing up one leg and crossing it over the other. I know in that one brief glimpse that he feels just the same as I do. Though he's better at hiding it.

Anton has managed somehow to bury his pain, for Rose. This side of him, the thoughtful, generous side is as new to him as it is to the rest of us. He's not touched any drugs since that day he almost overdosed and Rose nursed him through the aftermath. She's done what no other woman, doctor or therapist has been able to do, and he's not going to balls it up by shooting up and killing himself. Besides, he knows Rose will kick his arse into touch if he so much as tries. Well, as soon as she's fucking healed, that is.

Goddamn it.

"I'm going to sit here," Erik says, sliding onto the bed next to Rose. A statement, not a request. He stretches out beside her, his hand seeking out hers automatically, as though he can't bear to be near her and not touch her. The gravity of that simple act blows me away. Rose has managed to reach across the void and drag Erik back from the darkness of his past. I couldn't love her more for it.

"Ivan," Rose says, urging me to sit.

Pulling up a chair, I flank her left side, resting my elbows on the armrests and leaning my chin against my clasped hands.

We all wait, knowing what's coming.

"Tell me everything. I won't accept anything but the truth," she says, looking between us.

Silence smothers us all like an oily cloth, making it hard to breath.

Anton is the first to speak. Of the three of us, he's less emotionally attached to Ms Hadley. She might have been his nanny in his formative years, but her close relationship with his father meant that he could never allow himself to love her. Those feelings were only ever reserved for Erik and me, and now Rose.

"Ms Hadley is in a secure unit for the mentally ill. The case won't be going to court. She won't be going to prison." He looks directly at her, not flinching as her expression changes from shock, to incredulity, then rage. White hot rage. It rips outwards, eviscerating the silence.

"What the fuck?!" she shouts, sitting forward, her body jerking involuntarily.

Erik places a hand on her shoulder, squeezing. She flinches, her nostrils flaring as she sucks in a sharp breath, pain lancing across her face.

"Erik, her shoulder," I warn.

He removes his hand, muttering an apology.

Anton leans over, resting his hand on Rose's ankle. "My father's a powerful man, Rose. He knows people… I'm sorry."

"But she *shot* me. She tried to fucking *kill* me. Doesn't that count for anything. Does my life mean so little? Am I that fucking worthless?"

Real pain cuts through her words, shredding my heart. I reach for her, then realise I don't have permission to touch her. I've already pushed that boundary today. Instead, I scrape a hand over my face before locking eyes with her.

"You are not worthless, Rose. Don't you ever think that. Viktor has friends in very high places. He protected Erik when he was a kid. Paid off the authorities for Anton and covered up Svetlana's suicide so the paparazzi wouldn't descend hell on us whilst we grieved. For whatever reason, he's chosen to protect Ms Hadley too even though we all know she doesn't deserve it."

"And Erik's mother? What about her?"

This time it's Erik's turn to explain. He looks grim, tired. Fucking wrecked if the truth be known. "Back at the farmhouse we found some old photos, and letters…"

"What letters?"

"They were love letters from a man who signed them with just the initial 'S'. Letters sent to my mother…"

"Ms Hadley?" Rose asks.

"No, my real mother, Isabelle."

"But why would that make you think Ms Hadley murdered her?"

"Because the letters told a story of a love between not two people, but three. Ms Hadley, Isabelle and this man only known as 'S'. Except an agreement had been made, one in which 'S' had to choose who he loved more. Ms Hadley or Isabelle. He chose Isabelle, and I'm the result."

"And you think Ms Hadley killed Isabelle out of jealousy?"

"Yes. She almost killed you for the very same reason," Erik answers her, sighing heavily.

"Why don't you inform the police? It could change everything. We could get her put away."

I shake my head. "It won't work, Rose."

"Why the hell not?"

"Because they're just love letters. There's no real evidence. All of this is supposition. Us reading between the lines. It would be thrown out of court," Anton says, not liking the truth but speaking it anyway.

"There must be a way…" Rose looks between us, pleading with her eyes.

Erik grasps Rose's hand once more and presses a lingering kiss against her knuckles before pulling away. "Ms Hadley might have gotten away with murdering my mother, but she sure as fuck isn't going to get away with hurting you."

"What do you mean?" Rose asks, twisting her body to look at Erik.

"It means I will somehow make her pay. I don't know how, or when. But she will, Rose. I fucking promise you."

Her lips press in a hard line. I know she wants revenge just as much as the rest of us, but I also know Rose, and she won't want Erik to put himself in a position he can't come back from.

"And Viktor, what about him? Why would he help her? She could've killed any one of you. Can he not see that?"

"Honestly, I don't know why my father would protect her. They've always been close but knowing my father there's more to this than any of us are able to understand right now."

Rose listens but it's as though she's no longer taking anything in. Her thoughts are somewhere else, somewhere dark. Her past crawls up her spine and wraps around her throat, choking her and drawing out the sobs she's held in all these weeks. All these *years*.

"I thought I was going to die," she mutters, gritting her teeth and swiping at the tears. "I lay there, whilst the sound of the gun firing rattled inside my head and warmth oozed from my shoulder, and do you know what I'd thought?"

"What, Rose?" Erik asks, his face stony.

"That I'm glad it was me she shot and not any of you. That this was my penance for watching my father die, for not helping him."

"Rose," I begin, failing to find the words she needs to comfort her.

"The world was fading into the kind of darkness that you don't wake up from. Ironic no, that I was shot in an act of passion. Ms Hadley did it to save Erik, just like my father had shot Roman to save me. In her eyes I was just as much a predator as he was."

"Enough!" Erik snaps. "That might be her reason, but don't you dare lump yourself with that fucking man, not after what he did to you. You were just a fucking child, Rose. I'm a grown arse man, you *saved* me."

I watch in shock as he rears upwards onto his knees and

turns towards Rose, grabbing her hips and sliding her down the bed, straddling her. She lets out a cry of pain as he grasps her wrists in his hands and pins her arms to her side.

I stand abruptly, the chair falling backwards behind me.

"What the fuck, Erik?" I shout.

Anton stands, reaching me before I can yank the bastard off Rose. She's not fucking healed. What does he think he's doing?

"Wait," Anton says, holding me back. "He won't hurt her."

"He already fucking is!" I snarl, trying to shove Anton off me. "I won't watch him do it."

"Just wait, brother. Wait," Anton soothes, hauling me backwards a little.

The only reason I don't knock him out is because of the way Rose is looking at Erik. Her eyes are trained on him, a sense of relief flooding across her features.

"Please," she begs, but she isn't asking him to stop, she's pleading for something *more*.

Erik nods once, then turns to Anton and me. "Get over here. Rose needs to understand she's fucking worthy of our love."

"Love?" I grind out, seeing how tightly his hands hold onto her wrists.

"Yes," he snaps, "We all know you love her, Ivan. We all fucking do. Anton has finally found a reason to live in the real world and not a drug fuelled haze, and I have a woman pressed beneath me with my cock harder than stone. Rose is the only woman who isn't afraid of our kind of fucked up. Of course, I love her. There isn't another woman on this planet who I would've walked out of that glass prison for."

"Erik…" Rose chokes out.

"She's not ready. She isn't healed. You could hurt her," I protest.

"Not today. Today we're gentle. We think of Rose's needs. Can you do that?" he looks at us both, waiting for an answer.

Can I? What a stupid fucking question. I might need Rose's dominance, I might need to feel pain, but that doesn't mean to say I can't be gentle, that I can't give her pleasure through more vanilla means. If there's anyone we need to be worried about, it's Erik.

"Well?" he pushes, glaring at us both.

The answer is a simple one, and we both voice it.

"Yes."

CHAPTER 6

ROSE

I look at Erik's profile as he addresses Ivan and Anton, at his strong jaw and sharp nose. He's a beautiful man. They're all beautiful, and just as complicated as each other.

"Don't just fucking stand there," he barks out.

His command is as much as a challenge as it is an order, which they both react to in different ways. Ivan scowls, giving Erik a *fuck-you* look. He hates to be told what to do by his peers, his natural tendencies to be submissive in the bedroom clashing with his dominance everywhere else. He won't back down to Erik, his pride can't, won't accept it. Anton reacts completely differently, with a calmness that tells me he'll do what Erik orders not for his best friend, but for me. If he didn't agree, he would refuse with little fuss and would not be swayed.

"You're being a fucking tyrant, Erik," Anton says with a wry grin, not in the least bit perturbed by his demands.

"Just do it," he retorts, turning his attention back to me.

I'm only just beginning to understand their dynamics and my place within them. This whole experience is new to me and like them, my trust isn't given lightly or just to anyone.

Funny, given their needs and their inner demons, that I trust these three men implicitly. This could all go horribly wrong and push back my healing for weeks. The sheer fact that Dr Smithton said that any sort of 'vigorous exercise' should be avoided tells me that this might not be the best idea we've ever had. But currently I don't give a shit.

It's been too long. I *need* them, and I never need anyone.

"What are you waiting for, Ivan?" Erik calls, the tenuous hold he has on the situation fraying.

"First things first, stop ordering me about, Erik. I might be Rose's submissive, but I sure as fuck aren't yours. Secondly, you might be some badass soldier, but I can still kick your arse," Ivan snaps.

"Then stop being a pussy and get over here," Erik says back, a grin pulling up his lips.

Beneath him, I hold in a nervous laugh as a thread of excitement overrides the worry that this is going to cost me physically. I already know I'm lost emotionally, even though none of these men are aware of quite how much. I still need to evaluate these feelings I have, and someday soon I'm going to voice them, but I refuse to delve beyond the here and now.

Erik releases my hand, then presses a delicate kiss against the pink mark wrapped around my wrist from his grasp. He looks at me as his thumbs circle my palms.

"There isn't anywhere on earth that I'd rather be than here right now with you. This, what we all have, is the *only* thing that will get me through the shitstorm that I know is coming. Are you going to weather the storm with us, Rose?"

"Until the storm breaks, or we do," I respond honestly.

The truth is, none of us know how this will pan out. There are no guarantees when it comes to us. Broken lives lead to broken people, the cracks harbouring the darkness. It's inevitable, and each one of us know this all too well. We have so much to lose if this goes wrong, and yet despite that, I'm with them every step of the way. I think I have been since the moment I walked into Browlace and came face to face with our nemesis, though I hadn't known it then.

Erik smiles then leans over and presses his lips against mine. I open my mouth, welcoming his tongue and the taste of bitter coffee and lust fuelled by love.

Love.

My heart stutters, trying to escape my chest. Erik admitted he loves me, and it cost him nothing to share it. I wish I could be as brave. He's so fucking brave.

This time our kiss is different to before; it's slow, warm and tender, like an evening summer breeze that you never want to end. He breathes life into me with every sweep of his tongue and groan against my lips, leaving me panting and breathless when he withdraws.

I watch him climb off the bed, feeling shaky with lust and slick between my legs.

"Undress Rose," he commands Anton, who simply nods, his gaze falling to me.

There's a light in his eyes I've not seen for a while, and I recognise it for what it is. Anton is memorising this moment, etching it into his memory to revisit later. I hope for all our sakes it encourages him to pick up his pad and pencil again, because I know that without his art, he isn't whole, and I need him to be. We all do.

Keeping his gaze fixed on me, he undresses until he's naked

before us, his long hair falling about his shoulders. He's leaner than a few weeks ago, and for a moment I worry he's taken to drugs once more, but the glow of health shining out of his skin assures me that he hasn't. My gaze roves over his chest and stomach and the shaded areas defining every muscle. He's not as built as Erik or Ivan, but he is just as sexy. Lower still, his cock is thick and erect, and it occurs to me that this is the first time we've not fucked hidden in darkness or half shadow. I squeeze my thighs together, welcoming the throb of pleasure that pulses between my legs in anticipation.

Besides him Ivan is still, his jaw tight, his eyes lowered, and I understand what he's waiting for; my permission. "Ivan. I want this. There isn't anyone I trust more than the three of you. Get undressed and join us," I order gently.

The tension in Ivan's shoulders releases as he blows out a long breath. He undresses slowly, giving me a striptease that has me biting my lip, my fingers edging to the spot between my legs, wanting release and seeking it out.

"Keep your hands still," Erik bites out. "You are not to touch yourself, understand?"

"Yes." Oh, I understand alright. My skin prickles with the anticipation his command brings. It's been a long time since I've wanted to submit... needed too.

Ivan keeps his eyes lowered as the exchange takes place. But this time, this time I need him to see me. Need them all to see me, because even though I can't express how I feel with words, I hope that they will understand what's in my heart through my actions. I'm theirs for the taking. If there's ever a time to find me at my weakest, it's right now.

"Ivan, I want you to keep your eyes on me. I want you all to *see*," I explain, the tenor of my voice taking on the same command as Erik's.

Immediately, his eyes snap up, meeting mine. The absolute devotion I see in them snatches my breath, detonating my already quivering resolve. The words I've yet to admit, just a whisper away. I slam my mouth shut, not ready to release them.

Not yet. Not yet.

Swallowing hard, I move my gaze to Anton who's standing by his side.

"I'll never take my eyes off you, Rose," Anton says, grinning. His smile bringing the light instead of hiding the dark like it had before.

Reaching over, he squeezes Ivan's bare shoulder then walks to the end of the bed and peels off my socks. He takes his time undressing me from the feet up, paying extra care as he removes my trousers and underwear. The gentleness with which he does so unhinges me, breaks me down, and I'm reminded of the way he had massaged me until I fell asleep in his arms all those weeks ago.

Today, I'm staying wide awake.

"You are so beautifully flawed, Rose," he says absorbing every inch of my skin, committing it to memory. His eyes rove over me, lingering on the ugly bruising around my knee. Kneeling on the bed beside me, Anton's fingers whisper across my bruised skin whilst Erik and Ivan watch.

"Is it wrong that the broken parts are my favourite?" he asks quietly, a frown drawing his eyebrows together.

"No, it isn't," I reassure him. "I love that you see beauty in the parts that I find so ugly, in the parts that hurt."

He nods, seemingly lost to his thoughts as his warm fingers run over my now hot skin. "Is this as black as it seems?" he asks, cocking his head to the side.

"Pretty much."

Anton files that piece of information away, then working his way upwards, he trails a finger over the dip beneath my rib cage running it along the bone that protrudes a little more than it had before. Like him, I've lost some weight over the past few weeks. I've also lost some muscle definition too, but I'm not worried. I'll get it back.

He bends over, his long hair falling across my stomach as he licks along the skin pulled taut over bone. My nostrils flare as his fingers slide up my inner thigh seeking out the tender flesh between my legs. I open them further, giving him access, loving the look of pure desire in Ivan and Erik's eyes as they watch me slowly unravel with every caress.

Anton's warm lips move upwards as he seeks out the scar from my shoulder surgery. The skin is still sensitive to the touch, and my nostrils flare as he presses a kiss against the raised skin.

"This one. This is my favourite. Not because of what she did to you, but because you survived it. You're a survivor, Rose, and now you're ours. If anyone can guide us through this fucked-up shit, it's you."

Anton's finger moves inside me as his hot mouth slides back down my body. Behind him Ivan's jaw ticks. He loves his best friends and he's accepted us all together, but he finds it the hardest to deal with.

"Get on the bed, Ivan," I manage to utter as Anton slides another finger inside me and closes his mouth around my nipple, teasing the nub with his teeth and tongue, and sending shockwaves of pleasure to my core.

Despite everything, Ivan doesn't hesitate. He stretches out beside me and waits for my permission, my instruction. Needing it, needing to let go of the control and the stress he feels at all times. I turn to look at him, reaching upwards with my free hand then pinch his nipple. Hard. He cries out, flashes of relief and lust zinging in his eyes. I lick my finger and swirl it over the spot I'd just pinched, chasing away the pain with pleasure.

"Kiss me," I demand, as Anton shifts between my legs and lowers his mouth to my pussy.

Ivan swallows my moans as he slides his tongue over mine, his fingers tangling in the length of my hair. My hips jerk upwards automatically as Anton replaces his finger with his tongue, pumping my swollen warmth.

"Keep still," he murmurs, pressing my hips into the bed and holding me down as he fucks me with his lips, tongue and fingers. I'm becoming boneless beneath them both, Ivan's kiss devastating me just as much as Anton's skilled mouth.

Amid all this pleasure, I'm very aware of Erik climbing onto the bed, and I reach out blindly to him. He captures my wrist, holding me tightly then pulls my index finger into his mouth, his teeth scraping over my skin, biting on the fleshy pad. The sensation is just this side of painful and draws me up sharp from my impending orgasm.

"You touch me when I say, Rose," he growls, the low rumble sending goosebumps scattering over my skin. "And that isn't happening today. This is about *your* pleasure. These fuckers don't deserve any release, and neither do I. This is our punishment. We won't leave you to your thoughts ever again."

In response, I pull on Ivan's hair, yanking his head back, panting. My need to submit, to dominate, to let go completely, twisting up inside of me until I don't know who I am anymore. Separately these men are dangerous, together they're a goddamn nuclear bomb.

Our eyes meet. Ivan's are stormy, raw, and filled with unending devotion.

Unspoken words bleed between us and my mouth pops open with the next command, only to be swallowed by a moan as Anton circles my clit with his tongue.

"I want you to let go, Rose. I'm *ordering* you to," Erik demands, towering above us all. He bites the delicate flesh of my wrists, before sucking the pain away and licking my skin.

My response to Erik's ministrations is captured by Ivan's brutal kiss.

And it is brutal, because he doesn't hold back, and I understand now why he refused to kiss the women who he'd once dominated. Ivan's kisses are devastating in their intensity. If a kiss could sear a soul in two, it would be his.

I let out a groan as he pulls away, then cry out as Anton nips my sensitive flesh. I look down at him, at my wetness glistening on his lips and beard.

"Don't stop. Fucking eat her out, Anton. Make her come," Erik growls.

Anton grins then slides his tongue provocatively over his lips before burying his head back between my legs. My back arches as I pull his head tighter against me, rocking against his mouth.

"Keep your eyes open. Look at them both, Rose," Erik says, as Ivan moves lower, wrapping his lips around my nipple and sucking hard just as Anton nips my clit between his teeth. I hadn't told Ivan he could touch me that way, but I'm too far gone to reprimand him. But then again, who cares? Right now, all the lines are blurred. They are so damn blurry that I wonder whether I'll ever see a straight line again. If I'll ever want too.

"Don't think, Rose. Just let yourself go," Erik says as watches us from above. His cock jumps in response to the whimpers of ecstasy that I'm unable to keep inside, and with every lick and every tug at my tender flesh I slide into a still unfamiliar place where emotions hold both allure and paralysing fear.

Because right now, I feel *everything*.

I feel the soul-stripping pleasure of their kisses, their touch. I feel intense pain in my knee and shoulder, both spots now throbbing in time to the frantic beat of my heart only serving to heighten the pleasure more. And the words I want to shout out? They're hovering on my lips. I'm close to freefalling into a place I've always dreamed of, but I know that once I voice them, I can't take the words back. When I utter them, I want to be sure that I have no reason to wish I hadn't.

Erik bites and nibbles at my fingers and palm, understanding that I need the pain to counteract the intense pleasure. I can barely see straight as Ivan and Anton work in tandem, their skilled hands and mouths relentless in their pursuit of my release.

My senses are overloaded. It's too much... it's not nearly enough.

Tipping my head back, I let out a long groan at the orgasm brewing deep within me. It swirls up and outwards from my core like a tsunami, building speed as it takes hold.

Ivan and Anton don't stop. Between them they draw out the most delicious, earth shattering orgasm that makes my eyes roll back in my head, but it's only when Erik grasps my chin and forces me to look at him, that I finally let go.

"Come!" he demands.

So, I do.

I come hard and fast, my body juddering as though it's been electrocuted. For the longest moments I'm filled with the kind of blissful release that I imagine only people in love feel.

Then I realise that person *is* me. I'm in *love*, and this magic, this is the result.

"I…" the unspoken words hover between us as my men find their space surrounding me, engulfing me in their arms. I feel safe. Safe in the arms of these men who have the power to destroy me like no other who've come before.

"It's okay, Rose," Ivan mutters, burying his face in my hair, breathing me in.

I'm wrecked. Satiated. Fulfilled, and utterly and completely exhausted. I don't manage to utter the final, most important words before darkness swallows me and I tumble into the blissful void.

"ROSE, COME BACK," Anton says, his voice as warm as fur wrapped around the softest leather. "You sure know how to scare the shit out of us."

I blink back the stars that pinprick my vision. Wait, did I just pass out after the most intense orgasm I've experienced in my life?

"What happened exactly?" I mutter, as all three men slowly come back into focus. Anton is sitting next to me, fully dressed and drawing circles on the back of my hand. Ivan is pacing up and down, stopping the second he hears me speak, and Erik is staring out of the window a tick in his jaw jumping.

"You came, then I think your body finally decided that enough was enough… Sorry about that," Anton responds, smiling ruefully. He's not sorry at all. In fact, I'm pretty sure his head has expanded more than just a few inches during the time I've been out cold.

"Dr Smithton did warn me not to do anything too strenuous…" I mumble.

"He warned *all* of us," Ivan adds, striding over to my side, and sitting next to me. "But we ignored him anyway. Not the smartest decision we've ever made."

"But the most fun," I say, with a small laugh.

Anton chuckles, but Ivan frowns, clasping my hand tightly in his.

"I'm *fine*, Ivan," I reassure him. "You gave me what I needed, don't feel guilty."

He seems to accept that, but the concern he has for me is heart-warming. Not so long ago, Ivan didn't allow himself to feel, choosing to find release with a knife cutting through his skin. All his scars are healed now, and I'm going to make sure he'll never have a reason to inflict more.

"Where did you go, Rose?" Anton asks me, cupping my cheek in his hand and drawing my attention back to him.

"The darkness," I respond softly.

He nods, understanding. "How was it?"

"Peaceful."

"Good."

Anton rests his head on the pillow beside me and continues to draw circles over my bare skin. Circles that turn into shapes. It's a good sign and following my blissful orgasm, the most positive thing to happen since I was shot.

Behind him, Erik is silently staring out of the window. He's pulled on his slacks, but he's not wearing a top and the muscles of his back are bunched with tension that I wish I could ease. He's suffering still, because of Ms Hadley. Because I'm not fit enough to submit so that he can feel in control.

"Erik?" I say carefully.

His shoulders tense. "We have a visitor," he responds,

turning around slowly to face us. His face is grim. Hard. Angry.

"Who?" Ivan stands, sensing the unease and the rage rolling off his best friend.

Erik's gaze flicks to Anton, whose face pales with realisation. "Viktor."

CHAPTER 7

ANTON

"What the fuck are you doing here?" I shout, pressing my finger into my father's chest.

He raises an eyebrow at me, peering down the length of his nose. He's always so fucking regal, like he's the king of every damn castle, and we're mere servants who should bow and scrape in his presence.

"That's no way to greet your father." A dismissive chuckle escapes his lips, a sound I've heard so many times over the years. But I refuse to be that kid he could belittle so easily and tear apart with a few choice words.

"Fuck you," I snarl, anger flooding my blood as I launch for him, landing a punch square on his jaw. The sound of his surprise is drowned out by the loud crack of bone meeting bone.

His hand flies to his chin, as his eyes narrow, and I swear to god, there's respect flooding within them. The sick bastard.

"I see you've finally grown a backbone. About fucking time."

I raise my fist again, but feel a firm hand squeezing my shoulder. "Anton," Ivan warns.

This time it's my turn to shrug him off.

"No, Ivan. He doesn't get to come here, not after what he's done!"

"And what's that, son?" my father asks, crossing his arms over his chest. "Protecting the woman who brought you up when your own mother was too high to do the same, too weak and pathetic to look after you? You're cut from the same cloth."

"You, cunt! Don't fucking talk about my mother like that. You made her into that person. At least now she's at fucking peace. I wish I could say the same about us, but you insist in pushing your way into our lives again and again. We don't want you, and we certainly don't want your little bitch in our lives anymore. Now, get the fuck out!"

"You heard Ant. You're not welcome. Don't make this any uglier than it needs to be," Erik says calmly. He steps forward, flanking my side, whilst Ivan flanks the other.

"I'm not here to see Anton. I'm here for you, actually," my father says to Erik, dismissing me with a flick of his wrist. Well, there's a fucking surprise.

I try not to flinch as though I've been slapped, but ever the perceptive man, my father notices and his lip curls up in an ugly smile. For years I've dreamed of wiping that smile off his face and now's my chance. I step towards him, but this time both Ivan and Erik grab my wrists to hold me back. All the pain I've felt over his lack of love and any kind of affection boils inside my chest. I want to rip him to shreds just like he's done to me repeatedly over the years. I want him to feel just a fraction of the hurt and disappointment that I've felt every second of my life being his son.

"I don't give a shit. Get your sorry arse out of here…" Erik snaps.

My father holds his hand up, arrogant as usual. "Wait. Let me say what I came here to say, and then I'll leave."

"No!" The three of us say simultaneously.

"I came all this way, and I'm going to say what I must. *Then* I'll leave," he repeats, stubborn to a fault.

"Are you deaf? They've asked you to leave, now *leave!*"

I spin around on my feet to see Rose at the top of the stairs, one hand leaning on a crutch, the other holding onto the rail. What the fuck does she think she's doing?

Ignoring the snort of derision from my father, I run up the stairs two at a time.

"What are you thinking, Rose? Do you want to break your neck?" I say when I reach her.

"Not mine, no," she responds, narrowing her eyes at my father.

"Let me help you back to your room," I say, tucking my arm around her waist. She leans on me, clearly exhausted from the short walk from her room to this point.

"Fuck that. Take me down. I have something I wish to say to your father," she retorts, angry on my behalf.

"Rose…"

"No. Either you take me down, or I sit on my arse and slide down the stairs," she responds stubbornly.

"You don't need to deal with him."

"Yes, I fucking do." She gives me a determined look, and I couldn't love her any more for it. This woman is the strongest person I know. She's carried us all through the darkness. She stood up to each of us and survived it. I'm proud to have her by our side.

Making an easy decision, I sweep her up into my arms and carry her down the stairs. The whole time my father watches, his face blank and without any emotion. The man's a fucking cold-hearted bastard. There isn't any warmth in him. Not one shard.

Both Ivan and Erik seem to haul themselves upright as we descend, finding strength in Rose's presence. I understand the way they feel because I feel the exact same way too. With Rose by our side, we're fucking invincible. Placing Rose on her feet between us, we face my father together.

"Still here I see," my father snarls, and the split second before I punch him for the second time, I wonder why he hates her so much. This time I draw blood, as the bone in my father's nose cracks, breaking it. I feel nothing but a sick sense of emptiness.

"Last warning!" I snarl, my voice hard, cold.

He laughs. He actually fucking laughs and there's an edge of madness to the sound. For the first time in years, I realise that we're finally getting a glimpse beneath his impenetrable exterior. Always so smooth, so put together but I've managed to crack his armour, or maybe that's just Rose, she's an expert at that. I'm just about to drag him out the door when Rose rests her hand on my arm, squeezing gently.

"Wait, there's something I wish to say, Anton."

My father just laughs again. I nod tightly, my fingers curling into my palms. Rose slides her hand into mine, calming me instantly.

"I don't know what you think you're going to achieve by

coming here, Viktor. The last time you graced us with your presence," she sneers, making it perfectly clear that it wasn't a pleasant experience, "You belittled your son and sent him to a very dark place."

"He's weak, always has been, always will be..." he says through his hand, trying to stem the flow of blood.

Rose steps forward and pokes her finger in his chest. We all move with her, Erik holding her upright with his arm wrapped around her waist, whilst I hold onto her hand still. That alone shocks my father. He knows about Erik's past, and for just a second, I see real fear in my father's eyes. It's harder to control a person when there are no weaknesses to exploit.

Rose's eyes narrow as she spits out the next words. "But you *didn't* break him then, and you're not going to break him now, and neither will *she*. You've underestimated Anton, *us*. We are stronger than the shit you want to drown us in. This *whore*, as you so kindly referred to me the last time you were here" she says, pulling her shoulders back and jutting her chin upwards, "is more than just a woman who can handle three powerful men. I'm more than a woman who can satiate them in the bedroom. I'm *the one*. I'm theirs and these men are *mine*. They don't belong to Ms Hadley, and they sure as fuck don't belong to you."

"Now, listen," he starts, blustering over the words as her sheer presence and anger makes him shrink just a little. It might be unnoticeable to someone who doesn't know him, but to me it's obvious. Momentous even.

"No! *You* listen," she growls, stabbing her finger into his chest with each word. "There's nothing and no one that will come between us. So, say what you came here to say, then leave."

This time it's my father's turn to flinch. Very few people have stood up to him, especially not a woman. Even Ms Hadley wouldn't dare talk to him like this, and my mother, she barely spoke a word to him the years they were married, let alone ever give him a piece of her mind. Perhaps if she had, perhaps if *I* had, things would be different now. Pride swells inside my chest, and I glance at Ivan and Erik. They too are glowing with it.

This woman, she's everything we need and so much more.

My father folds his arms across his chest as he calculates his next move. He lowers his hand, blood dripping from his nose and coating his lips and teeth, making him look even more unhinged than he already does.

"I suppose you're the one who *saved* Anton?" My father laughs again, blood and spittle flying out of his mouth.

"No. He did that all on his own. I just helped him to see what you couldn't. That his gift lies within the darkness he lives in every day."

"How pretty. You do have a way with words, Rose. I must admit, I'm surprised. Ms Hadley had you passed off as some brainless bimbo. I see the attraction though, but it's not enough. They'll tire of you, and when they do, you'll have wished you kept a little bit of yourself hidden away, protected. Tell me, Rose, how long did it take them to get beneath your skin? Have they made you fall in love with them yet because once they do, they'll ruin you."

To Rose's credit, she doesn't rise to the bait, she cocks an eyebrow instead, "Come on Viktor, you need to do better than that," she goads.

My father looks from me to Erik, then Ivan. The madness leeches into his eyes and this time he doesn't even try to hide it.

"You don't want to make an enemy of me, *Rose*," he spits, hatred so powerful I feel the force of it, we all do.

Rose tips her head back and laughs. Viktor's face turns puce. I've never seen him this unhinged before. "Rose," I murmur, squeezing her hand in warning. When my father sets his sights on someone to ruin, he will stop at nothing to do just that.

"I'm not scared of you, Viktor. I've met worse men in my life. Your *power*," she sneers, "comes from buying your way out of every situation. Didn't anyone tell you that money can't buy you *love*? Isn't that the real issue here? You're so fucking angry because these men, these wonderful, powerful, loyal men can't be bought. It stings to know that they love me, doesn't it? I bet you and Ms Hadley have plotted and planned together about how you can finish me, *ruin* us. It wouldn't surprise me if you were the *mastermind* behind all this. Using a bitter, twisted, old woman to do your dirty work."

Rose is breathing hard, her nostrils flaring as her accusation hangs in the air. Could she be right? Please, don't let her be right.

"She'd do anything for me," he snarls eventually, laughing hysterically now. He doesn't even try to deny it.

I drop Rose's hand as a violent kind of calm settles over me. My father's behind this.

My own fucking father.

For long moments time stands still as we all absorb his confession. He might not have said it outright, but we all know the truth. He may as well have fired that gun himself.

Darkness swallows me.

It isn't the same pitch black that has become a haven. No, this kind of darkness is the type you fall into and never return from. It's where all the rage lives, the pain and abandonment.

It's the black hole where survival is just a worthless notion and only destruction awaits.

I freefall into it, and there isn't a damn thing I can do about it. Not one thing.

I'm powerless to stop myself as it filters into my bloodstream.

Years of self-doubt, hurt, and betrayal rushes through my veins destroying any rational thought.

Stepping forward, I grip the man who's never loved me by the throat with such force that his feet lift off the ground. Anger blazes a trail up my arm as I squeeze tightly. I'm vaguely aware of Rose calling my name, but I can't answer her. I can't see straight through the rage that is peeling off my skin in layers, flaying me to the bone. My father's fingers grip at my hand, as blood vessels begin to pop in his eyes.

I'm going to fucking kill him.

And yet he still manages to smile no matter how hard I squeeze.

This time I'm going to wipe that smile off his face for good. This is the man he's made, and this is the man who's going to kill him for it.

"ANTON, STOP!" Ivan shouts, gripping hold of my wrist. "Brother, you do this, everything ends. Let him go, *please*."

Everything slows. The beat of my heart, the sound of my breathing, the whistle of rage running through my veins. I've never felt such dark hatred in my life. Nothing has felt worse than this moment right now. The void is so deep, so dark, so fucking bottomless that I'm powerless against it.

"He wants this. Let him go, Ant," Erik says this time, his hand folding over Ivan's. "Brother, don't give in to him. Don't do it."

Beside me my best friends try to persuade me to let go, and

even though I can hear them, I can't seem to stop myself. Years of hatred pours into my soul, blackening it further. There's no coming back for me at this point.

My hand tightens, death taking hold.

Then he does something I don't expect; he drops his hands and doesn't fight back.

CHAPTER 8

ROSE

I'm still clutched to Erik's side as he begs Anton to stop, and as much as I hate his father right now, I need to save Anton from himself. I can't let this man or Ms Hadley destroy us. If Anton kills him what we have will be over.

Twisting in Erik's hold I reach for Anton, wrapping my arms around him from behind and clutching him against my chest. Pressing my mouth against his ear I say the words I hope will draw him out of the darkness and back to me, to us.

"Anton, don't do this. I can't lose you. I won't. Let him go and look at me," I beg.

He doesn't respond, he's in too deep.

Sliding around his body with difficulty, I place myself between him and his father. Ivan makes room but doesn't let go of Anton's arm. Now we all surround him. Erik on one side, Ivan the other and me in between, his father's throat still gripped in his hand. None of us care about saving that man from what he deserves, just saving Anton from a life sentence.

Clutching his face in my hands, I force him to look at me.

"You do this, *he* wins. Let him go."

I swallow hard and make a leap into the darkness with him. Taking his free hand, I lift it to my throat, walking into his grip. I feel his fingers tighten automatically, shifting over my skin. Recognition flickers in his gaze, but still he holds tight.

"I'm asking you not to kill Viktor. Not to save *him*, Anton, but to save *us*. Don't let him, don't let Ms Hadley ruin what we have. Come back to me, Anton. We need you here. We can't do this without you," I repeat, my heart burning with conviction.

And just like that he lets go.

Behind us Viktor coughs and splutters, drawing in lungsful of breath. But he is insignificant in this moment. *Nothing* is more important than these men. I belong right here, surrounded by them all. I feel Erik and Ivan slide behind me protecting me from the man who came to destroy us, but only served to bring us closer together.

Together we are strong, unbreakable. We've fought to get to this point. Every single one of us facing the darkest parts of our souls and surviving it.

Anton grips my face with shaking hands, his whole body trembling. His dark eyes finding mine. "I love you, Rose," he grinds out, before crashing his mouth against my own.

Our kiss is earth shattering and loving in a way that reassures me that I was right to choose this man, *these men*.

Colours bleed into our kiss. The shimmering ghosts of our pasts and the dense white fog of uncertainty evaporating into the golden amber of a new dawn that's bursting with passion and *love*, streaks of red running through it like the blood pumping in our veins. In our hearts. I let the colours envelop me, falling helplessly into his arms, weakened by my physical state but feeling inordinately stronger for his love.

Eventually, reluctantly, we part ready to face his father once more.

Anton draws me against his chest as my arms slide around his waist. Erik and Ivan step aside, revealing Viktor who stands at the open door. Outside the night sky is dark and oppressive. But I'm not afraid of the man who looks at me with deep hatred. I refuse to let him scare me.

"This isn't over," he snarls, his voice hoarse, raw.

"Yes, it is." Erik crosses his arms, stepping forward. "Get the fuck out. Next time we won't stop him. Next time we'll help."

Viktor nods, a strange kind of acceptance passing across his features before he grips hold of the door frame. I'm sure I'm not the only one to notice how he holds on so tightly. His knuckles white.

"Erik, I came here to tell you that your mother is dying. She's *dying*," he chokes out, and for a moment the tiniest flicker of pain flashes across his face before he shuts it down quickly.

Erik stiffens, but that's the only outward reaction he allows himself.

"Then you'd better return to her, Viktor, because not one of us will be following you to do the same."

With nothing left to say Viktor walks out, the front door slamming shut behind him.

WE SIT TOGETHER in the parlour. A fire has been lit in the hearth, but I can't seem to get warm. Curling into Anton's side,

I stare at the flames sparking and cracking, consuming the logs.

Erik is standing by the fire, his hands sunk deep into his pockets. Ivan is by his side, his hand resting on Erik's shoulder. A comforting gesture that warms my heart even when the cold harsh reality of the last few weeks begins to set in. Ms Hadley had tried to kill me, and Anton's father had been behind it. Their hate for me is overwhelming. I've no idea what I've done to deserve it.

"At least I don't have to kill her myself, the cancer should do a good enough job of it for me," Erik mutters, finally giving us an insight into his thoughts. I know he hates her right now, but I'm not fool enough to think that there's no love left for her. She was his mother, she brought him up, and in her own twisted way loved him fiercely. I don't condone her behaviour, and god knows I despise her, but love isn't something you can switch off so easily, no matter how much you want too. I understand that all too well.

"Here's hoping," Ivan responds, his own voice dark and contemplative.

All three of them have been quiet, thoughtful, and I've not had the energy to start the conversation we must have in order to move on from this.

"Could this all be some elaborate ploy?" Erik asks for the third time since Viktor left.

"I wouldn't have put it past them both. But there's no denying it's true, Erik," Anton responds heavily.

After Viktor left, Erik made some calls. Ms Hadley has stage four metastatic breast cancer and all I can think is that I'm glad. I can't summon up any sympathy for the woman who tried to destroy us. It doesn't matter who the true mastermind behind it was, she lifted the gun, she took aim and fired. That witch is going to get her comeuppance in the worst possible way, and I don't have an ounce of empathy for her. Not one tiny bit.

But I hurt for Erik, for them all. Betrayed by the people closest to them, they're left reeling, cast adrift and now it's up to me to give them purpose, to provide them with shelter and security. I can do that. I *will* do that.

"Erik, will you sit with me?" I ask gently, shifting on the sofa.

Anton eases his arm from my waist, then gets up. "I'm going to ask Fran to fix us some supper. None of us have eaten all day. I'll be back in a second."

"I'll go," Ivan says. "There's something I need to grab from my room anyway." He glances at me, smiling tightly, stress tightening his jaw.

"You okay?" I ask. A stupid question, of course. None of us are okay.

"I will be," he responds cryptically, before heading out of the room.

I watch him leave, worry fizzing in my stomach. This afternoon has taken its toll and I know they're all finding it hard to keep it together. Ivan needs Domina, he's desperate for her and I feel helpless not being able to help him right now.

"He'll be alright, we all will," Anton reassures me.

Despite almost losing Anton to something he wouldn't have been able to come back from he's holding up well considering. I felt his rage, his anger. I understood it. We all did. But I'm grateful he had the strength to pull himself back from a future that would've left us all broken. Somehow, he's holding it together better than all of us.

"Erik, sit down. Take comfort from the one woman who has

the power to keep us together," Anton urges him wrapping an arm around his shoulder. "Come on, man."

I watch as Anton manoeuvres him towards the sofa. Erik lets him.

"Rose, I'm going to check on Ivan."

"Thank you," I respond.

"Be right back." He presses his lips on the top of my head, but I reach up to him and grasp his face pulling him in for a deep kiss. I'm so proud of him, of how he's dealing with everything.

"What was that for?" He asks when I eventually let him go.

"Just because, Anton."

He gives me one of his panty-melting smiles, then leaves us to talk.

The moment Anton leaves the room, Erik slumps forward, his head in his hands, a long painful moan falling from his mouth. He's tried so hard to keep himself together, to show us he isn't affected by the news, but of course he is. I know him better than he thinks, we all do.

"This is on me, Rose," he blurts out.

"What are you talking about?" I reach for him, my fingers gently stroking his back. He flinches at the touch, snapping his head upwards, a dark look looming in his eyes. I pull away sharply, recognising what's just beyond the thin resolve. The monster is there, waiting for the opportunity to bare its face. Still it haunts him, patient to the last.

"I'm sorry," I murmur, realising my mistake.

"No! Fuck, Rose. Don't apologise for trying to comfort me," he retorts, grabbing my wrists and drawing my cupped hands to his lips. He kisses each palm with reverence. "I'm just on edge right now. Too much to take in…"

"You think this is your fault, don't you?"

"It is," he responds tightly, still gripping hold of my wrists.

"You aren't responsible for their actions."

"Her love for me has forced her to do these things."

"No. Her jealousy has done that. Love is inherently giving, Erik. It might be painful sometimes, but it isn't selfish. Love has always been used as an excuse to perform the most heinous acts, but that *isn't* love. It can't be. Don't be fool enough in thinking that her love for you has caused her to act this way."

"Viktor used her to get at you, *us*. Why?"

"Power, control, ownership. Who knows what goes on in his head?"

Erik's hands grip a hold of me tighter, his thumbs pressing into the thumping pulse of my wrists as though checking I'm still alive, still actually here with him.

"But I want to own you too, Rose. Doesn't that make me the same as Viktor? Her?"

I shake my head fiercely. "No. You are nothing like them."

"You're wrong," he responds gritting his jaw and sliding his hands up my arms, gripping my shoulders, his fingers curling into my flesh. "I look at you and I *want* to own you. I want to control your desire and eek out your pain and pleasure. I want to bottle it up and binge on it for days on end. I want your submission, Rose. I want to hear the whimpers of your lust as you beg for release. I want you at my mercy... *Goddamn it*."

Letting out a soft laugh, the tenseness I've held in my shoulders relaxes at his words. Honestly, it's good to hear them and rather than striking fear in my heart, all I feel is a sense of belonging, *relief*.

"Tell me what you feel when Ivan and Anton touch me, Erik."

His eyes snap to mine at the question, searching my face.

"It's okay," I reassure him. There is nothing he could say that would stop me from caring about him. Nothing.

"On the surface, *lust*, Rose. It turns me the fuck on. I might want to dominate you but there is nothing sexier than watching those two bastards give you everything you deserve..."

A smile pulls up my lips at that, perhaps there's a little of the voyeur in Erik too.

"But beneath that," he continues, "*Envy*, because unlike me they're no longer inhibited by their fucked up pasts... Not in the same way I still am."

"And," I persist, knowing there's more. There must be.

"*Happiness*, Rose." He laughs at that, a little surprised by it. "I'm happy they have you. I'm happy *I* have you. That isn't a feeling I've experienced for a very, very long time."

"Now answer me this; would you destroy that happiness for selfish reasons? If you thought you could have me all to yourself, would you destroy what we have to get it?" I'm taking a risk here asking this question, but my gut tells me he would never betray his best friends. It isn't in his nature, in any of theirs.

"No, never." He lets out a long breath, relief softening the tenseness in his jaw. "*Never*," he repeats vehemently, searching my gaze, needing me to believe him.

"Then you are the man I've always believed you to be; loyal, courageous, strong. You can own me in the bedroom, Erik. You can control me and dominate me to satisfy your needs, my own but that isn't the same as wanting ownership of every part of me including my feelings for your best friends, or my life. You're giving by nature, accepting of us as a whole. You're selfless *not* selfish. You're nothing like Ms Hadley or Viktor. *Nothing*," I repeat, hammering my point home.

For a beat Erik just looks at me with admiration and awe.

Then he slides his hands over my shoulders and up my neck, cupping the back of my head before pressing his forehead against mine. "*Thank you*, Rose," he utters, his fingers gripping onto my hair.

"I'm only telling you the truth," I respond, smiling against his lips. "We promised each other in that glass cage that we'd always be truthful, and I *will* keep that promise. I will remind you everyday of the man I know you are if that's what it takes for you to shred this self-doubt. When you look in the mirror, I want you to see what I see and not the image of a man who once had the power to inflict such violence. You're a warrior, Erik, just like Ivan, just like Anton, just like me. That's *why* we belong together. That's why I…"

My breath is snatched from my lips, swallowing the words I was so ready to utter as Erik crushes his lips against mine. He steals my heart and sears my soul with his kiss. Like two warriors, battle worn and weary, we hold onto each other finding strength and a home in each other's arms. When we pull apart, both of us are ready to face the oncoming war.

CHAPTER 9

IVAN

Rose joins me in Svetlana's studio a few hours after I left her. Erik carries her into the room, Anton following them in with a tray of food. Despite having every intention of heading to the kitchen to request supper from Fran, I'd found myself returning here, a nagging sense of wrongness cleaving a hole in my chest despite Anton's efforts to get me to return to the parlour and the comforting arms of Rose.

Now he's returned bringing them both with him.

"I brought food. We've already eaten," Anton explains.

"I'm not hungry," I reply. There's no way I can consume food in this room, has he forgotten what happened here? Because I sure as fuck haven't. My mind has been going into overdrive thinking about what Viktor said, what Ms Hadley had done to Rose on his behest.

"Ivan, you should eat…" Erik begins, then stops when he sees my fingers graze over the darkened spot on the floor beneath me. We look at one another, and I feel a dark oppressive cloud looming overhead. It's been a while since I've felt this way, and I hate the fact I'm the one to break first.

"Leave the tray outside, Anton," I growl, casting my gaze downwards, not willing to argue the point further.

I don't look up as Erik approaches me, Rose now supported by his side. Right now, I can't look at the woman I put in danger because of my love for her, *our* love for her. She isn't safe with us. Viktor made a promise I know he has every intention of keeping. He's nothing if not a man of his word.

He always keeps his promises.

My thoughts stray to Svetlana and the day I found her bleeding out on this very floor.

Broken, ruined, *dying*.

So much death. So much pain.

Viktor had always been supportive of our relationship, the perfect prima ballerina and her talented husband, but it came at a price. Over the years of our marriage, he flaunted us to his colleagues and friends, doted on Svetlana and yet... I swallow hard, bile rising up my throat.

There had always been a measure of control with Viktor. He had no hold over me other than the fact I'd known him most of my life, but he had used the both of us as a tool to impress people. In the beginning, I'd gone along with it because I was too preoccupied with the highlife as a world renowned ballet dancer and everything that comes with it; the adoration, the women. But I also remember the arguments between Viktor and Svetlana when she'd refused to attend some dinner or other event he insisted we went along to. I always stuck up for my wife, supported her need to hide away from the public eye. It's why I bought Browlace Manor eventually, to get away

84

from the circus Viktor had always wanted to drag us into. Towards the end of her life, Svetlana refused Viktor more and more…

My chest tightens as panic seeps into my veins.

Could Viktor have played a part in her death too? Could Ms Hadley? It's not beyond the realms of reality that they had. We know what Ms Hadley is capable of and Viktor has shown that he's twisted enough to fuck with other people's lives. Svetlana might have slit her own wrists but he's always had a way with words. He's fucking *cruel*. Anton can attest to that. Add my infidelity to the mix and the fact that, for the most part, I wasn't home much towards the end, there was plenty of opportunity for Viktor and Ms Hadley to mess with her head. I was too busy fucking other women whilst Svetlana's mind went to dark places.

Fuck!

My fist slams into the hardwood of the floor. I wasn't there for her. I didn't protect her. I was a fucking bastard just as much as Viktor.

"I'm so sorry, Svetlana," I say, my hand pressing against the stain of her blood.

The days that followed her suicide might be a blur, but that night is seared in my memory. I'll never forget it. Even now, even after all this time, that night is as clear to me as the dark stain of blood beneath my fingers now. There was so much blood. I remember the sheer and utter disbelief seeing her lying on the floor, her white dress stained red, and the blind panic that followed. I didn't know how to help her. Perhaps I could've saved her?

Then I remember the gut-wrenching, soul-stripping pain and the *guilt*. The years and years of guilt. There's no way I'd survive Rose's death. The threat of harm makes me want to rip the world to shreds. I should've let Anton strangle his father. I should've fucking helped.

"You didn't come back, Ivan," Rose says softly, her bare feet just inches from my fingers. She stands on the periphery of the stain, the creamy skin of her ankles in stark contrast to the darkened wood.

"I needed a moment. I'm sorry," I apologise, hearing the hurt in her voice.

"May I have a chair please, Anton?" she asks my best friend.

I keep my head lowered as he moves about the room. A few seconds later, Rose is seated before me, Erik and Anton by her side.

"Look at me, Ivan. Tell me what you're thinking," she presses, seeking out my darkest thoughts, never afraid to face them head on.

Only her, only Rose can pull me out of the shadows. I raise my gaze to meet hers, flinching at the sorrow I see within her eyes. In the half-light of the room I notice the dark circles surrounding her meadow-green orbs and the exhaustion that has become a constant in her life now. She may be mentally strong, but she's physically weak and my instinct is to protect her from my dark thoughts and the pain that voicing them might inflict.

"Ivan, talk to us," she insists, worry pulling her lips into a frown that makes my heart sink like a fucking rock. As much as I want to protect her from the truth, I know I can't, shouldn't.

"It's Svetlana," I say, running my fingers over the stain. I can almost feel the warmth of her blood as though she's right here beside me bleeding out and not buried in the grounds of Browlace. Two years ago she'd died right here and until today

I'd believed it had been solely my fault. Her actions caused by my infidelity. Now, I'm almost certain that I wasn't the only one responsible for her death.

"It's just us, Ivan. Don't be afraid," she urges, reaching for me.

I feel the gentle touch of her fingers against my lowered head. Her presence gives me the courage to voice my fears. Heartache and pain overridden by a deep sense of loyalty to the woman who changed everything for me, for us.

"What if…" I find it impossible to voice my fears as a memory of that time flashes before me. Curled up on her side, blood drenching her white dress. Her skin so pale, her lips blue. Her eyes lifeless.

"What if," I choke out, not able to finish my train of thought. I look up at Rose pleadingly.

"Ms Hadley and Viktor had something to do with her death…" she finishes, always able to voice the most difficult of things.

Her words and my thoughts thicken the air around us, and now they've been voiced I'm more convinced than ever that they're true. For the second time today, the four of us are shocked into silence.

"They wouldn't…" Erik says, eventually breaking the silence. His voice trails off as I look at him. He knows as well as I do that his mother is capable of the worst kind of evil and that Viktor is just as bad. Rose has a scar on her shoulder to prove it and Viktor has practically admitted to his part in the whole fucking thing.

"Why?" Anton asks. "Erik's *her* son, and as incomprehensible as it is to us, we all know that Ms Hadley's hate towards Rose is because she can't bear to lose him. Svetlana wasn't Erik's, she was yours, Ivan. And my father?

We all know he's a twisted fuck, but what would he gain from Svetlana's death? He doted on her, or at least it seemed that way?" he questions me, doubt spreading across his face like ink in water.

"Don't you see? Ms Hadley has been a surrogate mother to Ivan since he was a child as much as she was to both of you. Viktor has been in Ivan's life for just as long. Over the years Ms Hadley's love had twisted into something ugly, and we now know that Viktor seemingly held all the strings, like some fucked-up puppet master. Why, I don't know, but he did, *does*," she corrects herself.

"Because he likes to control everyone, and everything. He always has," I sigh, everything falling into place. He lost control of Svetlana and as a result she became worthless to him.

"Yes," Rose agrees heavily. "You loved Svetlana, Ivan, and because of that she became a target. We have no proof other than gut instinct, but if we're right and Ms Hadley murdered Erik's mother, then it isn't too much of a stretch that she would be capable of killing Svetlana too, or at the very least be coerced into pushing her into suicide by a man we know has the capability of making Ms Hadley do whatever the fuck he wants. I don't trust that man anymore than I trust Ms Hadley."

"So you've come to the same conclusion too?" I ask Rose, my heart hardening with the knowledge. Rose might not know all the details about how Viktor had used Svetlana and I to progress his own businesses or that, towards the latter years of our marriage, how Svetlana had refused to kowtow to Viktor's demands, but she's smart. Rose knew of our marriage, we were the darlings of the ballet world and in the public eye a great deal. I'm betting that if we were to search hard enough Viktor would be in the background of some of those photographs taken of Svetlana and I at the many social events he dragged us along too. He liked the notoriety of being seen with us, just as much as all the other fuckers who used us to their own gain.

"I believe somehow between them, it's a very real possibility they could've had a hand in her death. We all know she was vulnerable because of what you..."

"What I did to her. It's okay, Rose, you can say it. I'm not innocent in this either. I'm just as fucking guilty."

I didn't protect her from Viktor. I didn't protect her from Ms Hadley, and I sure as fuck didn't protect her from myself.

Her shoulders sag with the weight of that truth. "I'm sorry, Ivan. I'm so, so sorry. When you're in a dark place a few twisted words can do a lot of damage..."

"Fuck!" Erik exclaims, dropping to his knees beside me. He wraps his arm around my shoulders, hauling me against his side. Anton joins us, falling to his knees too.

"I'm sorry, brother," he murmurs, holding on tight.

More lies, more deceit, more fucking secrets.

The more I think about it, the more I know it to be true. I have no evidence. I have nothing concrete that will confirm the worst possible scenario, but I know in my godforsaken heart that Ms Hadley and Viktor had a hand in killing my wife, and the only way to know for sure is to ask. Because although this house is filled to the brim with the lies Ms Hadley has weaved, although it creaks and groans, a mournful lament to us, the men who live inside its walls, it can't tell us what we need to know. Svetlana's memory, and the truth of her death is buried within the foundations, haunting the rooms she passed through when alive and staining the floor beneath us now. All of it is a constant reminder of the violence of her death and the secrets and lies that hide the truth from us.

In a moment of clarity, I know what must be done. If we

are to move on from this, we need to confront Ms Hadley before it's too late. We may be walking into a trap, some kind of far-fetched plan to destroy us all, but I know myself enough to know that I won't rest until I find out the truth one way or the other.

But there's something we must do first.

Reaching into my pocket I pull out my flip-knife. It's the same one I found Svetlana with. The same one I've used to cut my own skin over the years. Beside me, Erik and Anton withdraw slightly, uncertain as to where this is going, but they'll understand soon enough. I flip the blade open, running my finger over the blunt side.

"When we were kids, we made a pact. Do you remember it?" I ask Anton and Erik.

They both nod solemnly, understanding dawning. We had been fourteen, drunk and high on weed after Viktor had ridiculed Anton in front of his colleagues. As I recall, Anton had skipped out of his home dragging Erik along with him and met me at the local park. He told us what happened between lungsful of marijuana and mouthfuls of vodka. That night we became blood-brothers bonding over heartfelt words and the illicit taste of alcohol and drugs.

"What was it, the pact?" Rose asks, interrupting my thoughts. Her gaze flicks between the three of us and the knife. Her expression is curious, though a little fearful. I don't believe she's afraid of me hurting her, but more that I might hurt myself.

"We vowed to remain loyal, to always have each other's backs and to never let anyone come between us," Erik murmurs, watching me carefully. He tenses beside me, and even though I know he understands what's about to happen here, he's still readying himself to grab the knife should I try to do anything stupid. Always the soldier, the protector in so many ways. Which makes it so fucking sad that he wasn't able to protect himself from Ms Hadley, from his tormentor, from my father.

"We vowed to be honest with each other even if we couldn't be honest with ourselves, and above all else, we vowed to love each other. Pretty poetic for a bunch of drunk fourteen year olds," Anton continues, smiling at the memory. His face is littered with memories, the same as Erik. We've spent our lives as brothers and even now all these years later the pact remains.

"It's a good pact," Rose responds with a smile even though her eyebrows pull together in question. "The knife worries me though."

"Don't let it. Despite what I believe happened here, I'm strangely calm, Rose. It's an odd sensation, honestly," I say, wondering when the fallout will happen, when I'll buckle. Maybe I'm still hoping I'm wrong... I don't know.

"You're in shock," Rose says. "We all are... Put the knife down, Ivan." She reaches for me, but I shake my head.

"Don't be afraid, Rose. This isn't like the last time we were in this room together. I might be about to slice open my skin but not for the reason you think."

"Then why?" she asks, observing me as I peer up at her.

"A real pact can't be made without an exchange of blood. Today, we extend the pact to you, the woman we've chosen, the woman we *love*." I allow that word to permeate the air that's thick with tension. She needs to understand the depth of emotion that I feel for her, that we feel. "Do you trust me?" I ask, taking her hand in mine, the knife hovering over the fleshy skin of her palm.

She doesn't hesitate. "Yes, without any doubt."

"Good." I press a kiss into the palm of her hand before

quickly sliding the tip of the knife over her flesh. Blood pools immediately as she winces from the sudden slash of pain.

"Anton, Erik," I say, reaching for each of them in turn. They hold their palms up and I cut them both. Erik cups Rose's hand in his, Anton settles his palm over hers. Then I slash my own palm, placing my hand in a fist above them. Erik and Anton both look at me, then nod urging me to say the words we swore to each other all those years ago. Three boys who found a family with one another, now three men kneeling at the feet of their queen, *the one*.

"In the darkness when the lights go out," I start.

"When pain haunts our dreams and distance keeps us apart," Anton continues.

"We make an oath to always have each other's backs, to remain friends, brothers, *family*... until our last breath, " Erik finishes. He catches my eye, a glimpse of the boy I once knew dancing in his eyes.

"Finish it," he demands.

Turning my attention to Rose, I drop the knife, and cup their hands between mine, our blood mingling as I extend the pact, making a vow to the woman we love.

"Rose, you found us at our most broken. You dived into the darkness and you fucking absorbed it. You fought for us like no one has ever done before. Anton knew from the moment you came into our lives that you were the one, the only one who could save us from ourselves, to bind us together. He may not be right about many things, but he was right about that," I say, pulling laughter from Anton's lips and a smile from everyone else.

"This pact may have been made by three childish teenagers, but what comes next are the words of three men who love you completely, utterly, and without restraint."

She smiles tumultuously, her lips quivering, but there are no tears, just a deep sense of wonder in her eyes. "And now we extend this pact to the woman who completes us. The woman who danced into my life and helped me to see the truth of my heart," I say, dropping my gaze and submitting to her dominance.

"Who stepped into the darkness and filled it with colour," Anton adds.

"Whose strength and truth humbled me…" Erik murmurs.

"Rose, you're the one, the *only* one and we vow to protect and love you above all else, forsaking all others until our last breath," I finish, feeling inordinately stronger for it.

We are all silent as we watch our blood drip onto the floor below. It seeps into the cracks joining Svetlana's and marking a new step in our relationship, our future. I couldn't love Svetlana how she deserved. I couldn't protect her heart, couldn't protect *her*. But I won't make the same mistake twice and god forbid anyone who tries to harm what we have and take what is ours. Not this time.

After a minute or two, Rose cracks a wobbly smile, easing her hand out from between ours. She curls her fingers into a fist and holds it against her chest, wincing a little at the sting.

"If I didn't know any better, I would think we just got married," she says, her voice mixed with mirth and a heavy dose of emotion.

We all laugh, but not one of us denies it. This is a vow after all.

CHAPTER 10

ROSE

A week passes. In that time, I learn to use my crutches better and my knee and shoulder pain ease with every passing day from the strengthening exercises my new physio, Alicia, has taught me. The swelling is all but gone and the bruise is now turning an ugly shade of green with unsightly patches of yellow, turning my skin from black and blue to the same sludgy colour of the pond I stand before now.

Across my palm the cut is healing, the skin knitting together slowly. I'm hoping it will leave a scar so that I have a reminder every day of the vow we made together, the pact. To an outsider, it may seem a ridiculous thing to do, but it *has* strengthened us. It has secured the foundations of our relationship into something infinitely stronger, unbreakable. And God only knows we need that strength now.

"Thank you, Alicia," I say, smiling at my physio as she helps to ease me onto the bench and hands me a cup of coffee.

I'm feeling particularly crappy this morning and we both decided a bit of fresh air was needed to revitalise me. I'm pretty certain what I actually need involves the three men inside locked with me behind a bedroom door, but circumstance and other factors- namely a vicious old woman and a wretched businessman- have made that impossible right now. Their heads are elsewhere, and I can't blame them for it. I feel the same way.

"Not a problem, Rose. It might be colder than a penguin's arse out here, but you need a bit of fresh air. Being cooped up inside is the last thing you need. I'll stay with you for a bit, then I'll let one of the lads know you're out here, or I'll walk you back in. Either way, I won't let you turn into an icicle."

"Don't let them hear you call them *lads*, might hurt their egos a bit," I say, grinning. They're definitely men, I can't even begin to imagine them ever being laddish at a younger age. Though given the pact they made to one another, I know that they were just as fiercely loyal and intense back then as they are now. It's just as well, that's the way I like them.

"Pretty sure their egos would only take a bashing if *you* were to call them a name they didn't like. Ever done that, you know, in the bedroom?" she winks, already sussing out our unusual set up.

I can't help but grin, but I don't elaborate any more than that.

"You can't blame a girl for trying," she laughs, taking a sip of her tea.

We sit in comfortable silence for a while, watching the swans float across the lake. It may feel as cold as the arctic, but the lake hasn't frozen over which is a good thing because I'd hate for the swans to leave. It seems such a long time ago now that I stood here with Ivan having a conversation about the ballet Swan Lake. That day things fell into place for us both, and it has been a rollercoaster ever since. One I'm never going to get off no matter how tumultuous the journey might be.

"This place is beautiful," Alicia murmurs. "Pretty cool set up you've got here."

"It is, isn't it?" I agree.

Alicia is probably the nicest woman I've met. Well, girl really. I'm betting that she's not much older than twenty. But despite her young age, she has wit, charm and a sharp personality that matches her wild hairdo and makeup. Alicia is all the colours of the rainbow, from her pink and blue streaked hair to her purple eyeshadow, nose ring and customised trainers that poke out from beneath her scrubs. Ivan thinks she looks like a rainbow gone wrong, and from afar Erik thinks she's just plain odd, though he hasn't got close enough to really make a decision either way. Anton humours her, laughing at her terrible jokes whilst keeping me company through most of her visits. Today, he's locked himself away in his studio working on a piece he wishes to keep secret for now, and both Ivan and Erik are attending to business, so it's just been the two of us.

I'm not going to lie; it has been nice having a bit of female company. Besides, I like her, and beneath all the colourfulness of her clothes and personality she really is a very pretty, sweet girl. It's just as well then that my men are in love with me and she's young enough to be their daughter.

I smile at that, the knowledge of their love warming me far better than this thick woollen coat does. Alicia wraps her black hoody tightly around her, then turns to me, her brown eyes bubbling with mirth. She cocks an eyebrow.

"Spill it, ballerina," she jests, nudging me with her elbow.

"Spill what? I'll have you know this is the finest coffee

money can buy and I'm not about to spill a drop of it," I retort with a smirk.

She huffs, a blast of warm breath making little white clouds release from her mouth.

"Look, I get it. You've only known me a few days so you're not willing to dish the dirt on your set-up here and honestly you don't have to share a thing, I wouldn't be offended. But, unbeknownst to you I'm not unfamiliar with this kind of relationship or from being loved by more than one man. It's quite a feat to juggle them all, but women are the best damn multitaskers, so pulling it off ain't all that hard." She looks at me with a cocked eyebrow, her own eyes sparkling with mirth and secrets of their own.

"You mean..." This time I do manage to spill some coffee. Thank goodness for my thick woollen coat. "You're too young..." My voice trails off as I realise how *old* that makes me sound.

"Don't look so surprised, Rose. I might be young, but the shit that's happened has meant I've had to grow up, and fast. A life in care will do that to a kid. I was just lucky enough to fall in love whilst doing it," she shrugs, smiling over the rim of her cup.

"I know how that feels. Growing up fast, I mean." My childhood and my innocence were lost the moment I got involved with Roman. But a life in care? I can't imagine what it'd be like to grow up in those circumstances.

"Yep, life sure does stink sometimes...For a long time it did for me, until four years ago when I went to Oceanside. I'd thought that going to a reform school for a bunch of misfits would mess me up for good. It didn't." She lets that statement hang in the air before shrugging it off with a grin. Happiness seems to be a permanent state for Alicia, which is very refreshing given the small snippets of her past that she's shared with me.

"And those boys, are they still in your life?" I ask, curious to know.

"Yep, still here. Still mine," she grins, squeezing my arm. "Perhaps one day I'll introduce you to the four of them."

"Four?"

"Yep, with youth comes energy. Can't help it if I'm overflowing with it." She wiggles her eyebrows and we both burst out laughing. It's a sound I've not heard for a while.

"So, how did you get into physiotherapy…?" I don't say it out loud, but she understands the question that's hidden beneath this one. How does a girl who attended a reform school end up in this kind of profession? Her eyes darken a little, intriguing me further. In that brief glimpse, I see a past riddled with hurt and difficulty. I sense a kindred spirit in Alicia.

"Let's just say a couple of my *misfits*," she says, with a wry smile, "Had a bad habit of getting themselves involved in crap they shouldn't. That crap led to a lot of… injuries. I became the person to help get them through those times. Set me up for this job pretty nicely actually and it gave me something to focus on at Oceanside other than four boys who messed with my head before finally listening to their hearts."

"Sounds complicated," I respond. So, it hasn't always been rainbows and smiles then.

"Yep, complicated pretty much sums us up and I wouldn't have it any other way, but perhaps that's a story for another time, yeah?" she responds, glancing at her watch.

"I'd like to hear it," I say, honestly.

She catches my eye and nods. "And I'd like to share it. I figure us ladies should stick together. Honestly, I'm made of tough stuff. Pretty sure you are too, Rose. Growing up the way I have has made that an inevitability, and most days other people's snarky comments are like water off a duck's back, but living in such a small village makes it hard sometimes."

"I hear that," I agree. "I've probably got the nosiest neighbour in the whole of Cornwall. It's just as well that I'm holed up here and don't have to face her judgement."

"I'd stay here if I were you... pretty sure those lads would love it."

"I've no intention of returning home... I've just got to figure out what to do with my place."

Alicia turns to look at Browlace, a dreamy look passing over her features. "Me and the guys are working on getting a bigger home and eventually stop renting. But these things take time. One day soon, I hope," she says, her bright optimism back.

"I'm sure you'll make it happen," I say, already knowing that she's the kind of woman who will strive to get what she wants. "How did you end up in Cornwall? Your accent is very *London*," I say carefully, not wanting to offend her. I actually really like her accent. I'm also pretty sure she usually swears like a sailor but is on her best behaviour around me. This is her job, after all.

"I grew up in Hackney. We all did. This accent goes with the territory, *init*?" she jokes.

I laugh out loud. This girl is a breath of fresh air and exactly what I've needed to distract me from my current predicament and the heavy cloud that still hangs over us all. We all know that a confrontation is coming and we're not ready yet to face it.

"We moved here when things got a little messy back home..."

"You're not in trouble, are you?" I ask, suddenly worried that this sweet girl needs my help.

"Nothing we can't handle. You can take the kid out of Hackney, but you can't take Hackney out of the kid," she says by way of explanation.

"That's a little cryptic."

"That's all you're getting for now," she retorts with a wink. "Well, I'd better be off, Rose. I've got places to be. Don't do anything I wouldn't do."

"Wouldn't dream of it," I respond, a frown creasing my brow as I watch her walk back towards Browlace and Ivan, who's already on his way over. She holds her hand up for him to high-five as he strolls past, and to my delight he slaps his palm against hers, giving her a begrudging smile. There's something about Alicia that makes you see the world a little brighter than before. Her happiness is like a tonic, one we all so desperately need. I don't like to think that she's in trouble. I file that piece of information away, something to keep in mind over the coming weeks she'll be working with me.

Ivan sits down next to me with a look of bemusement on his face.

"What?" I ask, grinning.

"She's quite a character, that Alicia," he says, shaking his head and rubbing his palms together as though he can't quite believe he high-fived her like some teenager. He has a bandage wrapped around his hand, just like the rest of us. If Alicia noticed, she hasn't mentioned it.

"She sure is. I like her."

"Well, so long as she makes you happy, and gets you fit enough to walk without the damn crutches, then I'm all for her. Though, I swear if she refers to us as *lads* again I might just blow a gasket." He laughs, so I know he doesn't mean it.

Twining his fingers with mine, Ivan settles on the bench beside me. We both watch the swans glide across the pond. They stop in the centre bobbing together on the surface. The male cob leans over to rub his head against the female's long neck before she glides off gracefully, the cob following.

"Looks like she's the boss," Ivan remarks, drawing a smile from both our lips.

"Yep," I agree, with a light laugh.

Funny how a few short minutes with someone as upbeat as Alicia can change your outlook, but that lightness is short lived when Ivan breathes out heavily. I knew it was too good to be true. Our life is never straightforward, but then again why would it be?

"Erik's just received an interesting phone call..." He dithers, rubbing his thumb over the back of my hand rather than continuing.

"And?" I question, not liking the tone of his voice or his reluctance to tell me what the phone call was about. It must be bad.

"And someone from his past has just resurfaced."

I twist my body to face Ivan, not enjoying the look in his eyes one little bit. "Well?" I prompt, feeling impatient.

"It's Emmie. She'll be arriving tomorrow."

CHAPTER 11

ERIK

I wake up with a pounding headache, sleep yet again hard to come by. The only reason I've managed to get a few hours in was because I'd finally relented and snuck into Rose's bed. I've kept away, partly because I'm afraid I'll lose control around her, but also because she needs to heal completely before I let down my guard enough to be the man that she needs me to be and the man I want to be. Every day as she heals, so do I. My flashbacks might still be occurring, but I can manage them better with every passing day.

It's just my resolve, to not touch Rose until she's ready, that's waning.

God, I want her. It started as an ache and is now a sharp pain, the wound getting wider every moment I'm not holding her in my arms.

In her sleep she'd snuggled into my side, curling her body around my own. For a while I just lay there in shock at the normalness of it all. It's what I've been wanting, needing for years and it came at a moment I'd least expected. Eventually her soft breaths, her florally smell and comforting warmth meant sleep finally came. Now, as Fran walks in with breakfast, Rose is a little distant and not nearly as happy to see me as I'd hoped.

"Thanks, Fran," I mutter, watching her place the tray on the side table.

"No bother," she responds, glancing between us.

Out of the corner of my eye, I see Rose give Fran a grim look. They've become close and Fran already knows what such a look precedes.

"Want me to tell Ivan and Anton you're up?"

"Not right now. I want to talk with Erik in private. We'll meet them in the parlour in a little while before our *guest* turns up." Rose can't seem to help the sarcasm when it comes to Emmie and her imminent visit.

I get it. I too feel weird in my skin today. This isn't going to be easy for me, for any of us.

"Sure. Well, I'll leave you to it then," Fran says, bustling out of the room but not before giving Rose a look of her own. I'm pretty sure it's a look that says; *'go easy on him'*.

"Rose," I begin the moment the door shuts.

"Don't!" she responds, pulling back the sheets and sliding out of the bed. She hobbles towards the ensuite, not allowing me to explain. So much for her cuddling up to me in her sleep. Just goes to show she was pretty much unconscious when I slid into bed beside her. I had hoped she'd forgiven me for accepting Emmie's visit.

"For fuck's sake," I growl under my breath as she disappears inside the bathroom. I didn't *ask* Emmie to come. She sought *me* out, not the other way around. Frankly, I'm just as surprised and as shocked as Rose is. Emmie was the last person on earth I wanted to talk to, but she has something that might help us with Ms Hadley, or at least that's what she said. I'd wanted her to tell me over the phone, but she'd insisted she had to come and see me in person. I must admit that curiosity and a sick kind of fascination to see how the girl who'd broken my heart turned out had swayed my decision. But then again, I'm not entirely sure how I'm going to fucking cope with her in the same room as me, let alone listen to what she has to say. I hadn't considered that when I agreed for her to come. What I do know is that I need Rose on my side, because I can't fucking do it without her. I can't.

Leaping out of bed, I stride over to the bathroom and push open the door. Rose is struggling to get herself undressed, hopping on one foot and cursing under her breath at the same time.

"What are you doing?" I say gruffly. "Let me help."

"I can manage perfectly well on my own, Erik," she snaps, ignoring me and nearly toppling into the basin.

"Stop being so stubborn," I snap back, grabbing her by the arm and hauling her upright.

"I am not stubborn," she retorts, her cheeks rosy and anger blazing in her eyes.

"You're also being pissy."

She glares at me, yanking her arm out of my hold. "If you don't like it, you know what you can do."

"You're being intolerable, Rose. *Childish*. Snap out of it!"

Her nostrils flare, but this time she's not backing down.

"Childish? Intolerable?" she repeats, pressing her finger into my chest, whilst simultaneously sliding down her pyjama bottoms and somehow managing to wriggle out of them. I wonder if she realises that she isn't wearing any underwear. My cock stiffens, tenting my boxer shorts in response.

"Yes, all of the above. Jealous too, I might add."

Her mouth snaps open, then slams shut. She narrows her eyes at me. "And if I said an old flame I'd been in love with was coming to visit, how would that make you feel? I'm pretty sure you'd have trouble with it too. In fact, I'm more than positive you'd be a beast about it."

"You weren't truly in love with anyone before us, Rose. So, nope, wouldn't be jealous," I respond, this time holding in a laugh at the look of incredulity on her face. God, I never realised this kind of banter could be so much fun. She's always been so careful not to lose her shit around me, that doing so now is refreshing and a *massive* fucking turn-on. She's angry and feisty and I'm not losing my head in the slightest. Another huge step forward for me, for us both.

"Number one, that's not true, I *did* love Roman. You might not like that fact, *I* might not, but it's the truth."

Admittedly that cuts a bit, but the fucker's dead thankfully, and if he were alive it wouldn't be for long.

"Number two," she says, poking her finger into my chest, "Who said anything about me being in love with you all?" she huffs, leaning her pert arse against the sink and pulling off her t-shirt. Now she stands fully naked before me, and I see the spark of a challenge in her eyes. So, she knows exactly what she's doing then, provoking me like this. Our kind of dom-sub relationship was never going to be straight forward. She's too fiery, too headstrong to submit without a fight. And whilst I need her to submit to the punishment and the pleasure I dish out; I still need her to be strong enough to accept it. I like her fire. It's the kind of fire that heats me up without turning me to ash.

Folding my arms across my chest, I step backwards until my back hits the opposite wall. From this distance I run my gaze up and down her naked body lazily, before slowly meeting her gaze. The air is fraught with tension and lust, and I fucking adore her for distracting me like this.

"Number one, Roman is dead," I retort, mocking her just a little. Her nostrils flare and I have the sudden urge to wrap her hair around my fist and yank her to me. Instead, I continue to goad her, having way too much fun with this kind of banter. Is this what it feels like to be in a normal relationship?

"No shit," she retorts, spots of colour sitting high on her cheeks as she regards me. She's turned on, those rosy cheeks telling me as much as the sharp points of her nipples.

"Number two, you're not fooling any of us. Just because you haven't said the words like we have, doesn't mean it isn't true."

Rose huffs, muttering under her breath, mimicking me as she folds her arms across her chest, pushing her plump breasts together and forming a rather sexy cleavage that I have a very urgent need to lick or stick my cock between.

"You need to stop being so indignant and get over here," I say, opening my arms, expecting her to walk straight into them. When she doesn't, I frown.

"Why did you agree to her coming here, Erik?" she murmurs, her eyes dropping, evaporating all the fun from the room as she bleeds hurt and jealousy, her insecurities haemorrhaging.

I heave a sigh of my own. This wasn't exactly what I was expecting, but I've asked Rose to show me her truth time and time again, and I can't deny her my respect and my honesty when she bares herself so openly to me now.

"Various reasons, mainly because she has news about Ms Hadley, but also because I was curious to see how she turned out…" I admit, then wish I could take the words back when Rose flinches as though I've slapped her. "I didn't mean…"

"Save it," she retorts, trying to stride out of the room with dignity, but hobbling instead because her damn knee is still not healed enough to fully hold her weight.

"Wait!" I snap, a sudden flash of anger rearing inside of me now. Not anger at Rose per se, just angry at the situation and my stupid runaway mouth.

"Get out of my way, Erik," she mutters.

"No," I respond. Inside I can feel the part of me that's been kept at bay these past few weeks, rearing its ugly head. I reach out and grasp her arm realising I'm holding onto her tightly, but not able to release my grip.

"I've not given you permission to leave, Rose. So where the fuck do you think you're going?" I bite out, losing control of the situation and my emotions quickly.

"Screw you," she retorts under her breath, but she doesn't stop me when I haul her back against my chest. And she doesn't stop me when I rub my cock up and down the crack of her arse, only the thin material of my boxers separating us. My arm wraps around her waist and I lift her off her feet and place her before the mirror, lifting her chin so that she looks at our reflection. A flush of pink rushes up from her chest to her neck and cheeks, and I know I have her exactly where I want her. The pretty bloom of colour so like her namesake.

"Place your hands on the sink, Rose," I say, my voice lowering as I whisper the command into her ear. I bite her lobe, not once taking my eyes off her beautiful fucking reflection. Her body goes rigid, and for one awful moment I think she's going to deny me.

Then she lets out a whoosh of breath and nods, relenting to my will.

"I've waited long enough for this, Rose. I'm not going to wait a moment longer. Lean forward," I demand.

She slides her hands over the cold surface of the vanity unit, folding herself over the sink giving me a rather beautiful view of her plump, ripe arse and the pink slash of her pussy.

"Safe word," I grind out, barely able to restrain myself.

"Green…" she responds, a tiny smirk pulling up her lips as her eyes narrow at me.

I cock an eyebrow. "Because it's the colour of your eyes or the colour of your jealousy?"

"Both," she responds without apology.

"Green for jealousy it is then," I respond, grinning.

Running the flat of my palm over the curve of her arse, I enjoy this moment of tension before raising my hand and slapping it against her right arse cheek with a loud thwack.

Her body jolts forwards as she lets out a yelp, her creamy skin darkening a pretty shade of red with my handprint. My cock fucking leaps and it takes all my restraint to not yank off my boxer shorts and enter her with one hard thrust.

"You do know that you're mine, don't you, Rose?"

She doesn't answer me, and I punish her for it just like I know she wants. I've come to realise that silence is a weapon Rose wields to get us to bend to her will. A tiny smile flutters across her lips as a matching handprint blooms on her left arse cheek like two wings for my tortured angel.

"Do you understand what you are to me, Rose? You're my fallen angel. Broken and too dark to ever return to heaven, but strong enough to bear the weight of your sins and those sins of the ones you choose to love. You fucking lift me up, Rose, and I intend on doing the same for you."

She's fallen so many times that I find it incomprehensible that she's had the strength to pull herself up over and over again. Now that we're by her side, we'll always catch her when she falls. Every fucking time.

"I'm going to repeat the question. Do you understand that you are *mine*?"

Her head falls forward, as I slap her thigh this time, drawing a wave of goosebumps across her skin.

"Answer the question," I demand, pulling my boxers down, kicking them from my feet. My cock falls free, resting against her lower back between the two dimples that taunt me there.

"Until yesterday I thought I was. But now..."

"Emmie?" I ask her, my fingers trailing over the red marks, soothing the sting of my slap. I get just as much pleasure from soothing her pain as I do from inflicting it. She groans, pushing her arse back against me, searching for relief. Leaning forward, I adjust myself against her, my cock sliding against the slick wetness of her pussy but not entering; teasing and coaxing instead.

"Yes, of course Emmie. Who else?" she bites out, sarcasm bleeding from her voice between her moans of pleasure. That deserves another slap. Rose jerks forward, tensing with the pain then relaxing as I soothe her.

"You know that you're pushing it, Rose? Is that your intention or am I to expect this snarky side from here on out?" I stop my ministrations, withdrawing slightly. There are other ways to punish her.

Her head snaps up, a mixture of challenge, anger and acceptance in her gaze. "Look, you were right. I'm jealous, okay. I'm not proud of it, but I am."

"Jealousy is such an ugly sin, Rose," I remind her. She knows as well as I do the damage it can cause. I might tell her that she's mine, but she's also Anton's and Ivan's too. I accept that wholeheartedly. I'm not jealous of my brothers even though I would kill anyone else who tried to touch her.

My cock slides against her wet warmth rewarding her for her honesty.

"But you loved her *first*," she whimpers.

My heart fucking cracks whilst my soul soars. Rose is giving me her feelings readily, no longer bottling them up. Her honesty is a gift I intend on treasuring, but first she must understand what she means to me. Slamming my hand on the vanity unit next to hers, my fingers entwine with hers whilst I cocoon her body with my own.

"Look at me, Rose," I order. She lifts her head, her gaze meeting mine in the mirror whilst my free hand reaches around beneath her, searching for her sweet spot. I pinch her clit hard enough to draw out a squeak of surprise before I soften the shock with gentle rubs.

"Emmie means *nothing* to me, Rose…" I assure her, my voice a deep rumble of emotion. Even just feeling the warmth of her skin against mine is enough for me to blow my load. This woman turns me on like no other before.

"You've not seen her for years, you don't how you'll react when you see her now," she retorts, her face contorting between pain and pleasure as I pinch her clit again, then soothe the sting. She's so wet, that my fingers are covered in her juices.

"I tell you what I do know. I do know that she won't hold a torch to you. She won't make me feel inextricably strong, strong enough to walk out of a glass cage and strong enough to face my fears. And she sure as fuck won't make me feel weak for all the right reasons instead of the wrong ones," I say, rubbing more against her sleekness with my cock, not entering her but continuing to tease. Her wetness coats my dick and I feel a tingle work its way up from my balls. Jesus, she's going to ruin me.

"You can't possibly know that. You *loved* her..." she bites out, her head falling forward, the dark curtain of her hair covering her expressive face. I need to see her face.

"Don't hide from me," I grind out. Rearing backwards I grab Rose's hips and turn her around to face me. Pulling her roughly against me, my cock strains between us as I see the hurt brimming in her eyes.

"I *did* love her. I loved the girl she *was*, Rose. I stopped loving that same girl the second she betrayed me. Did you not believe me when I said that there was no one else on Earth that I would've walked out of that cage for except you?"

She presses her eyes shut, not allowing me to see the truth in them, the vulnerability, the fear that she might lose me to a girl from my past.

"Fucking look at me, Rose," I shout, not allowing her to hide from me now. Not like this. She opens her eyes, helplessness wallowing in them. I cup her face, holding on for dear life. "You are the only one for me, *understand?*"

She blinks, her jaw gritting.

"Understand?!" I repeat, sliding my cock to her entrance, teasing her there.

"Yes," she breathes, relief flooding her features. "Yes, I believe you."

"Don't ever fucking doubt my love for you again. I won't be so understanding next time," I warn her.

"Erik," she whimpers, clutching hold of me as much as I do her. "*Please...*"

Hooking her legs around my waist I finally give her what she wants, what I *need*, and slam into her, finding the only home I've always longed for right here in her embrace.

Our coming together is frantic, manic even and I skirt the edge of madness every single time our bodies part. I want to dive into her. I want to slide beneath her skin and stay there forevermore. I only feel safe, secure, *strong* with this woman. Even the thought of parting with her for a few seconds makes me panic.

"Rose!" I cry out, a hedonistic kind of frenzy taking over me as she submits herself willingly, needing my utter abandon as much as I need to release it. Supporting her with my arms and using the vanity unit to prop her up, I slam into her violently.

"Erik, don't stop," she utters, her voice as guttural as my own.

We move together in a frenzy, and for a time I forget about the fact she isn't yet healed. I forget about Ms Hadley, Viktor, fucking Emmie. Everything else disappears as I fuck her as though my life depends on it. She doesn't falter this time. She doesn't give in to her insecurities, or her fear of losing something so precious. Rose hangs onto me, welcoming every punishing stroke of my cock, every bruise-filled kiss and iron grasp on her body. I know my mark will stay on her skin for days to come, but I don't care. I want her to look in the mirror and see my handprints, see the level of passion and crazy I have for this woman.

How much *love*.

We make a mess of the bathroom until we fall, the two of us, together. An unending bliss opening within our chests, our two battered hearts beating the same tattered tune as we come.

CHAPTER 12

ROSE

Emmie arrives with another storm. It seems fitting somehow that this woman, who caused so much pain, is as dishevelled, fearful, and weary when she arrives as Erik has been since she screwed him over all those years ago. But whilst it blows a gale outside- the majority of Cornwall on an amber weather warning- inside I'm calm and ready to face whatever truth she's about to reveal. I'm not sure I can say the same for my men.

"Mrs Carrington is waiting in the parlour," Fran informs us, the top half of her body peeking around the door as though she's too afraid to fully step into the room.

"Thanks, Fran," I respond, given no one else seems able to. We're sitting around the dining table, lunch barely touched. Erik looks like he's about to throw up, and Ivan and Anton are stony-faced.

"Erik, you sure you can do this?" Anton asks, giving him a wary look.

Erik nods tightly. "I can do it, but I'll need Rose by my side at all times, okay?"

"You got it," I respond, gripping his hand.

"Whatever you need," Anton agrees.

Ivan pushes his seat back and stands. "Then I guess we should go hear what she has to say." He glances at me, the skin around his eyes tight. He's suffering right now and it's the first time I feel as though I wish there were more than one of me. I'm stretched thin, trying to be there for all of them is difficult to juggle. Ivan strides past, but I grab his arm, forcing him to stop.

"Are *you* okay?" I ask him, knowing full well that he isn't.

He presses his lips in a hard line, nodding sharply, trying to hide his feelings but failing.

"Ivan!" I warn.

He scrapes a hand through his hair. "Fuck, Rose. I need…"

"Domina?" I murmur, moving away from Erik for a moment.

"Yes," he admits, pressing his thumb and finger against his closed eyelids.

Grasping his face in my hands, I search his face. "Tonight, Ivan. Come to me tonight."

He breathes out slowly, tension releasing at the promise. Out of the corner of my eye I catch Anton watching us intently. I turn to him.

"You too." He hasn't come out of this unscathed and just because he appears to be handling the whole sorry state better than his best friends, doesn't mean that he is.

Anton licks his lips, then smiles slowly. "Can I bring my sketchpad?"

"You can do whatever you want as long as you're there." Our eyes meet, and though it isn't time for laughter and smiles, a glimmer of both are evident in his.

"Am I allowed to join the party?" Erik asks.

"That's up to you, Erik. But tonight Ivan needs Domina, I need to be her and she will *not* submit to anyone, not even you," I warn him. This is one line I won't cross. If Ivan needs Domina, that's what I'll give him. Erik cannot expect my submission in this circumstance.

"I understand."

Holding his hand out, I take it. "Ready?" I ask.

"As I'll ever be," he responds gravely.

The four of us leave the dining room and head to the parlour. Ivan and Anton enter first and when they stop abruptly before me, the sounds of their surprise filling the room, I get a sudden sick feeling in my stomach.

"*You're* Emmie?" Ivan says.

"Fuck," Anton mutters.

Squeezing between the two, Erik following behind me, I get a look at the woman who was once the girl that broke Erik's heart.

It's *Love*. The woman in the restaurant.

"You?" I whisper.

"Hello, Rose… Erik," she says, her gaze flicking between us both.

Behind me Erik stiffens, his hand crushing my fingers as he tries to maintain control.

"How do you know her name?" Erik asks, thrown by her familiarity.

"Besides meeting once in the restaurant in Kirkwall, the whole island now knows. There are some things the islanders like to keep hidden," she says grimly, looking at Erik. "And there are other things the gossip mongers spread like wildfire. I'm afraid you're the talk of Kirkwall. You *and* Rose," she explains, her cheeks flaming at his snort of derision.

"I see," I respond, when Erik can't or won't. "Idle gossip can lead to so much damage. I should know, I was the talk of this village for a long time when I was a teenager."

Emmie sighs, understanding flashing across her features. "Then we have that in common." She looks down, her fingers splaying over her wet jeans. "I was caught in the storm. The weather here is much worse than I've seen back home and that's saying something," she rambles. She grits her teeth, her body shaking with cold.

My gaze roves over this woman, and even though we've already met, I try to imagine the girl she was when Erik fell in love with her. She's attractive, still has a good figure, and seems to have a kindness in her eyes that doesn't fit well with the girl Erik had once described. But so much can change in the intervening years. I'm not the girl I once was, and I doubt she is either.

"Thank you for agreeing to see me," she says eventually, her cheeks flushing a deeper shade of red under our scrutiny. "I know this must be hard, what with everything…" her voice trails off as she swallows.

Behind me Erik curses. I squeeze his hand in mine then reach for him with my free hand, pressing my palm against his thigh, hoping it's enough to keep him grounded. He can't lose it now.

"I know I'm the last person you ever wanted to see again, Erik. I'm sorry if this hurts you…"

"Don't," he snaps, his resolve to remain calm fraying. "It's too late for that."

"Erik, if you can't do this, then you should leave," Ivan remarks, not afraid to say what we're all thinking.

"I'll be fine," he grinds out, his arm finding my waist as he pulls me back against him, using me as a shield between Emmie and the monster within him. I've faced it before and brought him back around. I can do it again.

"We appreciate you coming, but please excuse Erik if he finds it difficult to deal with this meeting… He's been through *a lot*." Anton says emphasising his point.

"I'm sorry for it," she responds, offering up her own apology for the part she played in his downward spiral. No one acknowledges her apology. I'm aware that it isn't fair to blame this woman for the mistakes of a child, but that's easier said than done.

Anton approaches Emmie first and offers his hand to shake. She takes it gratefully, some of the tenseness leaving her as he asks her to take a seat. She wraps her arms around her chest, turning her body slightly to the open fire to get warm.

Ivan looks at me, searching my face, then his gaze falls on Erik. I know he's trying to figure out whether Erik's strong enough to face Emmie, and whatever the fuck she's going to tell us.

"It's okay," I reassure him. "We've got this." We need a united front and Erik needs to know we trust him.

Ivan nods. "Stay over there, just in case," he says, motioning for us to stay put whilst he takes a seat next to Anton opposite Emmie.

She watches us all, trying to fathom what's going on. I imagine she has a lot of questions, especially about the glass cage and the fact that Erik was imprisoned in it, even if that imprisonment was self-inflicted. Whether Erik chooses to tell her is up to him, because there's no way any of us will.

"You said that you had something to say, something that was so important you needed to do so in person," Ivan starts, leaning forward a little in his seat. His body language tells me that he's just as interested in what she's about to reveal as Erik. Admittedly, now I've got over my own insecurities, I am too.

"I do. I came here to help. Ms Hadley... your mother, Erik, she's not a good person..." Her voice trails off at how obvious that statement is.

"No shit," he rumbles.

Emmie shakes her head and draws in a breath then looks directly at me. "I want you to know that I'm not here to get between you and Erik. I *love* Tim. I love him more than I've ever loved anyone." She pulls a face, wincing at that.

"There's no chance you'll be able to get between Rose and me, Emmie. I'm not the boy I once was."

"I can see that," she admits, a note of sadness in her voice. She pauses a moment as though deciding on what to say next. "I've spent years regretting my actions. I was a foolish child. A child that made a mistake. There isn't a day that goes by when I don't think about Layton, about what I did, about how I hurt *you*." She looks at Erik almost pleadingly, but he remains tight-lipped and steadfast behind me. His only reaction a tightening of his arms around my waist.

"I wrote a letter to you, Erik..." she leans over, fetching an envelope from her handbag. It looks old, the envelope torn a little at the edges, darkened with age. She places it on the table in front of her. "When I leave, I'd like you to read it. I wrote it a few weeks after you'd left the island. I should've posted it. I should've done a lot of things. I hope you can forgive me someday for my cowardice."

Her trembling fingers trail over the letter before she clasps them in her lap, looking directly at me.

"In the restaurant when I told you that secrets should stay that way for a reason, I had convinced myself that was preferable to the truth that could ruin lives. After all I'd kept my own secret for all these years. But the second I found out what Ms Hadley had tried to do, that she'd *shot* you, I knew I had to tell the truth no matter the cost. I owe Erik and Layton that much at least."

"Go on," Anton urges her, the rest of us unable to breathe, let alone able to prompt her to continue.

"I'd honestly thought you were a relative of hers, Rose," she continues. "I felt for you and the loss you portrayed so readily. I realised quite quickly after everything that came out about what happened in the outhouse that you'd lied too. Ms Hadley isn't your aunt, is she? You were there for Erik all along." Her eyes trail to his arms wrapped around me, and I nod.

"Did you know Erik was on the island?" I ask, tensing. Had she known that glass cage was for him? Had she turned a blind eye?

"No. I had no idea Erik had returned. Honestly, when Tim told me about the job, I didn't like to think about what that glass room was for, and I certainly would never have dreamed she had it built for Erik. Why would I? I hadn't seen or heard about Erik for years. As far as I was concerned, he was living his life somewhere far, far away from Kirkwall. Ms Hadley might've returned in the intervening years, but Erik never had."

"Okay," I respond, accepting her explanation. It might not be much, but somehow it makes me feel a little better about her as a person.

"As far as I was concerned you were there to find Ms Hadley, to heal a broken heart because you'd lost your father. That part about your father's death might not have been true, but you *had* gone there to heal a broken heart, hadn't you?" she says, smiling a little as she looks between us.

When I don't answer she continues.

"Only problem is, Ms Hadley has a way of breaking hearts, shattering dreams, destroying *lives*, actually, and I sent you right into danger. I won't forgive myself for that. Not now, not ever. I'd stupidly thought that perhaps I'd got it wrong, that perhaps she wasn't the woman I'd thought she was. The other islanders seemed to accept her and despite knowing I still lived on Kirkwall she never sought me out. I tried to warn you, Rose..." she says, realising how lame that sounds.

"Emmie, you've beaten around the bush long enough. Just say what you've come here to say and put us all out of our misery," Erik snaps, losing his ability to remain cool.

Her eyes flick to his, the blue depths brimming with tears of regret and shame. "I should've told you everything years ago. I should've sent that letter. I'm sorry I didn't. Perhaps your life would've turned out differently, perhaps Rose would never have gotten shot."

"Emmie...!" Erik warns, making her flinch. He's trembling now with the effort of holding himself together. Both Anton and Ivan shift uncomfortably in their seats, ready to stop Erik should he lose himself to one of his episodes.

"I believe your real mum was murdered, Erik," Emmie rushes out.

Behind me Erik grunts, letting me go. I turn to face him as his body goes slack and he stumbles into my arms.

"Erik!" I shout, barely able to keep him upright.

Ivan rushes to my side, helping to prop him up. His expression crumples with pain, his face a deathly white. "It's fucking true, it's fucking *true*, Rose," he mumbles.

I slide my arm around him, ignoring the shooting pain in

my knee and pull him into my arms as Ivan helps to prop him up, just as pale and in shock as Erik is. Anton is the only one of the three who's able to maintain a level of emotional control. We look at each other, knowing that we can't hide from the truth a moment longer. Before today our theories had just been supposition, the four of us making assumptions based on the small snippets of information we'd gathered. Having an outsider confirm our suspicions makes it all too real and a thousand times harder to swallow. We're all reeling. This is going to change *everything*.

It takes a good ten minutes before Erik is capable of speaking. When he does, he addresses Emmie directly. "Tell me what you know, and don't leave a damn thing out."

She nods her head, clasps her hands together and takes us back to that summer of 1998.

CHAPTER 13

EMMIE – KIRKWALL, LATE SUMMER 1998

I return to the dilapidated cottage two weeks after Erik left with every intention of taking a knife to my wrists and slicing into the delicate flesh.

Death is my only choice now.

Because I *can't* live with what I've done. Layton is in a coma fighting for his life and it's all my fault. If I tell Erik about his mother and what's she's capable of then she'll tell my parents *everything*. The truth would kill them.

So, in keeping Erik's secret, I keep my own.

Clasping the penknife, I head towards the bedroom and shove open the door, it creaks under the pressure, paint flaking off in strips. This is where Erik and I came to have sex. It had been his first time. He'd been so gentle, so loving. He had *loved* me that night. The first boy who ever had, unlike all the rest.

The *rest*... I laugh out loud. The sound of my voice

hysterical now. Tears stream down my face in bitterness and self-hate.

Ms Hadley is right. I *am* the local whore.

I sleep around. When you don't get any attention at home, when your parents are too busy mourning the older brother they adored above all else, you seek attention elsewhere. Peter had died in a boating accident three years ago. My big brother lost to the ocean.

His body was never found, and my parents lost themselves right along with him.

Sitting on the mattress, I pull out the letter I wrote to Erik earlier.

My feeble apology is blurred behind the tears which fall freely now no one is watching.

"I'm sorry. I'm so sorry."

Laying down on the mattress I close my eyes, trying to breathe through the wracking sobs of my sorrow and guilt. The last few weeks' events playing out in my head.

Ms Hadley somehow found out about what I did, and with that knowledge has prevented me from ever telling Erik about the hand *she* played in this whole sorry tale.

If I were a better person, I'd send the letter. But I can't. My parents can never know what I did.

The life *I* took.

I'm not sure how long I lie on the mattress, the letter clutched in one hand, the knife in the other. Eventually I hold the blade up, watching as the moonlight glints off the sharp edge. Outside a wind whips up across the shore, the cold slipping through the broken windowpanes and gaps in the floorboards. The sound is a bitter reminder of the mistakes I made and the decision that has destroyed three young lives, mine included.

Four if you include my unborn child.

A year ago today, I aborted the baby that belonged to Layton and me.

Sixteen and pregnant. I couldn't keep it. I didn't want it; the responsibility, my parents' disgust and disappointment. They would have disowned me, and I would've had even less than I do now. So, I did the only thing I could. I got rid of the baby.

And somehow, *she* knew.

"Tell anyone what Erik did and we tell your parents about the child you murdered," Ms Hadley had spat. Her words tearing me open. I'd felt ashamed because she saw me as a whore, a harlot. I felt desperately sad because I didn't want the baby. I would've had an abortion even if I had my parent's support to bring the baby up. That's the cold, hard truth. It was a mistake and I have to live with the consequences.

"As far as you're concerned Erik did what he did in self-defence. Understand?" Mr Sachov had insisted.

But Erik *hadn't* beaten Layton to near death in self-defence, he did it out of jealousy and pain. Of course, that's not what Mr Sachov had told the police. Maybe he'd bought them like he'd bought my silence, a sweetener to soften the blow. Ten thousand pounds to buy my silence, and a threat to reveal the truth to make sure I'd never ever speak of what really happened between the three of us that night.

I'd taken the money, but I haven't kept it. That too is lost to the ocean.

Turning on my side, I run my hand across the mattress. I'd brought Layton here too. He and I have been friends since we were kids. We fell into a relationship last year, two equally fucked-up kids finding solace and comfort in each other's arms.

It was short lived. I found out I was pregnant when he left for a job on the mainland.

I aborted our baby. He never knew. No one did.

Or least that's what I'd thought.

But somehow Ms Hadley found out. She threatened me even before the night Erik beat Layton up. She warned me off her son. Arrogant, stupid, a foolish girl in love, I'd ignored her.

I shouldn't have, because now look at me. Look at us.

Layton is in a fucking coma.

Erik's heart is broken, his life changed forever. I'll never forget the look on his face after he finally stopped hitting Layton. He felt the monster within his heart as much as I saw it beneath the blood smeared across his knuckles and cheeks. That beautiful, kind, loyal boy turned into something dark and hateful because of *me*, because of *her*.

Now look at us, look at me. Ready to end my life for the part I played in it all.

The sad thing is, I did care about Erik. So much. But his mother had made it difficult for me to believe in his words of promise and love. She'd told me that I was just a fling, a dirty slut he only wanted to lose his virginity to. She drip-fed me the poison of her words, and with low self-esteem and an already pretty fucking poor image of myself, I'd begun to believe them. That was even before she threatened to reveal my abortion. We were doomed from the start.

When Layton had returned to Kirkwall a week before Erik was due to leave, it was all too easy to return to his arms. It was wrong. I regret it. But in my fucked-up head I sought out the only comfort I believed was available to a girl like me. A slut. A whore. A girl who aborted her baby returning to the arms of its father. Another boy she'd once believed could love her but who would only abandon her too. I should've admitted the truth to my parents, to Erik, to Layton. If I hadn't been such a coward, none of this would've happened.

I was stupid, foolish, hateful, cruel.

So fucking cruel.

"I'm sorry, Erik. I'm sorry, Layton," I wail unable to keep my guilt in a moment longer.

Sitting up, I fold the letter I wrote to Erik and tuck it in my pocket. Then hold the knife over my wrist, lowering it to the delicate skin. Pressing my eyes shut, I feel the sharp sting of pain as the blade cuts into my skin, but the sudden sound of voices stills my hand.

"You should've destroyed them years ago, Clara. What the hell do you think you're doing?"

"This is all I have left of her, us, Stefan."

My heart beats loudly in my chest as I realise who's just entered the house. Why are they here? I leap up, looking for somewhere to hide. If they find me, I'm in deep shit. Tiptoeing over to the window, I open the latch and climb out. My feet hit the soft earth and I crouch down, listening, my heart racing in my chest. I'm still holding the knife in my hand, the cut on my wrist bleeding. Fuck it hurts.

"This is ridiculous, Clara. You should've burnt those years ago."

"It's all I have left of us, Stefan!" she repeats, her voice laced with the tinge of madness.

I can hear them moving around, but my heart is pumping so hard, I'm pretty sure they'll be able to hear it if they get too close. So I remain where I am, teeth chattering from cold and fear.

"I've built a new life, Clara. You are still a part of it, be thankful for that. But hiding the evidence risks everything. My wife, my sons, they must never know the truth. There is too much at stake. My wife's family are not the forgiving type and I *need* their money to keep my business going. This is foolish, crazy."

"Wanting to remember our love, that is *not* crazy, Stefan. I may not be able to have you the way I want, but I will have this!" she shouts.

"You got what you wanted when she died, Clara. You have your son and we have each other."

"He's *your* son, not mine. Barren and worthless, I could never give you what you wanted," she responds, her voice cracking.

"Yes, he is my first born son and will always hold a special place in my heart. Frankly, he's worth ten of his younger brother who's way too much like his mother for his own good. But for all intents and purposes he's *your* son, Clara. I cannot be his father. Not now, not ever."

"You chose her, Stefan. She bore you a son. You grieved when she died, would you do the same for me?"

"Of course, I would. I love *you*, Clara."

"That's a lie," she spits, real pain in her voice now. "I was never good enough. Even then, you chose *her* and now I have to live a separate life whilst you're married to *another* woman."

"I was wrong back then. I should've chosen you. She was weak, pathetic, but I made the right choice in the end. I chose *you*. I *still* choose you. Clara, you *are* my heart," he cajoles, his voice soothing and laced in the kind of darkness everyone should fear. There's truth in it, but there are also lies. Lies so hurtful it's a wonder she doesn't feel the darkness of them too.

"I loved her," she says, a sob filling her voice. "She was my best friend."

"She's dead. You have what you want."

"I have her son, but I never wanted…"

"What? For her to die? Don't pretend to be innocent in all of this, Clara. We did what we had to do. If it comes out about who his real parents are, then her death will be questioned too. Don't fuck this up now," he retorts angrily, a little of the façade slipping. When she doesn't try to correct him, he continues.

"It's time to put the past behind us. Leave this place once and for all." His voice is cold with no feeling. But hers, she cries bitter, painful tears that surprise me. Sobs fill up the derelict house and burst out of the window until they're swallowed by the wind.

Who is she crying for? What did he mean that she wasn't innocent? What had they done? All I have are questions that I know I may never find the answers to.

"Hush now," he says, trying to soothe her. "Let it go, Clara. Be the mother she could never be. Forget about her, come home."

Silence falls and even though I know it's stupid, I peek through the window. In the shadows, the two people I've come to loathe are wrapped in each other's arms kissing passionately.

I feel *sick*. Too absorbed in each other they don't notice me watching them. My fingers grip the knife tightly. They don't deserve to be happy, to love each other this way when they've destroyed everything. But what can I do? I'm just a kid.

Eventually they part, and I watch as she bends down, pulling back a loose floorboard, tucking something inside. He stands watching her but says nothing further.

"Let's go *home*," he insists, taking her hand as they walk from the room.

I wait outside, still crouched beneath the window until I hear a car pull away. Once I'm certain they're gone, I climb back in. With my heart in my mouth, I creep towards the spot they've hidden their secret. A huge part of me doesn't want to look, whilst another more determined part needs to know what the fuck they're hiding. Bending down, I use my knife to pull back the loose floorboard then reach inside the darkened hole.

My fingers wrap around some paper, and I pull it out. I find a letter, and a photo. On the photo is a younger version of the two people who were wrapped in each other's arms, and a woman I don't recognise holding a baby.

Flipping the photo over I read the back. 'Clara, Stefan, Isabelle and Erik – 1980'

Erik?

With shaking hands, I open the letter, only it isn't a letter, it's a birth certificate and on it the truth of Erik's heritage. He wasn't left on the steps of a hospital like Ms Hadley had told him. He wasn't abandoned at all...

His mother was Isabelle Ricci. His father, Viktor *Stefan* Sachov.

They'd lied to him.

And I'm pretty sure they'd murdered his real mother too.

CHAPTER 14

ROSE

Three things happen simultaneously. Erik lets go of me, stumbling backwards with a pained cry. Anton stands, reaching for the letter on the table, snatching it up and Ivan swears loudly striding towards Emmie who is cowering a little now. She looks between each of us, her hand rushing to cover her mouth, then bursts into tears realising the gravity of her confession and its effect on us all.

"I'm so sorry," she mouths, her words lost between Erik's cries and Anton's rage as he rips the letter out of the envelope.

"Where the fuck is it!" he screams, his eyes scanning over the letter as he looks for the birth certificate and photograph. Anton steps towards Emmie, Ivan holds him back. Both of them are shaking.

Emmie reaches for her bag with trembling hands and pulls out another envelope. Anton grabs it from her, pulling out two items. I watch as his eyes scan both.

"Bastard," he whispers, then stumbles backwards onto the sofa clasping his head in his hands, the birth certificate and photo falling to the floor.

For long seconds I stand unable to move, not sure who to go to first. I'm torn between the two. Both Erik and Anton are falling apart, and I'm helpless to do anything about it.

Ivan is the first to act. He wraps an arm around Anton's shoulders, pulling him into his side.

"Rose, deal with Erik," he says to me, shock widening his eyes. But beneath the shock I see a layer of rage that's apoplectic. I know that because I feel it too. God, how I feel it. I want to rip the world to shreds for all the pain these men have had to suffer.

There's a sick kind of all-consuming anguish opening up within me. It burns me from the inside out. How fucking could they? How could they keep this secret for so fucking long?

Viktor Stefan Sachov. 'S' from the letters. He's Erik's *father* and he and Ms Hadley killed Isabelle.

Motherfuckers.

All this time and they never revealed the truth of Erik's heritage, and of course now we know why. He only ever wanted to feel loved, to know he wasn't alone. Ms Hadley had let him believe he was abandoned like he was a worthless piece of trash. All his life he searched for love, only ever feeling betrayed by everyone he dared care about.

"He fucking never loved me and I always wondered why... now I know," Anton wails, curling his fingers into his hair, pulling at it.

"Shh, Ant," Ivan cajoles, trying to comfort him.

My god, Anton. How must this feel for him? Finding out from a stranger that not only is Erik his brother, but that his father thinks so little of him, reaffirming his poor sense of self-worth. Anton has been ridiculed and loathed his whole life, not realising that he lived in the shadow of Erik, never good enough for his father. One way or another, they've both been punished for existing, neither knowing the truth about each other or the real monster in their father's heart and Ms Hadley's.

My fingers curl into my palms as my hate for both Viktor and that witch grows to epic proportions. I want to scream until my lungs are raw. But I can't let that rage go. Not now.

Now they need me to be strong, but I'm struggling. I really am.

Twisting on my feet, I hobble towards Erik. He's slumped against the wall, his legs spread out before him, head hanging forward.

"Erik," I whisper, approaching him carefully. He's trembling so hard I'm afraid he's having an episode. If that's the case, then we're all in danger. "Erik, can you hear me?"

Ignoring the ache in my knee, I crouch down, reaching out to touch his arm gently. When he doesn't flinch or react badly, I squeeze his arm. "Erik, I'm so sorry. Let me help you up. Come with me, please."

"He's my fucking dad, Rose." Erik's voice cracks as he raises his head and looks at me. His amber eyes are swimming with shock and tears. One leaks from his eye and slides down his cheek. More pain.

My heart weeps with him.

"That fucking bastard is my dad!"

He stands abruptly, swiping at his face and strides away from me. For one awful moment I think he's going to hurt Emmie. Instead he sits down next to Anton and pulls him into his arms.

"Brother," he says with a trembling voice, wrapping his

arms tightly around him. Anton collapses against him, a pained sob escaping his throat.

Ivan folds both men in his arms, holding onto them as they all come to terms with this revelation and the other truths that have come out over the past few weeks. All I can do is stand and watch the three men who've taken my heart and made it beat again, weep in each other's arms. Too much has happened. There's been too much hurt, too much betrayal, that it's impossible for any of them to hold back the flood of their grief. If Viktor saw them now, I know what he'd think; he'd think them weak, pathetic.

But a crying man *isn't* weak. There is strength in showing your vulnerabilities, your heart. They've all taught me that.

Emmie is watching them with wide eyes. She's shaking violently now. Not knowing what to do next she turns to look at me, and I see the panic in her eyes. She's come into our home and dropped this bombshell. She's confirmed what we've all thought from the beginning and she's revealed a secret that has detonated their last ounce of strength. I'm scared for them, for us. *I* almost feel like an outsider watching their grief and pain bleed into the room, so Christ knows how Emmie must feel.

"Will you come with me?" I ask softly, not wanting to disturb my men as they come to terms with what has just been revealed.

"Of course," she responds, sniffing. Her own face is wet with tears, and I can't summon up any hate for this woman. She was brave coming here today, even after all this time. Yes, she might be twenty years too late, but I don't blame her for leaving it that long. It was never her responsibility to tell Erik. She'd been a scared child. Blackmailed into keeping the secret by two very dangerous people. She's lived with the knowledge and her guilt for a long time, that's punishment enough.

I usher her out of the room, only to find Fran approaching us.

"I should go," Emmie says, pulling on her wet coat. "I'm sorry if I hurt you all."

"No, you're not going anywhere in this weather," I say, taking her hand in mine. "You'll stay here tonight. Please don't worry about Erik, about any of us. You did the right thing in coming here."

She chews on her lip, her brows creasing together in concern. "I was a coward…"

"No," I respond squeezing her hand. "You were a child, a scared, confused child at that. This isn't on you."

"I slept with Layton. I *hurt* Erik…"

"You made a mistake, and you've paid for it. Thank you for coming. Thank you for telling the truth. They needed to hear it, no matter how hard it was to do so." I let go of her hand and turn to Fran who is looking more than a little confused. "Fran, please take Emmie to the guest room. She'll be staying with us tonight."

"Of course, Rose. Can I get you anything? Do *you* need any help?" she asks me, her gaze flicking to my leg. I'm standing awkwardly, holding my weight on my good leg and using the wall for support.

"No, I'll manage. When you've settled Emmie in, can you tell them I've gone to bed? I think they need some time alone together," I say.

Maybe it's cowardly to leave them alone like this, but right now I need to gather myself. I'm not sure I can be the woman they all need right now. I just need a bit of time to absorb everything. To think. To find the strength I'll need to pull them through. I promised to weather the storm with them, and I will do that. I just need a moment first.

Fran nods. "I'll take care of it," she says, before ushering Emmie down the hall.

CHAPTER 15

ROSE

Stripping out of my clothes, I get into bed feeling exhausted but unable to sleep with a million thoughts plaguing me. With each revelation a picture has begun to build. Ms Hadley, Isabelle and Viktor had once been lovers, or at least Viktor had slept with them both at the same time. Ms Hadley had loved her best friend it would seem, but her love for Viktor and jealousy had fucked that up, turning that bond into something ugly and tainted. Either she killed Isabelle, or Viktor had. Either way, they're both responsible for her murder and all the lies that followed it.

Erik had grown up believing he'd been abandoned by his mother. Anton had grown up not knowing he had an older brother but constantly living in his shadow, nonetheless.

Out of all this, one thing remains abundantly clear; jealousy has ruined lives.

Jealousy…

It's the kind of emotion that will change a good person into a bad one. It's the kind of emotion that can lead to murder. Ms Hadley is filled with jealousy and bitterness. It seeps through her veins poisoning her thoughts and twisting her love into something that is suffocating, oppressive, destructive.

There is no doubt in my mind that Ivan's love for Svetlana, no matter how screwed up that might've been, drew out Ms Hadley's jealous tendencies. Erik's love for me did the same, and she'd wanted to kill me for it too. I'm betting Amber would've had a similar fate had Anton actually loved her. As it was, he did Ms Hadley's work for her, sending Amber into a spiral of madness she's not been able to claw her way out of.

Now, here we are. Cast adrift and drowning in the repercussions of such a toxic emotion. And the worse thing? I've felt that same jealousy too. Yesterday when Ivan had told me that Emmie had called, that she was coming to visit, I had been blind with jealousy. I'd felt sick with worry that he would remember why he loved her, that he would cast me aside the moment he set eyes on her. Murderous thoughts *had* entered my head.

It's fucked up, but it's true.

Then, this morning when Erik had admitted he was curious to see how Emmie turned out, I'd wanted to do real fucking damage. Fortunately for me, I'd believed Erik when he had told me that I was the one for him. I still believe him, but that doesn't mean to say that I wouldn't have hurt Emmie if I thought for one second that she'd come back for him.

So what makes me any different from Ms Hadley? Can I honestly say that if Emmie had tried to get Erik back that I wouldn't have wanted to murder her, tried to? I'd watched my father die out of hate, bitterness and *jealousy* because my mum had loved him more than she'd loved me. That's the cold hard truth. That's who I am.

I'm no better than Ms Hadley, than Viktor.

"Fuck!" I exclaim, slamming my palm against the bedspread. Sleep isn't going to come anytime soon, so I pull back the sheets and get out of bed. It's not even that late, and even though I'm exhausted I know sleep won't come whilst I'm in this state.

So I do the only thing that helps. I get up and practice the five ballet positions. Alicia will kill me if she finds out, but I need to do something to distract me. Even if I'm not completely healed, I'm a damn sight better than I was five weeks ago. Besides I need the pain to centre me, to show me that I can bleed like all the rest. That I'm fragile. Human, breakable. That I *feel*. Somehow that keeps me sane.

Standing by my chest of drawers, I place my palm against the smooth surface of wood and turn my feet out before bending at the knees. Pain explodes. I inhale a breath, letting the pain wash over me. My racing heart calms a little more. Minutes pass as I move through the exercise, so absorbed by the movements and the pain that I don't hear the door open behind me.

"Rose, what the hell do you think you're doing?"

It's Anton.

"I needed the distraction," I respond, turning to face him.

He grits his jaw, running a hand over his beard. Behind him, Ivan and Erik walk into the room. They look like they've just returned from war. All three are pale, and in a state of shock. Much like me.

"Do you want to end up in the fucking wheelchair?" Erik bites out.

"Yes, that's the plan," I snap back, folding my hands over my chest.

"Jesus, Rose. What the fuck?"

It's Ivan now. He strides over to me, stopping short a few feet away. He reaches for me, his fingers hovering a few centimetres from my skin. I can feel the warmth of them as the electricity between us sparks and cracks like lightning on wet grass. A look passes between us; it's filled with need, with understanding and desire. Reaching for him, my fingers stroke the dark stubble of his jaw, the pad of my thumb running over his lips. I know what I must do.

"Take your clothes off and wait for my command," I order, my voice lowering.

Relief washes over Ivan's features as he begins to remove his clothes. Watching us closely are Erik and Anton. Anton has already taken a seat on the armchair in the corner of the room. He sits with his pad open, a pencil hovering over the paper. He looks at me, asking for my approval without saying a word.

I nod, giving him permission to document us this way.

His gaze falls to Ivan who is naked and standing beside me. I rest my palm on Ivan's arm. "You can choose what you'd like me to use. Grab whatever you need from the drawer then get on your hands and knees. Place the item on the floor beside you, " I tell him.

"Yes, Domina," he murmurs and the soft pad of his bare feet moving across the floor is strangely comforting.

Across the room, hidden half in shadow is Erik. He's leaning against the wall, his arms folded across his chest as he regards me. "You left," he says, making a statement.

"You needed time alone. I gave that to you," I explain, realising how feeble that sounds. In all honesty I'd felt on the edge of their grief this time, not a part of it. In that moment, I didn't feel able to stay. It was a private moment between three men who've known each other their whole lives.

"Bullshit. The truth, Rose."

I glance at Anton who is watching me intently. "Anton," I plead, not wanting to get into a conversation about this right now.

He places his pencil on the pad. "Answer the question, Rose."

"I didn't run. I just felt…"

"*What*, Rose?" Erik persists, striding towards me.

"You're family… you *needed* time alone with each other. I gave you that."

He stops before me, cupping the back of my head in his large hands. "For fucks sake, Rose. Don't you get it? Have you learnt nothing? *You're* our family, *you're* the beat to each of our hearts. You're the reason we didn't lose our shit downstairs. Christ, woman, what the fuck do we have to do to make you see that? We. Need. You," Erik grinds out.

"I get it. I'm sorry," I say, and I do. I really, really do. Because they are my family too. I know that now more than ever. There is nothing that will make me give these men up, nothing.

"Come here," Erik says, pulling me into his arms. He holds me against him for long moments, then lowers his mouth to my ear. "I told you the last time that if you were to doubt my love, *our* love, again there would be consequences…"

He lets that statement hang between us as he presses his hips against mine. I can feel the swell of his cock between us and warmth heats between my legs and beneath my skin.

"You're going to understand that I'm a man of my word."

Erik pulls back slightly, searching my upturned face. He

brushes a few strands of hair off my face with a sweep of his fingers.

"Be Domina for Ivan, soothe Anton's pain and then, then you're going to submit to *me*." He brushes a chaste kiss against my lips, his fingers curling into my hair before he pulls away sharply and strides back to his spot in the corner of the room.

For a few seconds it's all I can do but stand there and absorb the growing tension in the room. I let the anticipation fill me. Let their gazes scorch my skin.

Drawing in a calming breath, I turn on my feet and walk towards Anton. He watches me, waiting patiently. Bending over, I run my hand through his hair as I press my lips against his ear. "I know you don't take orders, Anton. But I want you to undress. I need you to be ready when it's time to fall into the darkness. I need you to fall with me, *please*."

Anton reaches up, his dark gaze meeting mine. "Every damn time, Rose," he responds, grabbing the back of my neck and pulling me roughly to him. Our teeth and lips clash as we kiss, a sweet kind of bruising pleasure. There's a sense of urgency from him, a need to be fulfilled, *loved*.

And the truth is, I'm so ready to love him, love them all.

When he pulls away panting, raw with emotion, a different kind of passion flares in my chest; one of solidarity, friendship, *family*. Not one of them has mentioned the conversation that took place in the parlour or Emmie's revelation. What is there to say? We all know the truth. This here, right now, is our way of healing each other. Of coping.

"For you, I'd do anything." Anton stands, undressing. I watch greedily, my gaze roving over every inch of his skin. He's beautiful and when he gives me one of his dazzling smiles, it's all I can do to remember to breathe.

"Don't keep Ivan waiting any longer, the man's about to

self-combust," Anton says with a smirk. The sheer fact he can be so generous, so selfless after the events of this evening blows me away, frankly.

He's right though, Ivan is tightly wound up. On his hands and knees beside me, there is a paddle waiting to be used. His head hangs low, his dark hair falling forward but his whole body is strung tight. Every muscle is rigid. Between his legs his cock is erect, the tip engorged from his desire and excitement. I have the sudden urge to slide beneath him and suck him off until he comes. But that isn't the kind of release he needs right now. Not yet, anyway.

Stepping into the centre of the room, I slip off my loose trousers, easing out of them, and let them drop to the floor. I remove my t-shirt next, leaving on my black lace underwear. My nipples pebble at the guttural sound that comes from the corner of the room and I allow myself a quick glance in Erik's direction, drawing in a breath at the force of his gaze.

Damn, I'm in so much trouble. But I do not look away.

If I'm completely honest with myself, there's a large part of me that likes to disobey Erik's orders, to push the boundaries between us. Deep down I had known that walking away from them earlier would have repercussions, but I did it anyway. I didn't do it to be cruel or heartless. I did it, for the most part, to give them that moment together. Yes, I had my own insecurities, that wasn't a lie, but I also knew that Erik would take it upon himself to make sure I understood that those insecurities would cost me.

When he looks at me now like he's about ready to devour me, I know he's going to fulfil his promise… and my core aches for it.

I *ache* for him and his firm touch and gentle caresses.

"Can you do this, Erik? I'm going to give Ivan what he craves…"

He nods tightly. "I trust you. But know this, the second they've got what they need, you're mine."

"Yes," I whisper, lowering my eyes, giving him my submission and a promise of what's to come.

But first Ivan and Anton. They need me too, and God knows I want them.

Tonight, I'm going to show them just how much.

CHAPTER 16

IVAN

R ose bends down beside me and picks up the paddle. Her long slim fingers stroking over the smooth leather and wood. I'm trembling, almost violently now, with the anticipation and need. I need this woman. I need Domina. It's been weeks since I've felt the reassurance of her firm hand, her confidence and surety.

It's been so tough watching her battle to get better and feeling so goddamn helpless. But yet again she wows us all with her strength and her resilience. Even now, still healing, she's stronger than we could ever hope to be.

She's so fucking strong.

"Ivan, I need you to lean on the bed. Get up, my love," she whispers, that word tumbling from her lips before she's able to stop it. I hear the sudden sharp intake of breath as she realises what she's just said.

My love...

The room stills.

No one moves, not even me, despite her command.

I hear the rush of wood moving through the air before the sound of the paddle cracking against my skin fills the space.

"Fuuucckk!" I cry out, jerking forward. My muscles tighten then relax as endorphins rush through my bloodstream. My fucking cock leaps.

"I said get up," she repeats, this time dropping the affectionate address. But it doesn't matter that she doesn't say it again. I heard it. We all did.

Pushing up off my palms I do as she asks and lean against the bed. My fingers find the cool cotton and I curl them into the material, readying myself for the next blow.

I don't have to wait long.

She smacks the paddle against my arse five more times, and with each blow I find myself letting go of all the stress I've felt over the last few weeks. She is firm and sure with each strike. She marks me, making me hers. It turns me on, more than I'll ever be able to express with words. I almost come with the final blow against my skin.

"That's enough," she says, dropping the paddle to the floor with a loud thud. Out of the corner of my eye I see her stumble slightly as she removes her underwear, she's still not back to full health and it shows.

Panting, I close my eyes against the bliss that always follows such intense pain. My skin burns, and I'm sweating but as her fingers caress the soreness, another kind of bliss unfolds, and I lose myself for a time in the quiet headspace that follows. This, this is what I seek. A peaceful kind of nirvana where no one but Rose and I exist. Her fingers smooth over the sore areas, working into the muscle of my arse and lower back. It's both painful and intensely erotic. Pain and pleasure combining, a high like no other.

"Ivan, get on the bed," she murmurs after a while, her gentle voice penetrating the quiet.

Crawling onto the bed, I lie on my back and wait for her instruction. She lies down next to me, curling into my side. Her mouth lifts to my ear and she whispers three words that both break me and put me back together.

"I love you," she says tentatively.

My fucking heart explodes. Rose has successfully detonated a bomb within me. I've known for quite some time that she's in love with me, with Anton and Erik, but to hear her utter the words is a blessing.

Turning my head to the side, I allow myself to lightly brush my lips against her forehead. As much as I want to kiss her, fucking love her back, she is still my Domina, and I am still her sub. That hasn't changed despite her words.

Tipping her head back, she presses a delicate kiss against my lips whilst her fingers burn a trail down my chest seeking out my cock. It twitches the moment her fingers wrap around the base.

"Before when you had made love to me, I wasn't ready…" she breathes deeply, a sense of serenity relaxing her features, her green eyes sparkling with hope. "But I'm ready now. I want you to make love to me, Ivan," she says, trailing her nails gently over my balls. My cock bounces against my stomach. I'm so hard for her, it's almost painful.

"I'm *ready*," she repeats. "There are no orders now, but that. *Love me.*"

We've come so far.

She doesn't have to ask twice. I will love this woman until the world stops spinning.

"Turn away from me, Rose," I say, gently brushing my lips against hers.

She frowns but does as I ask, facing away from me. I turn on my side, sliding one arm beneath her so that I can pull her tightly against me, drawing her back against my front. Cupping her breast in my hand, I trail my lips against the curve of her neck, seeking out the tender spot where I know she loves to be kissed. In my arms she melts against me, small moans of pleasure releasing from her lips as my fingers tease her nipple and my free hand slides down her side enjoying the dips and curves of her waist and hips. Her smell is divine, the most potent perfume that I'll never be able to get enough of.

"You've set me free, Rose. You've given me what I need time and time again. I will submit to you, always. I will love you every damn time we come together if you need me to. I'm yours. Whatever you command, I shall give it to you."

Sliding my hand lower, I seek out the warmth between her legs. My finger dips between her folds, caressing the wet warmth that greets me there. "Fuck, you're so wet..." I grind out, finding her clit and swirling my finger over the tiny mound of flesh. She parts her legs, bringing her knee up so I can get better access. I stroke her, taking my time to build the pleasure for her. Always her. She whimpers under my touch.

"I've got you, Rose," I whisper.

Rose arches her back against me, the crack of her arse sliding against my cock.

"Love me, Ivan," she moans, her voice pitched equally between that of Domina and of Rose.

It's the only command I need to hear. My own stresses satiated, I give Rose what she needs and angling my cock to her centre, I slide into her in one firm thrust. She so tight, so wet, so fucking mine. My eyes roll back in my head at the sensation and the feeling of deep, unequivocal love that I feel.

Holding her against me and anchoring her to my chest, I make love to the only woman who's ever understood the true depths of my nature. I love her with gentle caresses and soft kisses, firm strokes and blissful licks.

Right now, she doesn't want the frenzy of fast, lust-filled sex. She wants to know what it feels like to be *loved*, so that's what I do. I fuck her with every ounce of love I have. I fold her against me, my heart beating in time with hers. When she angles her head to kiss me, I respond with deep sensual kisses, our tongues dancing with each other's. There's no fight in this kiss, just acceptance and a sense of freedom. The silky smoothness of her skin against my own is a soft caress as I hold onto her tightly revelling in her warmth. As we make love, Rose responds differently this time, she grips my arms against her, her fingers digging into my skin, neither one of us wanting to let go. Her moans of pleasure, the way she pushes back against me, folding her leg back over my thigh so that I can fill her completely, cracks open my heart. Inside I'm fucking dancing, my soul soaring with every touch.

I revel in the sting that remains on my skin and the tight warmth of her body clutching my cock so tightly. Together we move, the gentle rocking of a boat on an ocean where new beginnings are just beyond the horizon. She murmurs her love for me, her words a gentle caress and a reminder of what we have become. We were once two lost souls, cast adrift and alone, fighting self-hate and pain with no hope of ever feeling whole again, and now… now we are so much more than that. Together we are a perfect fit, together we are something extraordinary.

"Ivan," she breathes. "Oh, Ivan… *I love you…*"

And I *feel* her love. I feel it in every single cell of my being. When she turns her head once more seeking out my lips, I swallow every breathless pant, every word that she utters, consuming her love, letting it fill me up and mend every broken part of me. Steadily, like the sun dawning, evaporating the dark clouds that have tried to ruin us both, we come together, the gentle lapping of our mutual orgasms binding us together with love, making us *whole*...

"Ivan, let her go."

I hear Anton's voice filter into my thoughts, my orgasm slowly fading away.

"Brother, may I?" he asks again, standing beside us both. Rose's own eyes flutter open as she turns her head once more, bringing her hand up to cup my cheek. She kisses me deeply, her fingers tugging on my hair.

"Thank you," she murmurs, smiling beneath my mouth.

I can't help but smile back. This feeling of completion fills me up as I look at Rose. Despite all the shit that's happened today, these past few weeks, I'm happy. So, fucking happy.

And now it's my best friend's turn to find that happiness too.

"Go with him. He needs you," I say, caressing the tip of my nose down the bridge of hers and pulling away from her gently. But she's not ready to leave my arms, not quite yet.

"Will you do something for me, Ivan?" she whispers, twisting her body so she's facing me now.

"Yes, anything."

"Will you lay some flowers at Svetlana's grave and make peace with the hurt you caused her? Will you finally let the guilt go?"

My response is caught in my throat, so I simply nod my head.

"You may have hurt Svetlana, but you *didn't* kill her, Ivan. That guilt doesn't belong to you. I need you to be strong when we face Ms Hadley and Viktor, because we *will* have to face them. Let the guilt go and be the man I see. The strong, passionate, courageous man who I'm in love with. Can you do that?"

There really is only one response I'm able to give her. "With you by my side, I can do anything, Rose."

CHAPTER 17

ANTON

Sliding my arms beneath Rose, I lift her off the bed. There's only one place I want to make love to her, and it isn't in this room. I lock eyes with Ivan who's lying boneless and satiated on her bed. He gives me a lazy smile, one that's filled with happiness and joy. She told him she loved him. I don't think she realised I heard her, but I'm happy for him. Truly, happy.

"I'll bring Rose back, okay?"

"You don't need to ask my permission, Ant. I'm pretty sure the only one in control here is Rose."

"You got that right," Rose says, grinning as she presses the flat of her palm against my chest. Her fingers scrape against my skin as she grasps my pec. "Take me to the darkness, Anton," she whispers so only I can hear.

Adjusting her in my arms, I stride towards the door.

"Where are you going?" Erik asks, grabbing hold of my

arm. The gravelly tone of his voice is pitted with questions I'm not particularly interested in answering. He wants to take control. I see that in his stance, in the way he looks at Rose. But not this time, not like this. He's my brother, my real life brother and that's both a wonderful revelation and a painful one because now I know why my dad has always favoured him. Erik was his first born son. I've always lived in his shadow, but even though he might be older by a few months, I refuse to kowtow to his demands and orders.

I need a moment with Rose. I *need* it.

Rose reaches for the door handle, opening it. "Anton and I are going to fall into the darkness, Erik," she responds for me, looking at him intently. I know she loves him too, but right now she understands that I need to be with her and *only* her. I'm so grateful for that, for understanding me.

"Then I'll wait," he says, turning his gaze to me. "Take care of her, brother."

"That's one demand I'm more than happy to fulfill," I respond before striding from the room.

ROSE and I lie together on the single bed in the room beyond my studio, shrouded in darkness. Her gentle breaths flutter across my skin, her lips burning a trail across my collarbone as she kisses me.

"How are you holding up?" she asks me, her fingers sliding into my hair as she cups my face.

"Like I've been punched in the gut." I've been hurt so many times over the years by my father that you'd think I'd be numb to his hate. But I'm not numb. I'm fucking dying inside. It *hurts*.

"You are worth a thousand of Viktor... *more*," Rose starts, tracing my face with her fingers as though a blind woman searching the face of the man she loves... does she love me?

"But not Erik, it would seem," I retort, hating the sound of my jealousy but helpless to stop it.

"It isn't a competition, Anton," she murmurs, brushing her lips against my closed eyelids.

"That's where you're wrong. It is. It always has been, even when neither of us were aware of it." I sigh heavily, feeling the weight of the truth pressing against my chest. My father loves Erik. He doesn't love me.

"I'm sorry. You don't deserve to feel this way. You're worth so much more than you believe."

She slides her leg over my thighs, hooking me against her as she sweeps her fingers over my chest, but I grab her wrist and flip her over, pinning her beneath me. Straddling her waist, I lean over pressing my forehead against hers.

"And Erik? Am I worth more than him?" I whisper, repeating my earlier question, jealousy for the brother I've always loved darkening my heart once again. Over the years, I've always been envious of him. Loving and hating him in equal measure. I thought I'd let those feelings go but finding out that Viktor is his father too has sent me spiralling. I hate being like this, but I can't seem to stop.

"You are both *everything*," she says softly, cupping my face in her palms.

"That isn't an answer, Rose," I retort. "Am I always to live in his shadow? Do I pale in comparison?"

"Fuck, no!" she exclaims, her fingers curling into my hair. She tries to pull me towards her, but I rear backwards out of her grasp.

"But you do love Erik like you love Ivan?" I ask, hating the way I sound but not being able to stop. She reaches for me again, but I hold her wrists, preventing her fingers from roving over my body and distracting me.

"Yes, I love Erik the same way I love Ivan," she responds, gently.

I let go of her hands and push up off the bed, backing away from Rose. I hear her scramble to sit up, her feet dropping to the floor.

"Anton, wait," she responds. And even though I can't see her, I know she's got to her feet and is searching for me in the dark. I step further away, moving as silently as possible, letting the darkness swallow me.

"Erik had my father's love, Ms Hadley's, Ivan's. He has *yours*," I say, breathing heavily, trying and failing to stop the jealousy leaking from my lips. "Ivan had Svetlana's and now he has your love. I've never had anyone. No-fucking-one, Rose. My mother tried to love me, but she too felt the absence of my father's love. It killed her in the end." I can't help but wince at the bitterness leaching into my words.

"You have me, Anton. My God, you have *me*," she says, almost desperately, pleadingly.

She moves towards me and I move away, side-stepping her. We dance blindly, two people relying on instinct and our other heightened senses now that we're once again shut in the pitch black together.

"I see the way you look at them both. Ivan who you've always admired, before as Luka the famous ballet dancer and now as Ivan, the man who can submit to you."

"Don't do this, Anton..." she pleads, still searching for me in the dark.

"Erik uncovered the truth about you. He was the one who

finally cracked open your heart. He did something I could never do, Rose. He made you fall in love with him…"

"Stop," she pleads.

This wasn't how I envisaged our time together. This wasn't how I wanted it to go, but I can't seem to stop the bitterness falling from my lips. How can I compete with a man like Erik? Gifted, brave, a fighter. How can I compete with Ivan? Talented, clever, determined.

I'd never thought I'd be this man, and honestly until this afternoon's revelations I wasn't. I'd been happy for them both. I *am* happy for them both, but I'm also fucking jealous.

"Stop it, Anton. Stop this right now. I won't hear you pull yourself apart, I won't. You mean everything to me!" Rose shouts, angry now.

"But not enough," I mutter. I saw the way she looked at Ivan, at Erik. I know that what she feels for them is more than she'll ever feel for me.

"You're wrong. So, fucking wrong," she protests.

I move in the darkness, stepping away from Rose as she brushes past me. "Anton, stop this!" she snaps, the air moving as she reaches out and grabs my arm. "Don't you dare doubt me. I walked into the darkness for you. I succumbed to my deepest fears for you. I held you whilst you battled your addiction. I stayed by *your* side forsaking everyone else. Don't you dare belittle how I feel for you. Don't you fucking dare!" she shouts now, anger blazing.

"Rose…" I start, feeling ashamed, foolish.

"Look, I get it. You're only human. I felt much the same way earlier when I thought Erik would leave me for Emmie. But if there's one important thing that I've learnt today it's that there's no place for jealousy between us. If this is going to work, you need to trust in my feelings for you *all*. There was a time I believed I could never love another person again. Now look at me, in love with not one, but three men. Three beautiful, dark, broken men who I adore above all else and *forsaking all others*." She says, her voice quavering a little at that marriage vow reference. My fucking heart soars.

She grasps me by the shoulders walking me backwards until I hit the wall with a soft thud, then she pushes herself against me, her naked body flush against mine. "You think I would have got through that time in the cage without you? Do you honestly think that I would have survived it without you by my side? I never got to thank you, Anton, but now I'm going to... Thank you for staying with Erik and me. Thank you for looking after me when I was shot. Thank you for sharing your past with me, for being brave enough to introduce me to Amber. But most of all, thank you for loving *me*... because I know you do. I *feel* it." She lets out an uncertain laugh, and I realise I've never said those words to her. Suddenly it's important that I do, right this fucking second.

Grasping Rose by the waist, I lift her off her feet and twist us around so that now she's pressed against the wall. Leaning in close, my cock pressing against her stomach, I crowd her, boxing her in. "I don't have a big speech planned, Rose. I'm not a man of many words. I've always expressed myself through my art but know this, I *do* love you. Very fucking much."

"Well, that's just as well, because I love you too, you fucking idiot," she responds, a laugh bubbling up from her lips. It bursts into the air bringing light and *hope*.

We hold onto one another, not able to see each other in the dark, but trusting in the happiness that lives there. Rose trails her fingers through my hair then tugs gently on my beard. She presses a light kiss against my lips, not trying to deepen it more than a gentle caress.

"Anton. You complicated, beautiful man. You intoxicate me. You keep me sane, grounded like no other. I need you. Ivan needs Domina, Erik needs submission, but you. You've always just needed me, and I love you for it."

Relief floods through me at the lightness of her words and the truth behind them. She fucking loves *me*. Laughing, I lift her up, wrapping her legs around my waist. "What now?" I ask her.

"Now you fuck me like you mean it, Anton," she responds, digging her nails into my skin and kissing me urgently.

So that's exactly what I do. I side into her welcome warmth and fuck her like a man who finds peace in the dark with the only woman who's capable of brightening his life. Gripping her hips, I press her against the wall sliding in and out of the sleekness of her pussy whilst around us the pitch black swallows us into it's deep embrace. Her soft moans and gentle breaths quicken as I become more and more frantic in my need to conquer her, to prove my love for her.

I need this. I need the connection, the release.

I need *her*.

Our hips slam together, her desire as potent and as heady as my own. I'm still an addict but instead of injecting heroin and snorting cocaine, Rose has become my drug of choice. She's intoxicating, mind altering and *mine*.

I've searched my whole fucking life for this feeling of belonging and found it at a time in my life when I'd given up on ever being happy. Because of Rose, I no longer seek colour in the way I did before. She's taught me the gentle peace that can be found in the dark, in the shadows of daylight. Rose is the colour that makes my existence a piece of art. She's every damn colour of the rainbow and as long as I have her, I'm free.

So, I fuck Rose like I paint, with every piece of my heart

and soul. There's nothing I wouldn't do for this woman. Nothing.

"Anton, I'm coming," she pants, drawing my face to hers, biting on my bottom lip as she grinds against me. A scream releases from her lips as she comes, my own release following shortly behind hers and I swear to God, for one moment I see every damn colour of the rainbow.

CHAPTER 18

ROSE

I awake to the sound of someone singing a pretty tune. The woman's voice is so beautiful that for a moment I just lay listening, my eyes shut. The melody is a soft wave as it washes over me, her voice soothing in a whimsical kind of way. Stretching a little, I allow myself the time to wake up slowly, enjoying the way my muscles feel relaxed, and my head free from worrying thoughts. It's been a long time since I've woken up this way.

Anton must have the radio on in his studio, he often likes to paint with music playing in the background, says it helps his creative juices. I make a mental note to find out who the singer is so I can buy their album.

When the singing stops abruptly, I rub my hands over my face and sit up, surprised to find myself back in my own bed and not in the hidden room beyond Anton's studio. How the hell had that happened?

And then I remember.

I'd made love to Anton for hours in the dark then fell into a deep, satisfied sleep wrapped in the warmth of his arms. We both needed that time alone together. Anton needed to feel loved, adored and I needed to be Rose and not Ivan's Domina or Erik's submissive.

It had been beautiful and exactly what we both needed to soothe our souls.

Scraping a hand through my hair, I try and fail to hide the stupid grin on my face.

"Good night I take it?" Fran asks, stepping out of my walk-in wardrobe holding a set of clean clothes. I feel my cheeks warm. She chuckles.

"You know I went into Anton's studio this morning to take him breakfast and the man was dancing to some awful tune with a grin a mile wide on his face."

"He was dancing?" I laugh.

"Yep. Surprised me to know end, given you all looked like someone had died yesterday!"

"What was the tune?" I ask, not willing to let on how close she is to the truth. The less people know, the better. It's safer that way.

"I don't know. Some crap that had him waving his hands about like a loon. He went as red as a beetroot when he realised I was watching him. Poor sod."

"Oh my god, stop it. That's hilarious."

"The silly bugger couldn't stop smiling. I guess love does that to you."

"Yes, I guess it does," I respond, feeling inextricably *happy*.

She places my clothes on the bed, sitting down next to me. "I brought you some clean clothes. Figured it would save you the struggle of grabbing them from the wardrobe yourself."

She passes them to me, and I take the pair of dark jeans and white t-shirt gratefully. "Hope that's okay?"

"Thanks, Fran. Good choice," I reply casting my eye over my favourite pair of jeans and a soft cotton top.

"It's no bother. I'll start getting brunch ready now that you're awake."

"Brunch? What time is it?" I ask, glancing out the window. It's a bright day, the sun is so golden you could be forgiven for thinking it's the middle of spring and not winter. Perhaps that's a good omen? I always feel so much better when the sun's out.

"Eleven. The boys let you have a sleep in, given you're so worn out. Besides…" Fran's smile wavers a little.

"What is it?"

"I hate to be the bearer of bad news, Rose, but whilst you've been sleeping our guest decided to leave. Ivan tried to persuade Mrs Carrington to stay, but she wanted to get back to her husband. Erik is a little upset."

"Because she left?" I ask, worry creeping up my spine.

"No, not about that. Honestly, I think he was more relieved." Fran pulls at an invisible thread on the bed cover, a frown creasing her brow.

"So, what then? Should I be worried?"

"Erik's a little out of sorts today, quite the contrast to Anton. Ivan is teetering somewhere in the middle. Erik seems close to succumbing to an episode. I admit I'm worried about him."

"Shit!" I exclaim, pulling back the blanket and twisting my body, my feet slamming onto the floor. "Fuck!" I exclaim when my body reminds me it's not completely healed just yet.

"Hey, don't panic, Ivan's been with him, and now Anton has joined them both. They have it under control… I think."

"I should go too," I say, ripping off Anton's delicious

smelling top, not caring that I'm completely naked before Fran. Snatching up the t-shirt she grabbed from the wardrobe for me, I yank it over my head. Fran shifts her body, casting her gaze away to give me some privacy as I pull on a clean pair of knickers and the pair of jeans. It's still a little awkward to get dressed, but I'm far more flexible than I have been in weeks, the physio sessions with Alicia are paying off.

Sliding out of bed and being careful not to put too much pressure on my knee, I stand. Fran gets up too, handing me my hairbrush. She smirks eyeing the bird's nest that is my hair.

"Those were the days," she remarks, chuckling.

I brush it quickly, wincing a little at the knots. Passionate sex most definitely equals messed up hair. Warmth spreads up my chest and neck as I remember how Anton had fisted my hair in his hands and fucked me with holding anything back.

"You're going to make yourself bald, tugging at that beautiful hair like that. Here, let me," she offers, holding her hand out for the brush.

I hesitate, giving a little frown. It's such a motherly thing to do, and certainly not something I ever experienced from my own mother. I hand the brush to Fran without thinking too much about it.

"I need to be with him. He shouldn't go through this alone," I say, turning my back to her so she can work her way through the knots.

"Take a few deep breaths, Rose. Don't go in there this wound up. It won't help you and it certainly won't help Erik."

"Shit, you're right." Filling my lungs up with air, I breathe in and out slowly, forcing myself to calm down. She continues to work out the tangles and the action soothes me. Somehow she knows just the right thing to do.

"There we go, all done."

"Thanks, Fran. You're so kind to me," I respond gratefully.

"Shouldn't I be?" she asks tipping her head to the side, as she regards me with wise eyes.

"Kindness isn't something I'm used to, honestly. I seem to bring out the worst in people."

Fran waves her hand about. "I don't believe that for a second. Look what you've done for these boys. You've brought out the *best* in them."

I sigh heavily, feeling a little lost all of a sudden. Being strong all the time is draining.

"Look, Rose, I don't need you to tell me what happened in the parlour yesterday, but I do want you to know that I'm there for you if you need me." She gives me a sweet smile, and for a moment I see the woman she was hidden beneath the greying hair, wrinkles and pretty pale blue eyes.

"I might only be a housekeeper, but I do care about you all. And I'm no prude, Rose. Believe it or not I have lived a colourful life of my own. I'm glad they have you."

"You're not *only a housemaid*, Fran. You're my friend and I appreciate you. Thank you for telling me about Erik. I'd rather know when he's in pain than have it hidden from me."

Fran pats my arm before letting it go, a wistful look shadowing her features. "Once upon a time I knew a man who was very similar to Erik. He too had opposing forces within him. It took a great deal of care and love to make him feel at peace with himself. Like Erik he was bullish and headstrong, but he was also gentle and incredibly thoughtful. You have it within you to help Erik, Rose. You've already done so much, but it will take time to get to a place where you're no longer concerned that he's going to fall into that dark place again. There might be weeks, even months, when he'll feel better and then out of the blue something will happen, and he will be knocked back to the time that haunts him the most. It won't be easy, but you're strong. Be firm, be there for him always and you'll make it through."

I nod my head solemnly. "Thank you, Fran... I think I needed that reassurance."

She pats my arm. "No bother, Rose." She walks to the other side of my room and picks up a pile of dirty clothes, placing them in the wash basket. "Brunch will be ready in half an hour," she says heading towards the door.

"Wait! Who was that on the radio earlier?"

"Radio?"

"Yes. When I woke up, I heard singing. I figured you had the radio on."

Fran laughs, a smile brightening her face. "That wasn't the radio, Rose. That was *me*."

"You? I didn't know you could sing," I respond, a little gobsmacked in all honesty. That voice sounded like it belonged to a girl much younger than the seventy year old woman standing before me.

"There are many things that you don't know about me. But, yes, that was me singing."

"Fran, your voice is beautiful! Seriously, I had no idea. Did you ever sing professionally?"

For a moment Fran's eyes glaze over as she remembers some long forgotten moment in her past. "Not professionally, no. There was only one night that I ever sung willingly in front of an audience bigger than a handful of people. That night changed my life forever," she sighs, her eyes tearing up.

"I'm sorry if I've upset you. I should learn not to pry."

She shakes her head. "You haven't upset me. It's been a while since I've thought of that time in my life. I didn't even realise I was singing," she says, swiping at a stray tear. "I miss it, I miss them."

"Them?" I ask, my brows pulling together.

"The *Seekers*... I was their captive, their little bird, Avery, and they were my heart."

"Fran..." My voice trails off as I see the hurt flash across her face. What does she mean she was their captive?

"It was a long time ago, Rose."

"Where are they now, the *Seekers*?"

She smiles shakily at me, straightening her spine. "That's a story for another day. Right now you need to go to Erik. Be with him. Then when you're *all* strong enough, deal with that witch and that monster, Viktor. Make. Them. Pay," Fran says, her kind eyes darkening. In them I see a glimpse of a past that isn't so very different from my own.

I HEAR SHOUTING the second I step into the corridor leading to Erik's private wing. Leaning on my crutch, I hobble as fast as I can to his bedroom door.

"She stays here, that's the fucking end of it," Erik roars, pushing his finger into Anton's chest as I fling open the door.

"No! She comes. She's safer with us. I don't want her stuck here on her own," Anton retorts, standing his ground.

"Hey! What's going on in here?" I shout, raising my voice over the din. Erik and Anton turn to face me. Both are breathing heavily with anger. *Shit.*

Ivan is the first to break the tension. He rushes forward, wrapping his arm about my waist. I lean into him, grateful for his support.

"We thought you were resting," he says, pulling a face as I wince at the sudden rush of pain.

"I was, and then Fran informed me Erik wasn't feeling too great. I thought she meant you were having another flashback, though I can see now that isn't the case," I say, addressing Erik directly. "What's going on here?" I ask looking between my two angry men.

"Erik wants you to stay here when we confront Ms Hadley and my… *our* father. I'm not keen on the idea. I don't want you leaving our side. If we confront them, we do it together or not at all."

"And I don't want Rose within ten feet of those murdering bastards!" Erik snaps, anger a violent tick in his jaw.

"I see," I retort, both touched by their thoughtfulness and a little pissed off, to be honest. "Ivan, would you help me to the sofa, please?" I ask him.

"Sure thing, Rose."

"Okay, looks like we need to have a little chat about a few things. Can you both keep calm enough to do that?" I ask, looking at them both as I make myself comfortable on the sofa. Ivan is pouring me a cup of tea, keeping busy whilst I give Erik and Anton my most severe *'don't mess with me'* look.

"Here we go," Ivan says handing me a mug, smirking a little when he sees the look on my face. "Uh-oh, you two are in deep shit now."

"Shut the fuck up, Ivan," Anton snarls, crossing his arms defensively. I've not seen him this angry before. I don't like it.

"This is a joke. You're staying put, Rose. That's all that needs to be said," Erik pitches in, glaring at Anton.

"This is not a dictatorship, Erik." I say as calmly as I possibly can. "I have a right to make my own decision, but I'm not fool enough to do so without hearing your thoughts first.

Because believe me, this isn't going to be the last time we'll have to decide something important together. If this is going to work, we need to talk and *listen*, got it?"

I look at each man in turn, waiting for a sign that they at least agree with this.

"Sure," Ivan says, raising both eyebrows at his brothers in a *'I told you not to fuck with her'* look.

"Fine," Erik sighs.

"I can deal with that," Anton adds, perching on the corner of Erik's bed. He keeps his gaze firmly fixed on me and not Erik who is now pacing back and forth, unable to keep still in his frustration.

"Good, because we're not a bunch of kids. We're adults, and this is a relationship. We need to talk, and we especially need to talk about things like this. I won't be usurped. Do that, and I won't even bother to hear your opinions, I shall just make a decision of my own."

"That's fair," Anton concedes, scraping a hand over his beard.

"Fine!" Erik snaps for a second time. He's so wound up that I almost, almost feel fearful. Then I remember who he truly is, and the advice Fran has given me. I must be firm, strong, but ultimately there for him, *all* of them, no matter what.

"Okay then, let's sort this out."

CHAPTER 19

ERIK

"So there really isn't anything I can do to persuade you to stay here, to let *us* deal with those two on our own?" I say, gritting my teeth in frustration.

"I've made my mind up, Erik. I've listened to your point of view. I've given you the courtesy of hearing you out. I understand your fears, I really do, but I'm coming. There are things I need to address too, and I can't do that hiding away at Browlace. You asked me to weather the storm with you, and I made a promise to all of you that I would."

"Your safety means more to me than you breaking a promise, Rose," I persist.

"Until the storm breaks or we do… *remember?*" she reminds me, her gaze determined.

"I remember," I admit, but that doesn't mean I have to like it or that I should agree.

"Then that's settled." Rose looks at Ivan, addressing him now. "Can you make arrangements for our trip to London?"

"Sure, I can probably get the plane chartered to City airport in the next few days once the weather's cleared if you think you can manage it?" Ivan explains.

"I can manage it. I'm a lot more able now. Apart from the odd twinge, my knee is nowhere near as painful as it was," Rose responds, absentmindedly rubbing her palm over her knee.

"Then I'll get onto it straight away."

"How is Emmie getting back to Kirkwall given no flights are leaving the airport at the moment?" Rose asks suddenly.

"I booked her first class on the train up to London, then on from there to Edinburgh. She's going to meet with her husband at a build job he's doing there at the moment. She was keen on talking to him…"

"I'm assuming about the abortion, and not about the fact Isabelle was murdered?" Rose questions Ivan, worry tightening her lips into a hard line.

"Not about the murder, no," Ivan confirms.

"And she really didn't want to stay? I feel like there was a lot left unsaid." Rose glances at me, an unreadable expression on her face.

"There was nothing more to be said, Rose. She'll live her life free from the burden of the secret she's carried all these years and we'll live ours," I say, shutting that train of thought down. I'm relieved Emmie's gone, in all honesty. I didn't need her here reminding me of the mistakes I made as a kid. As it is her letter burns a hole in my back pocket. I've still not read it, don't think I'll ever be able to.

"Despite my efforts to persuade her to stay another night, she was determined to get back to her husband," Ivan explains.

"Okay, I get that." Rose looks at me, her green eyes fixed on mine. I'd love to know what she's thinking, but this morning my head is too full of my own frantic thoughts to try and work her out.

Looking away from Rose, I glance out of the window. Last night I had gone to Anton's studio a few hours after they'd left the bedroom. I'd wanted to have my moment with her. But when I'd heard their laughter and the sounds of their lovemaking, I didn't have the heart to disturb them. Unknowingly or not, I'd already taken Anton's father away from him. I couldn't take Rose too. So, I'd returned to my room, locked the door and exercised all night. I've not slept at all, and it shows. I'm fucking wired.

Rose finishes her cup of tea, then places it on the floor by her feet. She looks at me, seemingly making her mind up about something.

"Fran has made us all brunch. It should be ready now. Ivan, Anton, will you do me a favour and tell her to keep mine and Erik's warm, we won't be joining you."

"No?" Anton questions, looking between Rose and me.

"No," she says softly. A look passes between them and Anton nods.

"Okay, Rose. See you later?" he questions, getting up and pulling his hair up into a bun.

"Absolutely," she smiles, a splash of pink warming her cheeks.

"Then we'll get out of your hair. I think that's our cue to leave, Ivan."

"Right, sure," Ivan says, jumping up. He slaps me on my shoulder before bending down and pressing a chaste kiss against Rose's lips.

"I thought they'd never leave," I mutter, breathing out a sigh of relief as they leave us alone, *finally.*

"They're looking out for you, Erik, be grateful for that at least," she remarks, scolding me.

I flop onto the sofa next to her. "I *am* grateful, but I'm also fucking wound up like a spinning top, Rose. I've not slept a wink…"

"I didn't realise, you should get some rest," she says, moving to stand.

"Rest?" I laugh, placing a hand on her arm. "I don't need rest. I need *release.*"

She looks at me cocking an eyebrow. "Didn't you get that yesterday morning, Erik?" she teases.

"That was yesterday, this is today, and that isn't what I meant," I retort, a little sharper than intended.

"What *do* you mean?" she asks, her face expectant, a flicker of excitement and trepidation lighting her meadow-green eyes.

I heave a sigh and pull Emmie's letter from my back pocket. "This has been burning a hole in my jeans for the last twenty-four hours. I've oscillated between wanting to read it and wanting to burn the fucking thing. I can't do either."

"You haven't read it yet?" she asks me.

"No. I'm not sure I want to."

Rose reaches for my hand, grasping it tightly in hers. "Do you want me to read it to you?"

I look at the letter and shake my head. "No. Emmie wanted me to read it, and whilst I don't owe her anything, I do owe the boy I once was the apology that's twenty years too late."

"Okay." Rose settles back on the sofa, folds her hands in her lap and waits.

With shaking fingers, I pull out the letter. It feels thin beneath my hand, and when I unfold it, a small tear appears down the centre. For a few seconds I just stare at the unfamiliar handwriting. Seeing words but not taking in any meaning. Then I start to read.

When I get to the end of the letter, I feel surprisingly calm. I don't feel angry, or sad, or bitter. I feel a strange kind of nothing, and emptiness, I suppose.

"Do you want to talk about it?" Rose asks when a full five minutes have passed after I've folded up the letter and slid it back into the envelope.

"There isn't much to say. This is a letter written by a scared seventeen year old girl. Emmie has apologised, she's alluded to something underhand, but she hasn't said anything outright. This letter wouldn't have changed a thing even if she had posted it back then. It might have given me some closure, but it's still a letter of half-truths and secrets."

"Then why give it to you?"

"I suppose she needed closure too. She's come here and said what she's needed to say. Now she can return to her life free of the burden whilst we must live with the knowledge."

"Is it enough to put Ms Hadley, Viktor away?" Rose asks me.

"I don't think so, no. This is just her word against theirs, and whilst we might have the birth certificate, photograph and a few handwritten letters that Ms Hadley was never able to get rid of, it still doesn't prove anything. Without a confession, they get away with it."

"Then we get them to confess somehow…" Rose insists, leaning over and taking my hand in hers.

"That's easier said than done. Besides, Ms Hadley is in a home for the mentally unstable. Who's going to believe her even if she did confess?"

"She tried to kill me, Erik. It's not that much of a stretch…"

"I don't think it's that simple," I sigh, the same frantic kind of uneasiness prickling my skin. "Perhaps we'll never get justice."

Standing abruptly, I walk to the open fire and chuck Emmie's letter into the grate. I watch the paper burn, the flames curling the edges before devouring it, leaving nothing but ash. Placing my hands against the mantelpiece I lean forward, dropping my head. Inside, I'm a storm brewing at the unfairness of it all. Despite Emmie's confession, despite knowing what they did to Isabelle, to Svetlana, to Rose, nothing is going to change the fact that we have no concrete evidence to prove their guilt.

They're going to get away with murder, literally.

"Fuck!" I exclaim, a familiar rage unfurling inside me.

"Erik, try to calm down. We'll figure this out," Rose says, stepping up beside me. She places her hand on my arm and I flinch at the contact. Not because I don't want her touch, but because I crave it so much it scares me.

"Don't!" I snap, rounding on her.

She steps back, a flurry of fear scampering across her face.

"This isn't a burden you need to carry alone, Erik. We'll all shoulder it," she insists, determined not to let me sink into a pit of despair. When I don't answer, when I *can't* answer, Rose continues. "Earlier you said you needed release, Erik. I crave it too." She holds her wrists out towards me, palms upwards. "I trust you. Find your release, give me mine so we can face this together." She swallows hard, her throat bobbing. "Whatever the storm brings, I'll be right there beside you. Even here, right now, if that's what it takes."

Before I can even think about what I'm doing, my hands reach for her. Instinctively, I grip onto her wrists. I've wanted this for so long. Yesterday had just been a prelude to what was to come, but now I need her full submission, her trust.

"Are you certain?" I ask.

"Never more certain than I am now," she responds meeting my gaze with a steely determination of her own.

"What's the safe word?" I ask her, reaching for my side table and pulling open the drawer. Inside is a length of cord. Not as thick as the rope we used in the glass room, but similar in texture and hold.

"Green," she confirms softly as I wrap the cord around her wrists, securing it tightly.

Turning her away from me I walk her to the bed, my chest pressed against her back. I can already feel the rapid thump of her heart as she waits for further instruction. Pressing a kiss against her neck, I step to the side, climbing onto the bed. Grabbing hold of the other end of rope, I pull her arms above her head, tying the rope to the bedframe. It's a four poster bed, with curtains either side. Fit for a king, *and* a queen.

Rose stands before me, her arms stretched above her. She winces slightly at the tautness in her shoulder.

"Too painful?" I ask her.

"No. I'm good."

Grasping her chin, I force her to look at me. "Paddle, whip or my hand," I ask.

"Your hand," she responds instantly, a flush of colour rising up her chest and neck. There's no fear in her eyes, just acceptance and longing.

"Why do you stay, Rose? All of this, it's such a mess."

"I stay because I'm strong enough. I stay because I understand you better than you understand yourself. I stay because I *love* you, Erik."

"Rose..." I cup her face, unable to find the words to truly

reflect how I feel about this woman. The ridge of my scar presses against the softness of her cheek and I remember our pact, the vow we made to one another in Ivan's studio. Pulling my hand away I run a finger over the raised skin. Our eyes meet, and she smiles gently.

"Every time you mark my skin with your hand, that scar will serve as a reminder of our pact, that with pain comes the healing we both need. Pain is fleeting, Erik, but healing, friendship, love; that, *that* lasts a lifetime."

"I'm beginning to understand that," I murmur, pressing a gentle kiss against her mouth.

Moving to stand behind Rose, I press myself against her back. I'm so fucking hard for her. Wrapping my arms around her waist and grasping her breast, I grind against her then lower my mouth to the curve of her neck and bite the tender flesh there. She groans, stretching her head further to the side to give me better access.

"Too many clothes," I grind out, grabbing the waist of her jeans and undoing the top button and zip. "These are coming off."

Kneeling behind Rose, I slide her jeans over her hips, pulling her cotton knickers off at the same time. Helping her step out of them, I chuck the offending clothes across the room. But she still has her t-shirt on, and I need her naked.

Grabbing the hem, I rip it from bottom to top. Rose sucks in a sharp breath at the sudden, almost violent action. It's not fully removed, given her hands are tied above her head, but it satisfies me enough.

"Remember the safe word. It's sacred and that is what we both obey, understand?" I ask her, knowing full well she does. I've seen how she is with Ivan. I've witnessed that side to her personality. She knows what it is to be a dominant, and now here with me, she will fully understand what it is to be *my* submissive.

"I understand, Erik," she whispers, a heavy dose of lust blanketing us both.

Still on my knees behind her, I press my lips against the globe of her arse and bite her. Enough to make her leap forward, but not enough to draw blood. She sucks in a breath through her teeth at the rush of pain, then sighs as I kiss the little indents on her skin. With me she will only ever slide into pain that is welcomed and not endured. I'm nothing like Roman or the woman who tortured me. Wrapping my arm around her thighs and holding her steady, I twist my body to the side, raise my hand and bring it down on her arse cheek. Colour immediately blooms, and a tiny bit of tension releases within me.

"Arghh!" she grinds out.

I follow the sting of the slap with a firm lick, my tongue sliding over the warmth of her skin.

"More?" I question.

"More," she confirms breathlessly.

In quick succession I raise my hand, slapping every inch of her arse until it's beautifully pink. Every time contact is made, I feel the scar on my hand smart. Her pain and mine intermingle. Her release and mine bound together.

Rose begins to pant, a bead of sweat sliding down her back and pooling in one of the beautiful dimples that sit above her arse. Leaning forward, I lick the tiny dip of skin, tasting her saltiness on my tongue.

"Hmmm," I rumble, not recognising my own voice.

"Erik," she grinds out, arching her back and pressing her raw arse into my face.

Standing, I move around her, slapping her thighs as I do so.

The expression on her face is blissful. Her body slumps, her knees buckling a little as her head falls forward. Sitting on the bed, I pull her body forward between my thighs and lift her chin reaching up to kiss her deeply. She groans against my lips, her eyes pressed shut, her mind someplace else. Selfishly, I want her with me in the moment. I want to see into her fucking soul, this woman that I love.

"Look at me, Rose," I demand.

Her eyelids flutter open, a dreamy kind of look in her gaze, but her lip pulls up at the side showing me she's still here with me. When has she ever left?

"Don't take your eyes off me, okay?"

She nods, not able to speak as I lift up the front of her t-shirt and pinch her nipples between my fingers and thumb, soothing them after with my lips. I feel the heat of her gaze as she watches me lavish and suck at her tight buds. A low moan escapes her lips as my fingers seek out her slickness. With her nipple between my teeth and fingers between her legs I bring her to an orgasm that makes her body go slacken further, her wet heat covering my fingers as she unravels before me.

I let her come down from her release, fisting my cock as her juices slick my skin. My balls tingle with my own impending release, but I'm not done yet.

"Can you take more?" I ask her, hoping in my heart that she can.

"Whatever you can give," she utters.

Pressing another gentle kiss against her parted, breathless mouth, I stand once more, my hands sliding gently over every inch of her skin. When I reach her arse, I cup my hand and slap her several times. Each time my hand meets her bare skin, all the worry, all the pain, all the fear I hold inside evaporates until eventually I'm empty of it and filled with nothing but love and unending devotion.

"You fill me up, Rose. You make it all okay," I murmur into her ear, then slide into her as she clutches my cock deep inside, her words of love washing over me as we come.

Leaning my head on Rose's shoulder I pull gently out of her. "Baby, I got you," I say, wrapping my hand around her waist as I untie her arms. She folds herself against me as I lift her up and lay her gently on the bed, tucking myself beside her. She turns to her side instinctively, her arse still red from my slaps and her eyes at half mast.

Leaning over her, I press a gentle kiss against her ear. "Thank you, Rose, for being everything I need. For being there for me, for loving *me*. You have my word from this moment on I will take care of you for the rest of my days, and I will protect your heart always. I *love* you."

A gentle laugh escapes my throat as I shake my head at how wondrous this feeling is for me, a man who never believed he could love again here telling this women how fucking adored she is.

"I love you too," she mutters, her eyes fluttering shut as I gently stroke my hand over every inch of her skin. When her breath settles into the steady rhythm of sleep, I wrap myself around her and fall into a peaceful sleep of my own.

CHAPTER 20

ROSE

Fran passes me a cookie as we sit at the kitchen table chatting about everything and nothing over our mid-morning cup of tea. It's become a regular thing we do together. I like her company a great deal. I shift on the edge of my seat, my arse still a little sore from my time with Erik yesterday, but it only draws a smile from my lips as I remember the way it felt to let myself go, to let my guard down enough to trust Erik to take me to the place where pain and pleasure collide. To be able to trust Erik to take care of my needs and his own is huge for the both of us.

"You okay, Rose?" Fran asks, a knowing glint in her eye.

"Yup, just peachy."

She arches her eyebrow, smiling. "Uh-huh, I can see just how much. Need something for that?" Fran motions to the way I'm sitting.

"Absolutely not," I retort, grinning. "So, when are you

going to tell me about the *Seekers*, Fran?" I press, asking for the third time in as many days.

She smiles, patting my hand. "When you're ready to hear it."

"I'm ready now," I insist, grinning.

"You need to concentrate on your men and prepare yourself for when you have to face Ms Hadley and Viktor. I understand Ivan has a flight arranged for the day after tomorrow," she says, changing the subject.

"Yes, the forecast is better for Friday. This incessant rain has been crazy. I think we're all going a little insane being cooped up for so long."

"I hope not!" Fran laughs.

"You know what I mean. Seriously though, I'd love to hear about the *Seekers*, how you met them, how you ended up working here when you have a voice of an angel." She smiles at that, her cheeks colouring a little. "It would be a good distraction, honestly..." my voice trails off as I try to ignore the knot of worry in my chest. Despite the four of us becoming closer than we've ever been, I can't seem to rid myself of the churning sickness I feel in my stomach when I think about Ms Hadley and Viktor. We must face them, and soon. I know that we can't move on without doing that, but it doesn't make it any easier.

Fran regards me for a moment, her gaze tracing over my face "My story isn't for the faint of heart, Rose. I promise, I will tell you one day but that day isn't today." She gives me a no nonsense smile then stands, gathering the empty cups and teapot. She places them in the kitchen sink then looks at her watch. "Oh, damnit. Ivan asked me to send you to Anton's studio at eleven, I completely forgot." She pulls a face.

"He did? Well, I'll head there now, I'm only ten minutes

late," I respond, glancing at my mobile phone screen. "Same time tomorrow?" I ask her.

She grins. "Same time tomorrow, Rose."

As I approach the studio, I hear laughter. The deep gruff sound of Erik's, the almost lyrical notes of Anton's, and Ivan's understated chuckle. It warms me from the inside out to hear them so at ease with each other. Once upon a time these men lived entirely separate lives even though they were sleeping under the same roof. Their friendship and brotherhood had been stilted, buried under years of unhappiness and anguish. Rather than encouraging them to talk, to spend time with each other, Ms Hadley had affected their relationship by keeping them separated. Ivan under piles of work and women, Anton locked up in his studio taking drugs to cope and Erik locked in a glass cage.

Now that she's gone, we eat all our meals together and they choose to hang out with each other purely for the joy of it, rekindling the closeness of their youth and finding a new kind of normal. I'm happy for them, for us.

Pushing open the door, I step inside Anton's studio, my mouth dropping open.

"What's happened here?" I manage to say. All three men stand watching my reaction. All of them are grinning.

The space has been cleared of all the canvases, furniture and paints. On one wall is a run of mirrors, and a barre. Tucked into one corner is an easel, canvas, and a small side table holding some art material. In the opposite corner is a music stand and Erik's violin case.

"Do you like it?" Ivan asks tentatively.

"But what about your studio, Anton?" I ask, looking from Ivan to Anton. I'm flabbergasted. This is just... *everything*.

"I've relocated to another room in the manor. This is your space now... and ours, if you'll have us of course."

"But..." My hand covers my mouth as I look between the three. "You did this for me?"

"This and something else, but you'll have to wait for that surprise a little longer, Rose," Erik explains, looking entirely too pleased with himself.

"What are you up to?"

Ivan grins. "That's for us to know, and you to find out... *eventually*." He holds his hand out towards me, grasped within them are my pointe shoes. "Would you like to dance, Rose?"

"I... what? My knee..." I fumble, losing my ability to form a coherent sentence. I've always wanted to dance with Ivan, and whilst he'd made that promise to me, I'd only ever hoped he meant it.

"...Is much better. I spoke with Alicia, she said that as long as we're careful, and I support you as much as possible then you should be fine. Want to give it a try?"

"Yes," I say immediately, drawing a laugh from his lips, "But are *you* certain?"

"More certain than I've ever been." He grins and my heart gallops wildly. "Anton is going to draw, and..."

"...I'm going to play," Erik finishes, striding over to his violin and picking it up. His large hands run along the smooth wood of the neck before he tucks it between his chin and shoulder. My eyes widen. The last time I heard him play was in the glass cage. I've no idea whether he's able to keep his episodes in check now.

"I've been playing quite a lot lately, Rose. With Ivan's help it doesn't hurt so much anymore. As long as I don't play Mazurka in A Minor, I'll be fine."

"Ivan's help?" I question. Looking between the two. "How come I didn't know about this?"

"You sleep, we dance, paint and play. We've been healing so we can be strong, for *you*," Erik says fiercely.

My heart squeezes so tightly that I'm finding it difficult to speak. "You've done this all for me?"

Ivan nods his head. "Every day since you returned from Edinburgh, we've healed right alongside you."

"But I'd thought…"

"That we'd abandoned you?" Anton asks.

"Yes, why didn't you say anything?"

"Because we weren't sure it would work… Only, somehow it did. It *has*."

Anton strides over to his easel, picks up the canvas and turns it to face me. On it is an almost perfect representation of Ivan and Erik. Ivan is leaping in the air in a perfect jeté and Erik is standing in the background, his eyes pressed shut in concentration as he plays the violin.

"That's beautiful, Anton," I choke out, my eyes trailing over the different shades of grey, white and black. It really is outstanding, so perfectly *them*, so perfectly *him*. All that beauty and not a shard of colour. "I'm so proud of you," I say, striding over to him as he places the canvas back on the easel.

"Hey, anyone would think you're in love with me." He laughs as I throw my arms around him and bury me face in his neck. I laugh with him. I'm so goddamn happy. So happy.

"Stop hogging Rose, just because we're not Michael bloody Angelo doesn't mean you get to have her all to yourself.

"Fuck off, Erik," Anton curses, but it's filled with laughter and absolutely no malice.

Giving Anton a quick kiss, I meet Erik in the middle of the room as he strides towards me. With one arm he scoops me up around the waist and crushes his mouth against mine. We kiss with restraint and not an ounce of embarrassment. This feeling of being so wholly theirs is freeing.

"I can't wait to play for you, Rose. Get those pointes on and dance for me, for *us*. Our Rose, our muse," he says gently, putting me back on my feet as he pops his violin beneath his chin and runs the bow lightly over the strings. The sound peels over my skin scattering goosebumps as it goes. He returns to his corner of the room and waits, watching Ivan and I intently.

"So, you want to dance with me?" I say, a little shyly now. My heart is thumping so hard, I can feel it trying to escape my chest.

"I'm a little rusty. Are you sure you want to dance with me?" he responds, grasping me behind my back and pulling me flush against his body.

"Yes," I breathe.

He presses a kiss against my cheek, then whispers in my ear. "First you need to get out of those clothes and into something more… appropriate."

"Oh, yes?" I respond, warmth flooding through my veins at the innuendo.

"I'm talking about those," Ivan says, pointing to some new black dancewear laid out on the chaise. He hands me my pointes and grins, shooing me away. "I'll just warm up whilst you get changed."

"You want me to change in the open?" I tease, pretending to be coy. He just responds with a wink.

Glancing at both Anton and Erik, I can see by the intense way they're staring at me that they're just as eager for me to undress. Well, if it's a show they want, then it's a show they'll get. I can't deny them anything. I don't want to.

Throwing out a sexy grin, I sashay as gracefully as I can to the corner of the room. Keeping my back to them, I drop my pointes to the floor and pull off my thick cable sweater and t-shirt. Stroking my fingers lazily over my skin I undo my jeans, sliding them slowly over my hips and down my legs, stepping out of them. Beneath, I'm wearing a grey lace thong and matching bra. Their little noises of appreciation set my skin on fire.

"There's my sexy muse," Anton mutters, drawing a smile from me.

These days, my colour choice of underwear doesn't vary much between varying shades of black, white, and grey. I do it for Anton so he doesn't ever feel like he's missing out. Of course, when I'm alone with just Erik or Ivan, that might differ. Often it's red for Ivan and a deep emerald green for Erik.

"Jesus Christ, Rose, you might not get out of here alive looking like that," Erik grinds out.

I look at him over my shoulder, chewing on my bottom lip teasingly before responding. "Bite me," I say with a slow smile.

"Oh, I promise, that's coming later," he retorts.

Holding back a giggle, I lean forward and pick up the black leggings sliding them on. Next, I grab the short sleeved leotard. When I'm comfortable, I turn to my men and curtsey, sweeping up my pointes on the way back up with a flourish.

"You look beautiful, Rose," Ivan says from the centre of the room. He stands with his back poker straight, wearing a loose pair of trousers. Whilst I've changed, he's removed his t-shirt and is bare-chested and glorious. Now, it's my time to suck in a breath.

"You're looking pretty gorgeous yourself," I respond pulling on my pointes and lacing them up my legs. I point each foot, flexing and stretching, getting used to the feeling of wearing them again. They feel like another skin, so well worn and perfectly moulded to my feet.

"Ready?" Erik asks, violin pressed against his chin, bow hovering over the strings.

I glance at him, there's a lightness in his eyes I've never seen before and absolutely no fear or any kind of worry. He's perfectly relaxed. Looking away from him, my gaze meets Anton's as he sits behind his easel, a fresh canvas before him. He grins, holding up some charcoal. Lifting his fingers to his forehead he salutes me, smiling that soul-shattering smile of his.

Finally, my gaze rests on Ivan. "Let's dance."

The first note releasing from Erik's violin has my steps faltering as I watch him. His eyes are pressed shut in concentration and bliss. My throat bobs as I swallow my fear that he's going to suddenly lose control. But he continues to play without any sign of falling into despair. In fact, he plays with surety and confidence. Slowly he opens his eyes and looks at me, his amber orbs glittering in the soft morning light. He dips his head once, then plays in earnest, his body swaying with sharp movements that match the quickness of the bow sliding over the strings, and the skilled fingers as they find the right notes.

"Come here, Rose," Ivan says, holding out his hand to me.

I take it and this time he bows deeply, dipping before me. His eyes meet mine, and something indescribable passes between us. Something magical, at least that's what it feels like. When he grips my waist and lifts me into the air above him, I let go of any thoughts of inferiority and just go with it.

For the next hour we dance together, moving fluidly and without restraint about the room. We don't follow any particular ballet, we just dance, somehow synchronising our movements. Ivan knows me body and soul, as I do him, so it's little wonder we can be free like this together.

Occasionally, as we dance, I capture glimpses of Erik lost to his own wonder and happiness, and Anton, a pencil gripped between his teeth as he sketches us. In this room, together, the four of us are free.

And my heart fucking soars.

CHAPTER 21

"You know you're taking the piss, don't you?" Alicia says, as she feels around the tender joint of my knee.

"I don't know what you mean," I respond, innocently.

Alicia raises her eyebrows and gives me a stern look.

"Oh, all right, I might have pushed it a little, but it was worth it." I chew on my bottom lip as I remember how it felt to dance with Ivan. That was a dream come true right there, made even more special with Erik playing the violin and Anton drawing us. If I were struck down by lightning right now, I'd die a happy woman.

Alicia pulls down my trouser leg, then stands. "Just know your body, Rose. It's going to take time to be fully back to normal. Plus, your medical condition complicates things. Don't push it, okay."

"Okay, boss," I salute her, and she laughs. "So, what now?"

"Well, I reckon you'll be signed out of my care in a few weeks. You won't be needing me much longer," she gives me a half-smile, pushing her multi-coloured hair behind her ear. I think she'll miss me. I know I'll miss her.

"That's a shame. I'm going to miss our little chats," I respond honestly.

"You will?" she looks at me, her deep chocolate eyes surprised by that comment.

"I will. Why's that hard to believe?"

"It's not," she beams at me, her lip ring glinting in the afternoon light. We're in my bedroom sitting on the sofa. Outside the weather is still terrible, Alicia's only just about dried off after getting caught in the torrential rain. She's wearing a pair of my slacks as her own jeans are completely drenched and being dried off by Fran.

"You've grown on me too. Besides, there's no one I know who lives a similar life to me and understands what we have to juggle." She laughs ruefully at that, rolling her eyes.

"Trouble in paradise?" I ask.

"Something like that."

"What is it?"

She heaves out a sigh and drags her colourful hair into a high ponytail showing of her pretty almond eyes. There are tinges of an asian descent in the shape of her eyes and cupid's bow mouth. I'm curious about her heritage but haven't felt it appropriate to ask.

"I mentioned that I grew up in Hackney, didn't I? That I got sent to a reform school as a last chance to get me back on track. I was a naughty kid," she laughs at that, rolling her eyes. "I met my crew there. The boys who eventually turned into the men I love…"

"But…?"

"But we've never been able to shake off our pasts. Even here, all these miles away from the streets and the bullshit that happened back home. I'm the only one who's managed to get a permanent job and I have all these responsibilities, Rose... bills to pay, mouths to feed."

"I can help. Do you need a loan?" I say immediately.

She looks at me and shakes her head. "Fuck, I'm not looking for a handout, just someone to talk to. Forget I said anything."

Reaching out, I squeeze her arm. "This isn't a handout and it's okay, you *can* talk to me? It's tough out there, jobs are scarce down here. If I didn't manage to get this job, I'm not sure what I would've done."

"Sonny and Easton have had some luck getting adhoc work in Newlyn on the fishing boats, but Camden and Ford get turned away at every possible turn. They'll literally do anything. But if I'm honest they don't really fit down here, and I'm worried they're going to fall into old habits."

"Old habits?"

Alicia looks at me with worried eyes. "Underground fighting. I spent most of my time at Oceanside fixing those two up. They come with scars, tattoos, a shitload of baggage with a criminal record to match. They basically scare the shit out of most people even though they're good men. Loyal. I hate that there's so much judgement. If only people could see what I see. They saved me in a lot of ways, Rose. I owe them a lot. They followed me here even though Cornwall is so far removed from what they're used too."

Making a decision, I stand. "Come on, come with me a second," I say, pulling Alicia to her feet.

"Where are we going?"

"Ivan's office. He might be able to help."

"I don't want no charity, Rose," she responds, folding her arms across her chest in defence.

"Who said anything about charity? Ivan's a businessman and a savvy one at that. He has a lot of connections. I'm pretty sure he can make some calls, see if there are any jobs going."

"He'd do that for me?" she asks.

"No, but he will do it for me. Come on, if you don't ask, you don't get."

When we enter Ivan's office, he's sitting behind his desk peering at the computer screen with a scowl. Anton is with him and they seem to be having a rather deep conversation about a recent business transaction. I can't tell if it's gone according to plan or not, because the moment they lay eyes on us, Ivan closes his laptop and gives us both an even smile.

"Everything okay, Rose?" he asks me.

Anton grins at Alicia, "Hey, Rainbow," he says, giving Alicia a wink before turning his gaze on me. "You good, Rose?"

"We're fine. Alicia was just telling me to go easy on the dancing for a bit. I think we got carried away, Ivan," I chuckle. Easily done when I'm around him. Dancing is not the only thing we get carried away with.

"Shit, that's on me," he responds.

"Rose is fine. It won't be long until she's back to full strength. Just don't overdo it," Alicia assures him.

"So, what can we help you with?" Ivan asks, looking between the two of us curiously.

Before Alicia gets cold feet and makes something up, I speak for her, explaining her situation. By the time I'm finished, Ivan is looking at us thoughtfully.

"What do you think? Do you know of any contractors who need more guys on site?"

Ivan shakes his head. "All of my build projects are back in London. Unless they're willing to go there, I'm not sure how I can help."

"Alicia?"

"No, going back to London wouldn't be wise," she says, a little disheartened. "Thank you, anyway."

"Are you sure there isn't something?" I press.

"What about that small project in town?" Anton pipes up, giving Ivan a look. "Didn't you say help was needed on that?"

"What project?" I ask, feeling hopeful. I glance at Alicia and she gives me a weak smile.

"Just a small rebuild," Ivan explains. "You know what, we could use some extra hands, it'll get the job done quicker." Reaching into his jacket pocket, Ivan pulls out his business card and hands it to Alicia. "Get them to give me a call. I'm happy to meet them after our trip to London. How does that sound?"

Alicia takes the card, pocketing it. "*Thank you,*" she responds.

"You've helped Rose. Now we're returning the favour."

CHAPTER 22

ROSE

We arrive in London a few days later, finally leaving Cornwall on Monday, rather than the previous Friday as we'd hoped. The intervening days have been filled with a new kind of peace between us all. Erik and Anton have spent a lot of time in each other's company. They've been unravelling their past conflicts and building a new relationship where secrets are no longer hanging over them both and brotherhood bonds are forged in love and a mutual kind of pain.

I'm so proud of them.

Ivan and I continue to dance together in our newly repurposed studio. Sometimes we're joined by just Anton or Erik, sometimes both. I'm at my happiest when the four of us are together doing what we love. Somehow, we've found a new path where happiness rather than pain is what we strive for. It has been a blissful, healing time.

Now, in the blistering cold and bustling streets of central

London, we're ready to face Ms Hadley as a united front, stronger than we've ever been.

"The driver's ready to take us to the institute. Last time to back out," Ivan says, gripping my hand in his and glancing at Erik and Anton. The wind whips up my hair lashing it against my face. I brush it out of the way and shake my head.

"We do this together or not at all," I insist, softening the firmness of my response with a smile.

"Until the storm breaks or we do," Erik agrees, climbing into the taxi with determination. Of the four of us, this will be hardest on him, but I'm ready to catch him when he falls.

AN HOUR later we pull up outside a fairly nondescript building. It isn't set in the rolling grounds like the care home that Amber lives in. No, this institute is a large, ugly grey-brick building on the outskirts of a Buckinghamshire. It surprises me. I expected luxury, but from the outside this place seems far from luxurious. In fact, it's depressing and exactly what she deserves.

"I can see Viktor spared no expense," Ivan remarks with a huge dose of sarcasm.

"He might've been able to buy her out of a prison sentence, but this is a court ordered institute. I imagine he's biding his time before he can transfer her to another more suitable unit," Anton says, his face stony.

"If she lasts that long…" Erik mutters, reminding us all that she has a death sentence hanging over her head. I don't feel any sympathy for her, none, but I understand that Erik might still. She brought him up after all.

I take his hand in mine. Our fingers link together, my scar

pressing against his. "Come on, let's get this over with," I say, pulling him up the steps towards the entrance.

The inside is just as bleak as the outside. It's grey, dull and bland. A rather severe looking woman with short cropped hair and no makeup sits behind a glass screen.

"May I help you?" she asks in a tone of voice that suggests she doesn't want to help us at all.

"We're visiting Clara Hadley, my mother," Erik answers, unable to hide the distaste in his voice.

I squeeze his hand tighter, reassuring him I won't leave his side. Not now, not ever.

The woman runs her finger over the list of printed names before her until she finds Ms Hadley's. "Ah yes, Mr Erik Hadley?" she asks, looking from Erik to the rest of us.

"Yes, that's right."

She nods. "You may enter, but the rest of you have to wait here."

"What?!" I exclaim, glaring at her.

"I'm sorry that's the policy. This *is* a secure unit for the mentally impaired," she says, enunciating every word as though I'm stupid.

"Look, *lady*," I snap, anger curling up my spine. "We're here to support Erik. His mother's dying, for crying out loud. I'm his girlfriend and these men," I say, pointing to Anton and Ivan, "Grew up with Ms Hadley. She's like a mother to them. They need to say goodbye …" I add, my voice cracking, pleading to this woman's better sensibilities. The emotion is all bullshit, of course. But it's worth a shot. There's no way I'm letting Erik go in there alone. No fucking way. Besides, there are some things I'd like to say to Ms Hadley myself and I will not pass up the opportunity to do so.

The receptionist glares at me, then smiles a sickly sweet

smile that I want to smack right off her face. "Nethertheless, there are just two names on the visitors list; Mr Erik Hadley and Mr Viktor Sachov. I'm certain your name isn't Viktor," she says, snapping the book closed with a thud and crossing her arms over her chest. "Besides, I've already met Mr Sachov, so…"

"Bitch," I mutter, none too quietly.

The woman glares at me and I stare back, not breaking eye contact.

"What now?" Anton asks.

"I go in on my own," Erik says, pulling his hand free from mine.

"No, the fuck you don't," I snap, not willing to let him face Ms Hadley without us.

"We've got no choice."

"Let me deal with this," Ivan says, nudging us both aside and leaning on the counter. He taps the glass partition, getting the receptionist's attention. "How much?" he asks, pulling out a cheque book.

She cocks a brow but doesn't respond.

"How much?" he insists.

"You're resorting to bribery now?" she laughs, shaking her head.

"We need to see Ms Hadley. How. Fucking. Much?" he snarls, the nib of his pen spilling ink as he presses too hard against the cheque.

"Fifteen thousand," she responds quickly, folding her arms across her chest, grinning smugly like she knows the price is too high and he'll back down. But she doesn't know Ivan, and she certainly doesn't know that he's a millionaire.

Ivan nods tightly then scrawls quickly across the cheque.

"Here's thirty thousand. Fifteen to get us in, and fifteen to make sure we're not disturbed. Got it?"

The woman's mouth drops open in shock. Ivan slides the cheque towards her through the gap between the glass and the desk. She reaches for it, but he clasps her hand beneath his. "Don't fuck with us," he growls, letting go of her hand once he's sure she understands he doesn't make empty threats.

"Follow me," she responds, tucking the cheque in her jacket pocket.

Once through the security checks, which are no more than a quick pat down and a search of my bag, we're escorted to Ms Hadley's room. At the door the receptionist gives us a curt nod.

"You have two hours. That's as long as I'll be able to keep the hospital staff away."

"We won't even need one," Erik responds, attempting to push open the door.

She holds her arm out, preventing him from entering the room. "I warn you now, your mother is in a bad way. She's refused treatment and has barely eaten since she was brought here. The medical staff have had to force a feeding tube into her several times, otherwise she would've starved to death."

"And knowing all of this you were going to prevent my boyfriend from seeing his mother, only letting us in because we *paid* you. What kind of monster are you?" I snap, my eyes narrowing. Despite having no sympathy for Ms Hadley, it still doesn't mean I agree with this woman's actions. She has the good grace to look ashamed. Erik bares his teeth at her, and she moves aside. We file in the room behind him, not bothering to thank her.

The smell hits me first.

Disinfectant, death, decay, and the vague lingering smell of piss. The room is as bland as the building itself. There are no home comforts, just a hospital bed, and one of those uncomfortable armchairs you find in hospital waiting rooms situated beside it. The walls are painted beige and have seen better days, some of the paper peeling from the corners. It's as close to a prison as you can get.

"Who's that?" A feeble voice calls from the bed. I hadn't even noticed anyone lying there. But now that I look harder, I see the skeletal frame of Ms Hadley. She peers at us from behind the thin cotton sheet, her sunken eyes focusing solely on Erik. It's as though the rest of us don't even exist.

"*Erik?*" she whispers, uncertain he's actually in the room and not just a hallucination.

Her skin is sallow, her hair dull and wispy. The cancer has already done so much damage in such a short space of time. If she'd been someone we cared about, it would've been horrifying to see her like this. As it is, I feel nothing towards her.

"Erik? *Son?*" she cries out, her thin fingers lifting to her mouth in her certainty that he's real and not a figment of her imagination. "You came. He said you refused, but you *came*. I knew you would. I knew you wouldn't forsake me." Her voice wobbles with emotion as she struggles to lift herself upright.

A funny sound, pitched between a sob and a snarl, escapes Erik's lips. For a while he can only stare at her. I can't begin to imagine how he feels. This woman who brought him up, who betrayed him in the worst possible way. Why is it the people closest to us have the power to hurt us the most?

"Yes, Ma. I'm here," he says softly, and for a moment I wonder if he really is strong enough to do this. To face her. I step up beside Erik, taking his hand in mine and squeeze gently.

"You can do this," I reassure him. He looks down at with

me with such pain and so much love in his eyes that my heart bleeds for him. He cups my face in his hand and presses a delicate kiss against my lips before pulling away.

"No!" she half-shouts, half wails and I feel her hate, even before we turn back to face her. Despite the feebleness she displayed a moment before, she now grits her teeth and hauls herself upright on shaky arms.

"It's *Mother*," she snaps, keeping her gaze firmly narrowed on me even though she's admonishing Erik.

"That's where you're wrong, it's always been *Ma* to me. Or at least it had been until you chose to shoot the only woman I've truly loved." He steps closer to her, and I walk with him. Anton and Ivan each find a spot in the room and wait. For what, I'm not sure.

But they wait.

"She doesn't deserve you. She doesn't deserve your love. I do, *I do*!" she cries, slamming her hand against the mattress. We all flinch not because she has the strength to do any real damage, but because her hate is so heartfelt it's impossible not to.

Her nostrils flare as she breathes heavily, her gaze flicking between us both. She might not be strong enough to attack me physically, but I get a feeling she's still got the strength left to rip at us with her words. Sometimes that kind of hate is far more powerful. I pull back my shoulders, lengthening my spine, readying myself for whatever she has to say.

"You've taken him from me. I *deserve* his love," she repeats, her lip curling up in a feral snarl, her black eyes darkening further.

And right there I see the truth of her jealous heart. The love she felt for Viktor destroyed when Isabelle gave him the son she never could. The years of pining for a man who would never leave his wife for the woman he proclaimed to love. Ms Hadley is the product of Viktor's cold heart. She's so desperate for real love, *true* love that she's willing to wipe out any competition to get it. All the while filling her own heart with bitterness, jealousy and hate. It's a sad way to live. Isn't it interesting how hate can consume a person like it consumes Ms Hadley now? She burns with it, her desire to hurt me clear for all of us to see. I think if she had the strength, she would try to murder me with her bare hands.

"You don't deserve a damn thing… you killed my mother. You *killed* her," Erik chokes out.

"I loved Isabelle!" she exclaims, tears brimming in her eyes. Real hurt swimming there that for a moment I'm taken aback.

"And yet you still murdered her," Ivan says dryly.

There's a cold kind of calmness that settles over him. He doesn't take his eyes off her as he waits for her to answer. "Tell me why?"

Ms Hadley twists her head to face him. "Luka," she whispers, noticing him for the first time. "Such a sweet child. Such a good friend to my Erik. You understand don't you, why I did it? She wasn't good enough…" she mutters, her voice trailing off as her eyes glaze over.

"Who are you talking about, Ms Hadley?" Ivan asks, stepping closer to the bed. He stands on the opposite side to Erik and me, looking at us both over her skeletal figure.

She reaches for him, and inexplicably he takes her hand.

"She was so young and beautiful. I could never compete. She had this way about her, almost angelic, and so very kind. She reminded me a lot of Isabelle…" The faraway look on Ms Hadley's face softens as she mentions her best friend's name.

"Who did?" Ivan asks slowly, but we all know who she's talking about now. My throat closes over as we wait.

"Svetlana loved you so much," Ms Hadley says, her voice gentle. I watch as her thumb strokes the back of Ivan's hand, a comforting gesture from anyone else, but she's nothing but a viper about to strike.

"Ivan," I warn, but he gives me a look that tells me he already knows what's coming. That he's ready for it. Pulling her hand out of Ivan's grasp, she points a bony finger in his face.

"You killed her, you know... All those whores you slept with. She was so *lost*, lying there on the floor with one wrist slit. I wanted to help her, I really did, but then I remembered how she was so like Isabelle. Pure, beautiful, perfect, *loved*... So when she told me she'd made a mistake, when she begged me to help her, all I could do was promise that I would look after you. Then I slit her other wrist. Such a pretty colour, all that blood..."

"Oh, my God," I whisper, my eyes widening at the toxic truth spilling from her lips.

Ivan launches forward, his fingers finding Ms Hadley's throat. "You could've saved her. You fucking bitch!" he snarls, tears springing from his eyes as he squeezes.

Ms Hadley doesn't have the strength to fight back and for a horrible moment not one of us moves to stop him. Thankfully, Anton is the first person to pull himself together enough to react. He reaches for Ivan's fingers and somehow manages to pull him off her. Ms Hadley coughs, struggling for breath. Not one of us moves to hit the button behind her head to call for assistance. Eventually, her coughs turn to wheezes and then, finally, normal breaths follow.

"You killed Svetlana, and you killed my mother too, didn't you?" Erik asks, dropping into the armchair at her side. He grasps her hand, not because he seeks comfort, but because he wants the truth. Erik understands that she's so desperate for his love, that she might just give him the truth if he gives her some comfort in return.

"No, that was Viktor…" her voice trembles and a tiny slither of me feels almost sorry for her, this wasted, wreckage of a human being.

"Why? How? Tell me, Ma. I need to know," Erik says gently, trying to coax an answer. I know he'll never rest until he finds out. Leaving here today without knowing the truth isn't an option. But we needn't have worried because it appears Ms Hadley wants to purge her soul as much as we need to hear the truth.

"Isabelle was deeply in love with your father, but by the time you were born Viktor had already wooed Anton's mother and had got her pregnant too, leaving them the only option of marrying otherwise her family would disown her. Of course, Viktor couldn't allow that to happen, he needed their money after all…"

She sucks in a shaky breath, her eyes glazing over as we lose her momentarily to her past. Erik glances at me, the depths of his pain turbulent and raw.

"Isabelle was desperate to stop the wedding," she continues finally. "On his last visit to Kirkwall they had a huge row. In the end, Viktor promised her that he'd call off the wedding. Then he got her drunk and dared her to a swim with him in the ocean, something we used to do as kids… He came back alone… And I became your mother instead of her."

"Jesus Christ…" Erik stands, backing away from the bed. She reaches for him, her feeble arms shaking.

"Please, Erik. It wasn't me. I *loved* her."

"No. You could've done the right thing, but you let him get

away with it because you got what you wanted, me, *him*. You're no better than he is."

"Please, son."

"I am not your son!" Erik roars, before striding from the room.

Ms Hadley cries out, the sound like a wounded animal, but he doesn't return.

"My boy, my Erik," she whimpers.

Ivan moves forward, but Anton holds his arm out. "I have a question of my own," Anton says.

"Ms Hadley, there's something that's been bugging me for some time now. I have a memory that I'm not sure is real or not. I'm hoping it isn't…" He breathes in deeply, a great deal of pain washing over his features.

She looks up at him, there's no affection in her gaze. Nothing. Anton flinches, but continues regardless. "The day I overdosed in my studio, you found me first. I remember you leaning over me. You said something…"

"*Just like your mother…*" Ms Hadley says, her voice cold, hard.

"And then you picked up the needle, filled it up with more heroin and shot it in my other arm… Didn't you?"

She closes her eyes briefly, opening them again. A tear falls, rolling slowly over her paper thin skin. "I wanted you to need me. I was losing you all and I couldn't stand it. I've always looked after you, but then *she* took you from me…" Ms Hadley snaps her head around to look at me.

"You evil witch!" I snarl, my whole body shaking with rage. "You could've killed him!"

"It's okay, Rose," Anton says with a long sigh. He looks exhausted, weary, but relieved somehow.

"It's not okay, Anton. Nothing about her drugging you is okay," I retort.

"No, but I won't live with hate in my heart. Not anymore." He turns away from me and looks at Ms Hadley. "If you hadn't done what you did, I would never have fallen in love with Rose. I can only thank you for that."

Anton doesn't say another word. He simply walks to me, pulls me into his arms and kisses me gently, then leaves.

"Just like your mother, Anton. You're nothing more than a talentless addict," she spits, her vile words bouncing off the closed door he's just gently shut behind him.

Ivan glances at me and I know what he wants to do because I want the exact same thing. But murdering her in cold blood isn't why we came here, and I won't let him go to jail for this woman who's already done enough damage. Instead he leans over, and cups Ms Hadley's face in his hand, turning her head to face him.

"You will never be forgiven for what you've done, and any love we had for you. It's *gone*. I wish you a long, slow and painful death. Goodbye, Ms Hadley," he says, letting her face go as tears suddenly erupt from her eyes. When he reaches my side, he grasps my hand. "You coming?" he asks.

"Just give me a moment?"

"I'll be waiting outside." He squeezes my hand then lets it go, making sure that he too kisses me. The noise that comes from Ms Hadley is animalistic in her fury.

I wait for the door to close before approaching her. She watches me warily, suddenly afraid. "Are you going to kill me?" she asks, laughing hysterically now. Fear and madness coating the air around us.

"No, I think you're doing a fine job of that yourself."

"Then what?"

"I've come here to thank you too..."

"*Thank me?*" she spits.

"Yes, *thank you*. If you hadn't hired me, I wouldn't have met these beautiful, strong, brave men. I wouldn't have found my place in the world. I wouldn't have found happiness, *love*. It's funny, I no longer hate you. I *pity* you, Ms Hadley. You've done everything in your power to destroy any kind of happiness for them, but unwittingly bringing me into their lives you've done just the opposite. So, thank you for giving me these men. We're going to live a long, happy life together and you are going to die knowing that not one of them will grieve for you. That you'll be a nightmare finally laid to rest."

With that, I press a kiss against her cheek then walk out of her room, her screams of rage following me out.

CHAPTER 23

"You look stunning, Rose," Ivan says as his eyes graze over me appreciatively.

"Thank you," I respond, fiddling nervously with a stray strand of hair that's fallen free from my loose updo. Turning to face the mirror in the bedroom, I apply another coat of lip gloss trying to distract myself from the fact we're about to see mine and Ivan's old ballet company perform at the Royal Albert Hall. A surprise organised by Ivan, and one I'm looking forward to and dreading in equal measure.

It seems so strange to be doing something this extravagant after confronting Ms Hadley only a few days before, but like Ivan said, why should we curb our desires just because one woman sought to destroy us? What we choose to do together is entirely up to us, besides this may actually be our first real date together the four of us. In fact, I think it's our first real date, ever.

"I must admit, Ant, you do have fabulous taste. I'm impressed," Erik says as he leans against the door frame looking entirely handsome in his black tuxedo and bow tie. Our eyes meet in the mirror, and I flush pink at his intense appreciation. He's clean shaven, and his hair is slicked back off his face, a darker blonde with the gel, only serving to highlight his amber orbs even more. Erik really does have the most beautiful eyes.

"It's not bad," I joke, with a nervous laugh, dropping my lip gloss into my clutch bag and taking one final look at myself in the mirror.

Erik's right, Anton does have impressive taste. I've never worn such a beautiful dress or one as expensive. Made by some unknown designer, this black floor length gown is beautifully chic and understated. The top half is corseted with a sweetheart neckline that pulls me in and pushes me up in all the right places. The bottom half is a silk skirt clinging to my hips and thighs before merging into a chiffon material that floats outwards at my knees and trails behind me slightly. Sewed across the top half of the dress and dotted along the skirt are hundreds of iridescent pearl sequins that shimmer with colour when they capture the light.

"It's perfectly you, Rose," Anton grins, pressing a soft kiss against my cheek as he looks over my shoulder, admiring his choice of dress.

"Yes, and at almost one thousand pounds, this dress is probably the most expensive thing I've ever worn," I say, twisting my body to see the light catch the sequins sewn into the corset and skirt. In the darkness the dress is like a midnight sky without stars, but the second any light hits the dress a rash of colour spreads out across it reminding me of a shooting star carving up the night sky. It's truly stunning.

"Are we ready to go?" Ivan asks, glancing at his watch.

Up until two hours ago I was under the impression we

were leaving for Browlace in the morning, but Ivan said he had some business to attend to, and so our stay has been extended. Hence our first proper date this evening. Ivan organised the tickets for the ballet and Anton had disappeared for several hours this morning returning with this beautiful gown, albeit a little distracted. Throughout the day he's been disappearing off into the spare room to make hushed phone calls. I haven't asked him to tell me what they're about, I figure he'll do that when he's good and ready. Besides, neither Erik nor Ivan seem in the least bit bothered by his secretiveness, so I figure I shouldn't be either.

"As I'll ever be," I respond.

Anton slides his hand into mine and clasps my fingers. "There's nothing to be nervous about, Rose, you've got us remember?"

I squeeze his hand back gratefully. "If I'm perfectly honest, I'm not sure how I'll feel watching the dancers on stage knowing I was once part of the company."

"Me either," Ivan admits. "It's been a long time for me too. A lot of memories will be brought to the surface, most of them I'd rather forget," he winces, pulling a face.

"Remind me again why we're doing this then?" Erik asks as we head into the lift, pressing the button for the lobby.

"Because the company was a huge part of both of our lives, and I think Rose and I both need to lay some past ghosts to rest before we can truly move on." He glances at me, looking for some affirmation or reassurance for assuming this is the right thing to do and we shouldn't just head back into our hotel suite and forget all about it. Like Ivan, I've so much emotional baggage mixed up with my time in the Royal Ballet that I know this is going to be difficult, but Ivan's right, I do need to move on from that part of my life. Ballet will always be my passion, but it will never be my career again and I have to say goodbye to that somehow.

"I'm beginning to come to terms with the fact that I'll never get to perform in a ballet again, a small part of me had always hoped that one day I would get to perform again somehow... stupid, eh?" I say glancing at Ivan.

"Not stupid, Rose. Not at all," Ivan murmurs.

"But despite that... *loss*, I suppose," I say, trying to find the right word for how I feel. "I *am* looking forward to it, truly."

Ivan gives me a grateful smile, then steps in front of me dipping his head for a quick kiss before the doors open and we head out to the lobby and into the car waiting to drive us to the Royal Albert Hall.

During the intermission, I excuse myself and head to the powder room. Our private box has the perfect view of the stage and I've been so overwhelmed keeping my emotions in check whilst watching the ballet that I need a second to myself.

"Hey, you okay, Rose?" Ivan asks, following me down the corridor. He's removed his jacket and loosened his bow tie, and looks decidedly delicious in a rumpled, messed up hair kind of way. I can tell by his appearance that he's feeling as emotional about this experience as I am.

"I... I don't know," I say honestly, because that's the truth. Inside I'm a mixture of elation and sadness. Elation because the ballet is so utterly enthralling, reminding me why I love to dance so much, and sadness for all the obvious reasons. I never really had a chance to grieve the loss of my career. It's honestly like losing a loved one.

"Oh, Rose. Shit, I'm such a fucking idiot," Ivan responds, his worried eyes scanning my face. He looks up and down the corridor then clocking the powder room, grasps my hand and pulls me inside.

"Hello?" he asks, pushing open each stool to see if we're alone. I can already tell the room is empty, given there are no women applying makeup or making use of the little bottles of perfume lined up on a silver tray besides the run of sinks. Even the toilet is decadent, with red flock wallpaper and a chaise lounge situated in the corner of the room.

"Ivan, what are you doing?" I ask him as he flicks the lock on the powder room door and turns to face me.

"I didn't want anyone to interrupt," he says, shrugging.

"Interrupt what?"

"This," he says, striding over to me and pushing my body up against the sink, and pressing a hesitant kiss against my mouth. "Is this okay?"

"It's okay," I mutter back just before he captures my mouth with his and gives me a searing kiss that makes my knees go weak and my mind empty of all the mixed up emotions I've been feeling whilst watching the ballet.

When we part, both panting and flushed I can't help but grin. "You sure know how to distract a girl," I comment, turning around in his hold and searching in my clutch for a lipstick. Ivan steps back, grins and then bows. I watch him in the mirror whilst I apply a sheen of red lipstick before turning back to face him.

"My lady, Domina, Rose," he says with an affected accent that makes me giggle. "I am forever at your disposal." Then he drops to his knee before me, lowering his head. The atmosphere goes from playful to serious in an instant. Stepping towards him, I run my fingers through his hair, loving the feel of the silky smoothness, then give it a gentle tug, urging him to look up at me.

"I'm sorry if coming here has made you sad. I thought it was the right thing to do," he says, guilt brimming in his eyes.

My fingers trace his handsome face, my thumb brushing across his bottom lip.

"It was, it is. You can't stop me from feeling this way, Ivan, and you shouldn't. I've worked hard, you've all worked hard to open me up. I need to feel in order to heal properly. Thank you for bringing me here and thank you for being here right now."

"I love you, Rose," he says, drawing my thumb into his mouth and sucking on it gently.

"I know. I love you too." I press my eyes shut, allowing him to circle his tongue around my thumb and suck gently, then withdraw it before this moment gets too carried away. "I'd really like a drink, if you wouldn't mind?" I ask him.

"Sure," he responds, "I'll go to the bar and meet you back at our seats in a moment."

Ivan unlocks the door and steps outside whilst I use the toilet. Over the flush I hear the sound of the door opening once more, and as I adjust my skirt, the sound of the door locking has me grinning once more.

"The interval is almost over, Ivan, we can continue this discussion when we get back to the hotel suite," I say, smiling as I pull open the stall door. He's not there.

But another man is.

"This is the female toilets," I explain, my inner alarm bells ringing loudly in my head.

"Rose Gyvern?"

"No, I think you're mistaken," I respond, thinking on my feet quickly.

"I think not." He arches a brow, a snarl appearing on his face a second before he lunges for me.

I do the only thing I can, I fight back.

CHAPTER 24

ERIK

"Rose, Ivan said you'd be in here. What are you doing with the door locked?" I ask, turning the handle.

A muffled noise from inside has me pressing my ear up against the door. "Rose?" I ask again straining to listen. Another noise sounds; a male grunt. Then a scream.

"ROSE!" I bellow.

"Help!" she shouts back, her cry of fear sending a well of dread through me.

"Fuck! Rose!" I roar, slamming the force of my whole body into the door. I'm vaguely aware of Anton rushing towards me.

"Erik, what the fuck is going on?"

"It's Rose, find Ivan. Some motherfucker has her," I manage to bite out before throwing myself against the door for a second time. It rattles in its frame, but it doesn't open.

"ERIK!" Rose screams, before I hear another male grunt and a sound that's very much like bone meeting bone.

"Rose?" I shout, slamming my fist on the door.

Silence.

"You motherfucker!" I shout.

The red mist falls.

Someone has my Rose and they're hurting her.

That someone is going to fucking die tonight.

Pacing backwards to the other side of the hallway I run at the door, throwing all my weight and every ounce of rage against it. The lock gives way sending me sprawling into the room. Within seconds my brain has analysed the scene before me.

A huge burly man, dressed in a tuxedo similar to mine, is holding a frightened Rose around the waist, one hand wrapped around her throat. Her dress is torn at the knee, her hair dishevelled, and one shoe has come off in the struggle. She looks as though she's been fighting for her damn life.

"One move towards me and I snap her neck," he says.

I allow myself one moment to look into her eyes and my heart fucking breaks. She's afraid, yes. But she's more afraid of what I'm about to do. She knows that I'm going to kill this man.

"Don't, Erik," she manages to say, her eyes brimming with tears.

Her lip is bleeding from a small cut, and her right cheek swelling. Then I see the shiner already blooming around his eye and realise that whilst he might have hit her, she's given as good as she's got. A swell of pride widens in my chest.

"I'm giving you five seconds to let her go before I murder your arse," I bite out. My whole body is filled with a rage so deep that I'm about ready to rip this man to shreds for laying a hand on my love.

"What the fuck?" Ivan says from behind me. I hear a tray

of drinks smash to the floor as he and Anton enter the space beside me.

"Who sent you?" Anton bites out, his voice dark, deadly. Unrecognisable.

The man loosens his hold on Rose's neck, but not his grip around her waist. She sucks in lungsful of air, a tear springing from her eyes as she looks at us all.

"I asked you a question. Who. Fucking. Sent. You?" Anton repeats.

"No names. Just a target," the man shrugs, relaxed as fuck. Doesn't he realise he's about to die?

"Viktor," Ivan bites out, and we all know it to be true.

"First you're going to die, and then I'm going to kill that bastard," I bite out moving towards the man.

"No. Don't," Rose squeaks, shaking her head furiously.

"Better listen to your woman. You murder me now and the police will be on your arse in minutes. I figure that's the outcome my employer desires above all else. Looks like I'm as much a sacrificial lamb as this one," the man responds, releasing Rose from his hold.

The second he lets her go, she runs into Ivan's open arms. Her sobs are enough to shear my soul in two. "You, motherfucker, are going to pay for laying a finger on my woman," I grind out, before launching towards him. I manage to get in three bone fracturing punches before Anton pulls me off.

"Enough, Erik. This is what he wanted. There are other ways to manage this," he grinds out, panting from the effort of holding me back.

The man gets up on his feet and gives me a respect filled look. "I'll take those punches for upsetting your woman, but I am gonna walk out of here alive and you're gonna let me," he grinds out.

"You fucking cunt," I growl, desperately wanting to finish him, but knowing I can't when I see the crowd of people gathering outside the bathroom door. This set-up stinks of Viktor. Why do the job yourself when you can get someone else to do it for you?

"Nothing to see here," the man says strolling through the crowd. They part for him, not one of them trying to stop him. I move to go after the bastard, but Anton stops me once again.

"Not here, brother. Revenge is a better dish served cold. He'll get what's owed to him after we deal with Viktor."

Gritting my jaw, I nod tightly, knowing he's right. With a trembling body, I reach for Rose who's still folded within Ivan's arms.

"Come here, Rose," I say, needing to feel her touch, needing to know she's okay.

Ivan releases her and she steps into my arms, her fingers gripping onto the material of my tuxedo as she sobs against me.

BACK IN THE HOTEL ROOM, Ivan stays with Rose as she lies in the bath whilst Anton and I talk.

"This ends now," I say, knocking back a second shot of whiskey. I'm still murderous, and the amber liquid is doing nothing to take the edge off. "As long as she's ours, he will still keep coming after her. My question is why now?"

Anton slams his palm against the coffee table between us. "This is my fault. I fucking forced his hand. He might've left her alone had it not been for me."

"What do you mean?" I ask, stiffening.

He looks at me with deep sorrow. "I've been making some phone calls these past couple of days to business associates of Viktor's."

"About what?"

"About the real man behind the business mogul. About the dodgy shit he's been involved in over the years. Viktor is retaliating in the only way he knows how, by hurting the people I love the most. I should've fucking killed him when I had the chance."

"And we should've let you," I respond. A look passes between us, but we aren't able to discuss our thoughts further because Ivan and Rose enter the room. She's wrapped up in a thick plush bathrobe, her hair still damp and without a spot of makeup. My heart aches at the exhaustion in her eyes and the bruise on her cheek.

"I'm going to bed," she says, trying and failing to give me a reassuring smile.

Getting up, I stride over to her and cup her face gently. "How do you feel?" I ask her, running my hand gently over the swelling on her cheek and lip.

"I've felt worse," she says, bravely. "I'm glad he only managed to give me a slap and not a punch. Pretty sure he would've broken my cheekbone had he hit me any harder. Though I'm glad I didn't hold back in the same way. I think he was surprised I was capable of fighting back, honestly." She smiles at me, trying to protect my heart by making light of the situation.

"Fuck, Rose. He should never have been able to get to you at all," I respond, and I don't just mean the hired hand Viktor sent to rough Rose up, but Viktor himself. This was Viktor's way at warning Anton to back the fuck off. We should've let Anton kill Viktor. In fact, I should've helped. Pressing a kiss against Rose's mouth I look over at Ivan. "Take Rose to bed. Stay with her. I'll be with you both in a moment."

"Anton?" Rose asks, her gaze falling to my brother who is looking at us all with guilt and heartbreak. She's worried about him. Even like this, shattered and vulnerable, she's still thinking of everyone else. This woman astounds me.

"Please, go to sleep. I've got things to sort out," he manages to say, wincing at how cold it comes out. He looks at her apologetically. "I'm sorry. I just wish…"

"Don't do anything stupid. I *need* you," she says gently before turning on her feet and following Ivan into the bedroom.

"It's too late, I already have," he mutters, grasping his head in his hands.

"What are you going to do?" I ask him.

"What I should've done years ago, *ruin* him."

CHAPTER 25

ANTON

Looking out of the penthouse suite window, I gaze at the city lights of London stretching out before me. It's way past midnight, but the city is still buzzing and full of life. As I stand here steaming up the window with my breath, a sudden yearning for home and the quite peace of Cornwall calls to me. Apart from the last few years at Browlace, I've lived in London my whole life, but I don't miss the hustle and bustle in the slightest. My creative mind has always yearned for the quiet peace that only living in the countryside can fulfil. The sooner we leave the better, frankly. But not before I've settled a few scores. I'll never live with myself if I don't.

Padding over to the bedroom suite, I peer into the space that's illuminated only by the city lights peeking through the half closed curtains. Rose, Ivan and Erik are all sleeping, curled up on the bed together, the day's events exhausting them all emotionally. Erik is pressed against Rose's back, spooning

her with his body. Ivan faces them both, his arm thrown over
Rose and Erik, clutching them close. I wish I could feel as
peaceful.

But sleep evades me. I still have a debt to settle, and it's
been years in the making.

Snatching up my coat draped over the chair, I pull the door
shut and make a quick call to the hotel reception. Five minutes
later I'm sitting in the hotel lobby, drinking a whisky whilst I
wait for my cab. Swirling the amber liquid in the glass I think
about what I'm about to do. Is it wise? Probably not, but I'm
not leaving London until it's done. Another quick phone call
earlier has put things into motion, and I'm about to see the fall
out. I hope the effect is as nuclear as I think it's going to be.
Revenge will be sweet.

"Anton, where are you going?"

Shit.

Looking up, I see Rose approaching me, a look of concern
on her face. She's no longer in her robe and nightwear but fully
dressed with a determined look plastered on her face.

"I heard you leave. Where are you going?" she asks again,
as the concierge indicates my cab has arrived. I stand, pulling
on my jacket.

"Anton?"

"There's something I need to do, Rose."

"And you thought it best to do that in the middle of the
night, *alone,* after everything that's happened today? Let me
guess, you're going to finish what you started at Browlace?"

"I didn't start it, *he* did, but I'm sure as fuck going to finish
it," I retort, not willing or able to back down. This is non-
negotiable. I will not have her life threatened again. Too many
people have been fucked over by Viktor, I will not let him ruin
us too.

"Do you have a death wish?" She folds her arms across her chest, anger and worry tightening her jaw.

Sighing, I scrape a hand through my hair which is hanging loose around my shoulders. The length has always pissed my father off. It's a tiny show of rebelliousness that I use to my advantage. Besides, I like my hair down. He can go fuck himself. But then again after tonight, his opinion as to the matters of my hair won't be a fucking problem anymore.

"Not a death wish, no."

She cocks her eyebrows, not in the least bit convinced. "I call bullshit. You feel guilty about what happened, but you didn't send the brute to rough me up. Viktor did. Don't put yourself in danger for me."

"I feel guilty because I *am* responsible, Rose."

"No you're not!" she insists.

"I made some calls to several of his business associates. I've stirred up trouble and this is his response. He hurts me by hurting you. Well, after tonight he's not going to hurt another soul. Viktor's going to wish he never touched you."

"Then I'm coming. You're not doing this alone."

"No fucking way, Rose. I put you in danger tonight, I won't do that again."

"Tough shit, Anton. I'm coming," she responds, folding her arms across her chest and daring me to deny her.

"That makes three of us then," Erik says, stepping out of the lift, Ivan following him.

"Oh, for fuck's sake," I exclaim, throwing my hands up in the air.

"You think we'd let you do this alone? Shut-up and get in the cab," Ivan says, brooking no argument. "Besides, where Rose goes, we follow, and if she insists on going, then so do we."

Half an hour later we arrive in Chelsea outside my father's home, a large Edwardian house with a ridiculous number of rooms, hardly any of them used given he lives there on his own. It's my house too really, but I've not set foot in the place for years. I don't particularly want to enter now but I must. This is the last conversation I'm going to have with my father. After this he's dead to me, to everyone, hopefully.

Pressing the number combination on the lock, I push open the door. My father hasn't updated it for years; 02071980. Erik's birthdate. Not mine, *Erik's*. His first born son's. For years that hurt me knowing he used Erik's birthdate as the door code. Back then I thought it was because he loved Erik for all his talent, not realising the true reason. But it doesn't hurt me anymore because I no longer seek my father's approval, I don't seek his love or his respect because it's worth nothing to me now. Rose gives me all that I need, and Erik and Ivan are the only men I need in my life. My soulmate and my brothers.

Here by my side.

Knowing that gives me the strength to finish what I started by making those phone calls. Would I have acted differently had I known the outcome for Rose? Absolutely. There's no way on earth I would've knowingly put her in danger like that. But now that I've started, I can't stop. This ends tonight.

Stepping into the hallway, I push down the feeling of inferiority and stride towards my father's study. Growing up, he spent all his time in this room whilst my mother and I were relegated to other parts of the house. She and I used to spend a lot of time together in the den, reading, watching television and laughing. Then Ms Hadley arrived with a five year old Erik and everything changed. Granted, my father was still as aloof and cold with me as he'd always been, but it was my mother who changed for the worse.

The drinking started a week after Ms Hadley arrived with the boy who would become my best friend, the prescription drugs a month later. I lost my beautiful, kind-hearted mother many years before her body gave up on living. I grieve for her still, the mother I loved with all my heart, destroyed by the father who could never love me and the woman who brought up his first born son.

Stopping at the door to his study I draw in a deep breath, then push it open. As expected, my father is sitting behind his desk working. I'm not even sure if he ever really sleeps, either way the chair he's sitting on must be well worn from all the hours and hours of time he's spent here scheming, making money, losing money and expanding his many businesses. Not to mention all the lives he's ruined in the process.

He looks up as we enter. There isn't any surprise on his face, just an amused kind of acceptance, as though he's been expecting us and finds it all mildly amusing.

Tosser.

"To what do I owe the *pleasure*?" he says, his tongue curling around the words with distaste.

"Hello, Father," Erik and I say simultaneously.

There's a glimmer of shock in his eyes before he quickly covers it up with a slow smile. "So, you finally figured it out?" He leans back in his seat and folds his arms across his chest.

"That and quite a few other things," I respond.

"Is that so?" he retorts, an arrogant smirk darkening his face.

"You sent someone to hurt Rose and you're going to pay dearly for it," Erik snarls.

Viktor smiles slowly, taking great pleasure at seeing the

bruise blooming on Rose's cheek. "I have no idea what you're talking about," he says.

"Don't do that, you prick. We know you sent that fucking brute to do your dirty work. We know about Isabelle. We know you murdered her, that you married my mother for money, that all of this," I say, flinging my arms wide, "was built on lies, deceit and blood."

"I see Clara has been talking. You know you shouldn't listen to the ravings of a mad old woman. She's not in her right mind."

I laugh, the sound bitter and hate filled. "Do you enjoy torturing the women you profess to love? Do you enjoy watching your children suffer? Does that make you happy?" I spit out, trying and failing to keep my cool.

"Don't talk to me in that tone of voice, you know as well as I that you're capable of the same... Look at that poor girl, what was her name...?" he pauses for affect, tapping his finger against his closed mouth. "Oh, yes, *Amber.* Perhaps we're more alike than you think?"

"Cunt," Ivan bites out, stepping forward. I hold my hand out to stop him. This is my fight, not his.

My father snaps his eyes to Ivan, they narrow. "Or wait, how about you? Svetlana slit her wrists because of the hell *you* put her through. I'm not the only man to fuck with feeble-hearted women with ridiculous notions of love. How was the ballet this evening, by the way?"

"Shut the fuck-up, Viktor," Erik snaps. "You'll get what's coming to you."

He laughs maniacally. "Now, now, boys. Empty threats are just that. You know as well as I do that you have no evidence to do a damn thing, and even if you did, I have enough money and know enough people in high places to get myself out of any shit you attempt to mar my name with."

He looks at all of us smugly and I want to fucking kill him. I want to fucking kill him for all that he's done. For the lives he has ruined. For my mother who loved him despite his faults. For Erik's mother who trusted in his love and was betrayed in the worst possible way. For hurting Rose.

One way or another, tonight this cunt is going down.

Rose steps up beside me, her fingers twining with mine.

"I'm here," she reminds me, calming my fraying temper. She's so cool, so calm. So fucking strong. I'm doing everything possible to not lose complete control. It's imperative that I keep my head. I don't want to give him the satisfaction of seeing me losing my shit again. When he came to Browlace, I lost it totally and whilst it felt good to wrap my hands around his throat it only proved to him that I'm a man who allows his emotions to control him. Not this time. This time, I've come prepared. There are other, better ways to destroy a person. One phone call to the right person, that's all it's taken to ruin my father in the only way it'll really hurt him; through his wallet. I don't know why I didn't just do that in the first place.

"You've always underestimated me, Viktor," I say, not bothering to address him as father since he's never been one to me.

"And you've always disappointed me, Anton," he lashes back. But his words no longer have the power to hurt me, not when I know how it feels to be truly loved. The strength I find in that spurs me on.

Ignoring his look of disgust, I walk over to his walnut cabinet and open the drawer, finding the handgun he keeps in there still. Picking it up, I check to see if it's loaded. Finding that it is, I hold it up and aim it at my father.

"Anton!" Rose cries.

"It's okay, Rose. Trust me," I murmur.

Viktor barks out a laugh. "You don't have the balls."

Striding over to him, I place the gun against his forehead. "You've no idea what I'm capable of. But believe me, by the end of this conversation it won't be me firing the gun."

Viktor bites out a sharp laugh and sitting forward in his chair, presses his head against the gun. "What the fuck are you talking about, *boy*?"

Turning to Rose, Ivan and Erik I motion for them to leave the room. "Wait outside. I'll be with you soon," I say.

"I'm not leaving," Rose insists.

"Erik, get her out of here," I snap. He doesn't hesitate. Not giving her a choice, he picks her up and strides from the room. I wince at the sound of her anger. She'll get over it, she'll forgive us.

"Anton, I can stay," Ivan says, hovering at the door.

"No. No you can't. Go."

Nodding tightly, he too leaves the room.

"Isn't that sweet how much they care for you. Can't see the attraction myself, I only reserve my love for those who truly deserve it."

Laughing, I step back suddenly, placing the gun on his desk. "Uncle Saviano and I had a really long chat today. Looks like he's rescinded his investments in your companies. Every. Last. Penny. Fifty million pounds, I think he said."

"What?!" Viktor snaps, sitting up. Panic flashes across his face. He taps at his keyboard, his face turning a sickly white as the truth of what I've said becomes apparent.

"What the fuck have you done?" he whispers, unable to believe what he's seeing.

"Did you know that Mum was his favourite sister? Turns

234

out he never liked you, and he sure as fuck doesn't take kindly to his nephew being treated like shit or threats being made to my girlfriend. Without his money, you've nothing to keep your businesses afloat. Looks like your cash cow has finally dried up."

"He can't do that." Viktor says, panicking.

"He can do whatever the fuck he likes. You forget that you're not the only man with money and contacts in high places."

"I have other investors, they will cover the deficit."

I laugh, really laugh at his arrogance. "No, you don't. You married *into* wealth. All your contacts were made through my mother's family and there's no one left who'll support you now Uncle Saviano has decided to cut you off completely. Those calls I made yesterday that forced you to send that man after Rose, they were my first mistake. There was really only one person I needed to call, and now that's done, you're well and truly fucked."

"Do you realise what you've done?"

"I learnt a hard lesson today by not going straight for the jugular. Now that I have, this is over. You're finished."

"I will be back. Watch me," he threatens.

"Stop lying to yourself. The truth is, all this time you thought you had the power when really it belonged to me. *I'm* the last born son of the Ricci family. Their blood runs through *my* veins. The only reason they kept funding your businesses was because they believed I would take it over eventually, that you were building it for *me*." I laugh at that bitterly. "But that changed the minute I told Uncle Saviano *everything* you've done. There's *nothing* he doesn't know…" I say slowly, loving the look of fear running rampant over his features.

"You son of a bitch! Do you know what you've done? He'll kill me."

"It's no more than you deserve. You killed my mother, all's fair in love and war," I shrug.

"She killed herself. I didn't force feed her prescription drugs, she did that all on her own."

"Because of *you*, Viktor. You might not have murdered her yourself, but you sent her to a place she couldn't return from."

"After all this time, why act now? Because of that whore you call your girlfriend?"

"First thing first, motherfucker, she's not a whore," I snarl, reaching for his collar and yanking him towards me, spitting in his face, then pushing him forcefully back in his seat. "Yes, I do this for Rose, but I also do it for my mother, for *me*."

"I'll fucking kill her," Viktor spits, glancing at the gun on his desk. I can see the thoughts running through his head. He could pick up the gun and shoot me, shoot us all. But I know my father, if he's going to commit murder, he'll make damn sure he's not the one pulling the trigger. Yesterday proved that to me. If he fires that gun now there's no going back and he knows it. No, my father will try to wheedle his way out of this, still arrogant enough to think he can talk my Uncle around. Thing is, I'm counting on that arrogance. Rose is safe. He, however, is not.

"Empty threats are exactly that, Viktor... *Empty*," I say, repeating his own words back to him.

"You little bastard," he spits, his face puce with rage.

I bite out a laugh. "You've treated me like your bastard son my whole life, you've destroyed lives and you tried to take Rose from me. This is the consequence, Viktor. As of now you're a pauper and no longer a part of this family. Like Ms Hadley, you have *nothing*."

"I still have assets. I have this house. It's worth a few million. I'll sell it."

"You could try but believe me when I say there is *no one* who wants to do business with you now. Besides, even if you did manage to sell, it won't be enough to cover the millions you're in debt, and you know it."

Viktor flinches, real panic littering his face.

"Well, there's really nothing left to discuss. Goodbye, Viktor. Enjoy an eternity in Hell." I say, turning away from him.

His silence is deafening.

Half of me expects him to pick up the gun and shoot me in the back, but I know that he won't risk pulling the trigger until he's checked for himself that he really, truly has no chance of getting my uncle back on side. No, he'll try to spin this all on me. I'm more than certain of that fact. Leaving the room, I pull the door closed, clicking it shut behind me. A few seconds later I hear him begging my uncle for forgiveness.

But forgiveness isn't something he'll ever get from the Ricci family. The fact of the matter is, if my father doesn't pull the trigger on himself, then Uncle Saviano has his own hired assassin waiting to do just that. When my feet hit the pavement outside, I hear the muffled sound of a gun firing. I don't look back.

Instead, I walk towards the only future that's worth having, I walk towards my heart, my brothers, safe in the knowledge that Viktor will never be able to hurt us again.

CHAPTER 26

ROSE

W e hear of Ms Hadley's death a few weeks later.

Like Viktor, she died alone. There was no one holding her hand, no one whispering comforting words as she left this world. She'd been dead two hours before the nurse made her rounds. We didn't mourn her loss, there were no tearful laments, or talk about what a wonderful woman she'd been. The day had passed like all the others, with laughter, happiness and love. In fact, the sun had shone so fiercely that we all took a walk in the grounds of Browlace, accompanying Ivan as he placed a bouquet of flowers on Svetlana's grave. We mourned her, not Ms Hadley, and then moved on.

This morning, as I warm up in my dance studio, Erik tuning up his violin, and Anton sketching, I feel a sense of deep, blissful peace.

"Penny for your thoughts?" Anton asks as he places his

sketchpad on the floor and pads silently over to me on bare feet.

"I'm thinking about us, this," I explain. "Until I met you all, happiness was an emotion I didn't often feel. I feel so fortunate..." My voice trails off as I think about what Anton's been through these past few weeks, years even. Knowing that Viktor shot himself in the head, blowing his brains out across the back wall of his office isn't a comfort, not really. I mean he's out of our lives for good, and I'm glad about that, but it doesn't detract from the fact that he got away with Isabelle's murder. If there is a hell, I hope he's fucking burning alive day in day out on a perpetual cycle for all the hurt he's caused.

"Hey, don't do that. Don't think about him," Anton says, reading me well. "I'm just glad that he'll never be able to hurt anyone ever again."

"Me too," I agree kissing him gently.

When we finally stop kissing- which I must admit, is a good five minutes later- Anton scrapes a hand over his beard, grinning. I lean over and give it a gentle tug. "It's getting quite long. I'll have to start calling you grizzly from now on," I say with a light laugh.

He captures me in his arms, pulling me close so he can graze his beard over my cheek. "You weren't complaining last night when my head was between your legs. Nothing like a bristly beard to heighten the pleasure, hmm?" Anton teases, brushing his lips against my ear.

I giggle, laughter bursting free as he picks me up and spins me around.

When he settles me on my feet, his face becomes serious once more.

"What is it?"

"I've just received my father's will. He left the house to

Erik," he says, glancing over at Erik who is staring at us both with a sombre gaze.

"I told you, I don't fucking want the house. Any of it. It's all tainted," Erik says, tucking his violin into its case.

"I'm sorry, Anton," I say softly, cupping his face in my hand.

"I'm not. Besides, we're going to give the money for the sale of the house to charity. At least some good can come out of this fucking mess."

"That's a good idea. What charity?" I ask him.

"I've been talking to one of Ivan's business associates; the Freed brothers. They fund a reform school called Oceanside for kids who've taken the wrong path in life, they wanted to help those kids who everyone else has given up on. The sale of the house will be going towards funding more spots at the school and extending it to meet the growing needs of kids who've ended up the wrong side of the tracks."

"Wait, Oceanside?" I exclaim, surprise and happiness lighting my face. "That's the school Alicia went to, her and her boyfriends."

"It is? Small world," Anton agrees, smiling broadly. "Well then, she turned out pretty great, despite her weird choice of hair colour. So I guess that has been a good decision well made?"

"Pretty certain she's a fishwife in disguise," Erik laughs. "Her swearing can rival any hardened sailor."

"Pretty sure she's going to be a friend for life," I retort, knowing in my heart I'm right. "So, what are your plans for the day?" I ask Anton and Erik.

"Ah, well, interesting you should ask that question," Erik says, approaching us both with a naughty look on his face.

"Oh, yes?" My cheeks heat under his scrutiny, as his eyes rove appreciatively over my body.

"Now as much as I adore that look you're giving me, I'm not talking about sex, Rose."

I pout, and both Anton and Erik laugh.

"Remember a few weeks back we mentioned a surprise?" Erik asks.

"Yes," I say carefully, glancing between them both.

"Well, it's ready," Anton finishes for him, just at the same moment Ivan strides into the studio. He's dressed in soft black trousers and a button down grey shirt. I've not seen him all morning and I greet him with a hug and a gentle brush of my lips against his mouth. "Morning, beautiful," he responds pausing momentarily, still surprised at such overt affection that's normally kept hidden behind closed doors, at least between us two. Though even that's changing now, evolving I suppose. I'm still his Dom in the bedroom, that will never change, but where once before there were rules around being affectionate outside of our private time, that has changed. I'm more than happy for him to touch me and kiss me how he sees fit and in return, I do the same. It works.

"What's this I'm hearing about a surprise?" I ask, chewing on my bottom lip trying to suppress a squeal of delight.

"Well, we've all been working hard on something I think you're going to really appreciate!" Anton says with a wink.

"Stop teasing me and fess-up. I need to know!"

"First things first, you need to get dressed," Ivan says. "Wrap up warm and meet us on the drive."

"Where are we going?"

"That's a surprise. Now go on, get that peachy arse dressed," Erik says, giving me his most smouldering sexy looks.

My arse happens to be his favourite part of my anatomy given he loves to spank it so much.

"Eek, should I be worried?" I ask, pulling off my t-shirt, revealing my tight fitting leotard.

Anton and Ivan groan almost simultaneously, a look passing between them. Erik shakes his head, capturing their heated gaze. "There's plenty of time for that later," he admonishes with a wink.

"Spoilsport," I mutter making sure I sway my hips as I walk away, a huge grin spreading across my face at the sounds of their appreciation.

CHAPTER 27

"What are we doing here?" I ask, frowning as we step out of the car and onto the promenade. The sea is surprisingly calm for a winter's day. Christmas is still a few weeks off and usually the December tides are rough and squally, not today. Today, it's the same slate grey as the cloud filled sky, tiny waves tossing the surface gently.

"You'll see," Erik responds, pulling out a length of black silk from his pocket.

"What's that for?" I ask.

"It's part of your surprise. Turn around, Rose," he commands.

Of course, I can't deny him, though I can't help but comment. "This takes kinky to a whole new level, are we exhibitionists now?"

Erik laughs, ignoring my remark and guiding me forward. "Take Ivan's hand, Rose. All will become clear."

"This is verging on creepy," I snigger, linking arms with Ivan and letting him lead me blindly onwards.

"Watch the steps," he says, steadying me as we descend one at a time.

"What have you been up to?" I ask.

This clearly has something to do with my old ballet studio, or rather the wreck of it that I've owned since Sylvia left it to me in her will. I miss her, she was a wonderful teacher and a friend to me growing up. The shell left behind is all I have left of her and the only happy memories I had as a child dancing in her studio whilst the ocean crashed against the shore outside.

"What's going on?" I repeat, feeling a little anxious now as Ivan removes the blindfold. He has me facing away from the studio, my line of sight out to sea and toward the tiny fishing ships far away on the horizon.

Ivan pulls out a key from his jacket pocket. His cheeks are flushed from the cold and something else, excitement maybe? "Happy Christmas, Rose," he whispers, handing me the key.

"Christmas is weeks away." I point out.

"Well, happy *early* Christmas then," Anton says as he and Erik catch up with us.

"Turn around, Rose," Erik says softly, his amber eyes alight with joy.

"You haven't?" I say quietly, glancing between the three of them. It suddenly dawns on me just what they've done. "You didn't! It's too much." My eyes fill with tears before I'm even able to see what they've done to the studio.

"Rose, nothing is ever too much for you. Turn around and take a look," Ivan urges, squeezing my arm.

My breath catches as I look at my old decrepit dance studio, that is no longer weather worn and derelict. It's been completely rebuilt, painted a brilliant white and almost exactly how I remember it looking when I was a kid, except for the sign above the door.

"Do you like it?" Anton asks, pointing to the sign. On it is a painting of a ballet dancer that looks exactly like me, written next to it in beautifully artistic cursive are the words; *Rose's Ballet School.* It's not graffiti writing exactly, but it's similar in style and unlike anything I've seen Anton produce before.

"Are you trying out a new style, Anton?" I ask.

"I painted the ballet dancer. The signage was done by someone else."

"It's stunning... who?"

"A friend of yours... *Rainbow,*" he grins.

"Alicia? I had no idea she was artistic."

"Turns out she's quite the graffiti artist. Her work is *dank,*" Anton says, smiling with mirth.

"Dank?" I laugh, "As in damp and cold?"

"No, as in 'awesome', 'cool'," he explains. "I've learnt quite a few new words from Alicia."

I shake my head in wonder, my attention drawn back to my refurbished ballet studio. It's beyond anything I could have ever dreamed of. How have they managed to pull this off? We've spent so much time together.

"This is just... You did this all for me?" I have no words as a sob escapes my throat. Emotions flood my chest, making my heart burst with affection, with love. I'm so full of it, so damn happy.

Anton wraps his arm around my waist, pulling me into his side. "You deserve this and so much more, Rose."

"But I already have a job," I blurt out suddenly, glancing at Ivan. Well, at least I think I do. I've not actually worked as his personal assistant for weeks now. His office is filled with tons of paperwork and a shedload of filing, and even though I've returned pretty much to full health, Ivan hasn't asked me to return. If the truth be known, I haven't wanted to either. Not because I don't want to spend time with Ivan, but because working in an office isn't really my thing. Before I needed the job to survive, and whilst I still want to find my own way to earn money, I don't want to do that behind a desk with the man I adore as my boss.

He grins. "You were a pretty great assistant, but you're going to be a wonderful ballet teacher, Rose. Sylvia left this studio to you for a reason. Now you can continue to do what you love in the place you loved to dance the most."

Tears spring from my eyes as I walk into Ivan's arms and hug him. "Thank you," I breathe, overwhelmed but inexplicably happy.

"Come on, let's show you inside," Erik grins, holding his hand out for me to take.

The studio is as beautiful on the inside as it is on the outside. A new run of mirrors line one wall, a brand new barre of smooth oak wood attached to it. The floor is shiny and buffed to perfection. But the most stunning thing of it all is the huge mural painted across the back wall. I see it reflected in the mirrors and turn sharply to gaze at it.

"Anton," I breathe, my voice cracking with emotion.

Before me is the most stunning black and white painting of the four of us. In the centre Ivan and I are dancing, we look so graceful. Ivan is lifting me upwards at the waist, his face gazing up at me as I look down at him. The look that passes between us is captured perfectly. There's no doubt we're in love.

"I don't know what to say…" I feel my men watching me as I stare at the mural, utterly enthralled by it. "This is just…" I can't form the right words to express how I feel because there aren't any that would fully give justice to the emotions bursting inside me right now.

Anton steps up behind me, wrapping his arms around my waist as he presses a kiss against the curve of my neck.

"You like it then?" he asks.

"Like doesn't even begin to describe how I'm feeling right now," I respond, softly.

"Do you think I've captured the likeness?" he asks me, genuinely wanting to know.

"Yes. I'm half expecting them to climb out of the painting. It's incredible."

To the right of Ivan and me is Erik, his eyes are pressed shut, his face blissful as he plays the violin. It's a beautiful copy of the man who has fought to overcome the darkness within him.

To the left is Anton's self-portrait. He's sitting before his easel, his head tipped to the side a pencil gripped between his teeth, one hand raised as he draws. I walk forward, running my hand over the mural, needing to touch it, wanting to connect somehow if that makes sense?

"I think I'm better looking in my head," Anton smirks.

"You are exactly as good looking as you think," I confirm, with an astounded laugh. This man's talent is unbelievable.

"Don't give him more of a big head," Ivan remarks laughing.

Twisting in Anton's hold, I reach up and kiss him deeply. "Every time I'm here, I shall always be reminded of our love. Thank you," I say.

"You're very welcome, Rose," he responds, then he jerks his head towards Ivan and Erik. "But these two arseholes had a hand in all this too. It was Ivan's idea, of course, and Erik actually did some hard manual labour alongside the men we hired. The man's a beast."

"My favourite kind," I grin, walking over to them both, and

holding out my arms. They both walk into them and we hug, the three of us. When Ivan starts kissing me, Erik mutters something about getting a room. We all crack up laughing. Once we've all calmed down Ivan walks over to a run of hooks holding several pairs of ballet slippers and selects a pair, bringing them over to me.

"Are you ready for your next surprise?" he asks, glancing at his wristwatch.

"There's more?"

"Several, actually," Anton grins as the door to the studio opens as two rather grumpy looking boys walk in, followed by a handful of girls in the full stereotypical ballet get-up; pink leotards and tutus. So much pink!

My mouth pops open as they gather in the studio looking between us all.

"Looks like you've got a class to teach," Erik winks before pressing a soft kiss against my mouth and taking a seat in the corner of the room. Anton and Ivan move aside too, chatting as I regard my new pupils. The girls are aged between about four and twelve, all of them have their hair pulled back in a tight bun. My heart squeezes at the excitement on their faces as they look about the studio and see themselves in the mirror.

"Well hello, Prima Ballerinas," I sigh, my heart warming at their responding giggles, and shy smiles.

"Urgh, so many girls," one of the boys says, drawing my attention their way. They both look uncertain and a little pissed-off actually. The younger of the two looks like he's about to bolt out of the door. Both are wearing clothes that are entirely unsuitable for dancing. I make a mental note to buy some suitable dancewear for next time. If there is a next time given neither look like they particularly want to be here.

"Hey," I say to them both. "Want to tell me your names?"

"I'm Sebastian, and this is George. We're brothers," the older of the two says rather proudly. He can't be more than ten himself.

"Well, hello to you both. Thank you for joining my dance school."

"Oh, our older sister made us. I ain't no prissy dancer," the younger boy, George, says.

"Is that so?" I ask smiling widely at him. I like his honesty. Behind me Erik chuckles, but all the girls in pink just glare at him. It's quite amusing, actually. I'm pretty sure there's more than a few prima ballerinas in this lot.

"Shit, sorry, Rose. He's got a mouth on him that one." Alicia walks in and cuffs George lightly around the head, giving me an apologetic smile as he scowls at her. "What did I say, Georgie? Don't be rude!"

"These are your little brothers?" I ask, straightening. "I didn't realise you looked after them." "Yep, I'm sister *and* mum, and these are the *responsibilities* I was talking about a few weeks ago. Little sods have given me shit all morning. Thought they might enjoy a bit of discipline." She pulls a face and I laugh.

"Well, you're more than welcome at my ballet school," I say to them graciously.

"So do you like it?" she asks, and I can tell by the look on her face that she isn't just talking about the studio we're standing in, but her artwork on the signage outside.

"I love it. You're very talented," I say, giving Alicia a hug.

"So I've been told," she responds with a wink.

I roll my eyes and address my new students, paying particular attention to the two boys who look like they'd rather be rollicking in the freezing ocean than be here with me.

"Just give it a try. You never know, you might enjoy yourself," I say to them with a gentle shrug of my shoulder.

Alicia mouths a thank you as she moves to sit beside Erik. This time there's no sudden panic he's going to attack her because of his past and fear of women. On the contrary, he's able to talk with Alicia without breaking out in a sweat. How times have changed.

"So, class, thank you for coming. My name is Rose, and I'm your ballet teacher," I say, addressing the group. There are several smiles, Sebastian is biting his lip with nerves and uncertainty and George is just plain scowling.

"George, what is it?" I ask.

"Dancing is for girls, I'm not a sissy. Laters!" he says to the room before twisting on his feet and walking straight into the arms of a young, tattooed man with long floppy blonde hair and a grin that hides a multitude of sins. Behind him another man leans against the doorframe. He's tall with skin the colour of mocha and a large scar that runs from his left temple all the way to his chin. He catches my gaze and my mouth drops open at the blueness of his eyes as he regards me. They're the colour of topaz and utterly enthralling. I smile and he nods his head sharply in acknowledgement, his gaze sliding over to Alicia. The look that passes between them is electric.

"Now, now, little troublemaker. Stop right there," the blonde says.

"Oh, piss off Camden. You can't tell me what to do!" he retorts puffing out his chest

"George!" Alicia shouts, her face turning pink with both embarrassment and lust as she looks at the man clutching hold of George, and the one standing just behind him like a sentinel at the door.

"What did I say to you, Georgie? Dancing is just like boxing; you need to be light on your feet and as strong as a lion. Ain't that right, Ford?" the blonde says casting a look over his shoulder.

Ford looks at George, his bright blue eyes twinkling with mirth. "Camden's right, but I have to say, there ain't no better feeling than winning a bare knuckle fight. Tights just ain't my bag."

"Ford!" Alicia exclaims.

"Just speaking the truth." He shrugs, giving her a wink, then heads back outside. All the little ballerinas seem to release a breath the moment he steps outside.

"If the truth be known, I wasn't much of a fan of the tights," Ivan smirks, crouching before George. "but if you become a principal dancer like I was, then you must have enough strength and stamina to perform the whole ballet. Some go on for hours and hours. I'm basically a ballet version of Mohammed Ali, and we all know he isn't a sissy."

George crosses his arms and glares at Ivan, unconvinced.

"Don't believe me? Okay then," Ivan says, pulling off his jacket, and kicking off his trainers and socks. For the next ten minutes Ivan shows George just what it means to be a male ballet dancer. The girls' ooh and aah, and Sebastian's eyes light up with delight. George still scowls, but by the time Ivan's finished there's a grudging respect in his eyes and a hell of a lot of love and adoration in mine.

"Now all of you grab a pair of ballet slippers. You too, Sebastian and George, and line up by the mirror, Miss Rose will be with you in a moment," Ivan says, striding over to my side.

"You hired them then?" I ask, glancing at Camden who is chatting to Alicia and Erik on the other side of the studio.

"Turns out Alicia's lads are some of the most hardworking men I've ever had the pleasure to meet. A bit rough around the edges, sure, but good workers, nonetheless. I'm thinking of hiring them for some other small refurbs I've got coming up."

"You are?" I look up into Ivan's midnight blue eyes and grin.

"Yep. There's a market down south for smaller refurbs. A lot of people are buying up land and empty barns and looking to convert them. That's where Sonny and Eastern are now, scouting out some new projects."

"You're pretty incredible, you know that, right?"

"I've been informed of that fact a few times, yes," he grins back, brushing his lips gently against mine. "Now, we have a class to teach."

"We?" I question.

"I meant you. I'll just give some pointers. Keep that little George in check," he winks, striding over to the rabble of excited children.

Folding my arms across my chest I watch Ivan as he gathers the group of dancers, paying particular attention to the scowling George. Behind me Erik stands, then strides to the office at the back of the room disappearing for a moment. He reappears with his violin, gives me a gentle smile, then begins to play. The children's mouths drop open as he wows them with his brilliance and the fast movements of his fingers as they slide over the strings drawing out sounds I imagine most of these children have never heard before.

"Bet you thought you'd never see the day these two asshats would be entertaining a bunch of kids," Anton says, stepping up beside me, his sketchpad in hand.

"It is rather surprising, yes," I agree, feeling suddenly overwhelmed with happiness.

Anton wraps his arm around my waist and hugs me to his side. "Mind if I draw, Rose?"

"Of course not, please do. I'll need evidence that this actually happened," I respond, tears welling as I watch enraptured as Ivan and Erik work their magic.

And that's how, twice a month, Ivan joins me in my studio teaching ballet right alongside me whilst Erik plays the violin and Anton draws us all.

Taking one step at a time.

EPILOGUE

SEVERAL YEARS LATER.

Stepping into the dark, I take up my position in the centre of the room. Curling up on the dancefloor, my hand is pressed against the stain of blood that still blooms there. My dress pools around me, the deep red of my skirt just like the blood spilt from Svetlana's wrists all those years ago. My fingers slide over the surface as my heart drums a wild staccato beat for the woman who died here, bleeding out in pain and grief over the man I've sworn to love for the rest of my life.

This dance is as much for Svetlana as it is for the four of us; the single parts of one whole.

Without one another we're simply lost individuals, cast adrift, misunderstood, lonely.

Together we are the sum of all those parts. Strong, dedicated, happy.

In the past few years we've grown closer and we're

stronger than we've ever been. I never, ever believed I could be this happy.

This in *love*.

But here we are, and I wouldn't change a single moment of the path we took to get here.

Beyond the veil of darkness, Erik stands with his violin pressed between his chin and shoulder. As the first note lifts into the air, goosebumps scatter over my skin and I unfurl my body slowly like a rosebud blooming in the moonlit night. Stretching my hands above me, I stand onto my pointes then move with the music, letting it fill me up, letting it dictate what steps to take. Spinning and twirling, my red skirt billowing as I glide across the dancefloor, the length of red chiffon around my waist begins to unfurl, representing the layers of protection I'd built up around my heart. It spreads out across the floor, a trail of heartache and pain left in my wake. I stop moving, taking small steps on pointe as I wait for the man who started this journey…

Ivan.

He steps onto the dancefloor, the top half of his face covered in a mask made of black velvet as a pool of soft light illuminates him too. For a moment we just gaze at one another before he steps towards the discarded chiffon still connected to my waist and tugs gently. Spinning around on my toes, Ivan unravels the rest of the material, unveiling the red basque and knickers that I'm wearing, a thin see-through red skirt the only other item hiding my modesty.

I see his nostrils flare as he looks at me, the tension between us filling the space with an energy that would be overpowering were it not welcome.

I hold my arm out, reaching for him.

My breath catches as he strikes out with his left foot,

pirouetting towards me. His black shirt rippling as he moves showing off the defined muscles of his chest and stomach. Beneath the mask his eyes are smiling.

When he reaches me, he takes my hand and bows deeply waiting for my instruction. Squeezing his fingers, my chest rising and falling in anticipation, Ivan rises, his hands slowly moving up my arms and across my bare shoulders. Stepping close so that his body is pressed against mine, Ivan leans down and brushes his lips across mine.

"I love you," he murmurs, so quietly even I have trouble hearing the gentle caress of his words.

When the music picks up tempo, Ivan kisses the back of my hand, his chest heaving with the emotion and energy of the dance, then he walks off into the darkness only to be replaced by Erik as he strides towards me, playing the violin as he moves.

Erik.

Dark, talented, irresistible, courageous.

He plays for me now.

The man who fought his darkness and overcame it. The man who walked out of a glass cage for me, the girl who unravelled the fear inside his heart as much as he broke the walls surrounding hers.

Every time I hear him play, I understand another part of him, and every time he watches me dance, I reveal more of my soul. Neither one of us taking without giving in return.

The man with a lion's heart and courage just as admirable.

And beyond Erik, encased in darkness is Anton.

Anton.

I feel him watching us now, just like he watched Ivan and I only moments before. A piece of my heart will forever belong to him and the darkness that he surrounds himself with. For us it has become a place of peace and tranquillity, a place where we come together in the quiet silence of our own beating hearts and breathless kisses. Where neither light nor colour penetrates. A place of peace.

But our love doesn't exist separate from one another. The four of us have a love that is tangible, visceral. We have an insatiable longing that is quelled only by our mutual passion and friendship. What we have isn't the kind of love many people can understand or even comprehend. It hasn't been an easy path, but it has been ours. As the years passed, we've never once stopped striving for the kind of love and happiness that will continue to play long after our hearts cease to beat.

This is our story, this is our symphony and now, now it is yours.

THE END

Coming Soon

I'M the kid your parents warned you about…

Eighteen months in prison or three years at Oceanside Academy.

Reform school has met its match in me, even if it is full of young offenders. Thieves, graffiti writers, drug runners and other petty criminals reside within the walls, and I'm just like them.

But what they didn't tell me was that I'd be one of only a handful of girls in a hoard full of boys. It'll take more than just street smarts to keep my wits about me.

Everyone here has a chip on their shoulders, and I'm no different. Mine's one of the biggest, that's why they call me Asia because I have one as large as a continent.

Rules or not, these bad boys are about to discover I've earned my label for reason...

I'm the biggest misfit of them all.

Pre-order Delinquent #1 Academy of Misfits and meet Asia, aka Alicia, who had a brief cameo in Symphony!

AUTHOR'S NOTE

This series has been a real labour of love and I'm going to miss these characters a great deal. When I started writing Steps last August during my kids' summer holiday, I never dreamed it would be as well received as it has been. I had an idea, followed by a dream and these four books are the result.

For almost a year now I've lived and breathed these characters and it's going to be hard to let them go! I may or may not have shed a few tears putting the final touches together. I sincerely hope you feel the absolute love I have for these characters and their story within the pages of these books.

If you've read my previous author notes or are a part of my Facebook reader group - Queen Bea's Hive, you'll know that the idea for Steps came after watching Sergei Polunin dance to Hozier's 'Take Me To Church'. I happened across the video on YouTube in June last year and must've watched it several dozen times on repeat. I was mesmerised. Enthralled, actually.

What you might not know is that same night I dreamt of an

old manor house and a room filled with a run of mirrors, on the middle of the floor in this room was a woman curled up in a pool of her own blood. Morbid, yes indeed, but that dream (nightmare) gave me a backstory to the man I'd already envisioned - Ivan Sachov. Pretty soon, Ivan's story evolved and his wife's suicide became the catalyst to this series.

Whilst this story has some very dark themes; depression, suicide, torture, PTSD, rape, child abuse, drug abuse, murder, it also has so much *light*.

All four characters are broken and defeated in so many ways but together, somehow, they find a place to belong. Throughout writing these books, my heart ached for each of them and the battles they had to face to become whole again. Ultimately, this series is about finding hope within the darkest parts of ourselves, finding redemption and a place to belong.

And, of course, it's about love. I hope that shines through.

If you're still with me and still reading, then you would have met some new characters in this book. Alicia, aka Asia. You can read Asia's story in the Academy of Misfits trilogy which is complete And out now! This is a gritty, angsty, knock 'em dead tale about a girl who's had a tough life and finds love in the unlikeliest of places, namely Oceanside Academy (a last chance reform school for those who are a step away from prison). Asia is an absolute tough nut. and I adore her. I hope you will too! Well that's it from me for now! Thank you so much for taking the time to read my books and my ramblings!

Much love Bea xx

DELINQUENT

ACADEMY OF MISFITS BOOK ONE

BEA PAIGE

PROLOGUE

Alicia Loi Chen which loosely means *Great Noble Thunder*… or some such crap like that.

That's me. That's *my* name. Pretty fucking great, yeah? At least my mum thought so given the amount of times she tried to convince me it was.

In her more lucid moments over the years, when she wasn't messed up on some drug or other, she'd loved to weave magical tales about far away countries filled with dragons and other mythical creatures. For a long time, she had me convinced that she'd been a concubine to the Emperor of China, and I was their lovechild spirited off to England for safekeeping, my name chosen because I was born to some great Chinese dynasty.

Of course, I realised pretty soon that she was full of shit.

My empty stomach, threadbare clothes and dirty, flea-ridden flat we called home had proven that. Our true story, the one she tried to hide from, has only ever been a tale of woe… and it's about to get a whole lot worse.

Born on December 26, 1998 during one of the worst hurricanes to hit the UK for years, my fucked-up, drugged-up, heroin addict mother actually named me after the storm that raged beyond the single glazed windows of our shitty rundown council flat in Hackney. Her wails of pain from pushing me out of her ravaged, undernourished body matched those of the hurricane that wound its way through the feeble mould-ridden walls of our home. Tracy Carter, mum's best friend and my surrogate mum growing up, had cradled my head as I slipped into the world wailing, my lungs bursting with rage at being born, my tiny little body already addicted to heroin. An angry baby junky, courtesy of my messed-up junky mum. Born with thunder inside me, thunder rolling outside, my name was fitting back then, I suppose. Except now I've shredded that name like a dirty threadbare jumper. I don't live a fairy tale life and I'm not some emperor's daughter, real or imagined.

I'm just *Asia*. A name *I* chose for myself, not because of my heritage. And certainly not because of my mother's addiction for the opium produced in the Golden Triangle of Southeast Asia that finally killed her on my fourteenth birthday.

Nope.

I'm called Asia because the chip on my shoulder is as large as a fucking continent, and with good reason. I started my life fighting to live, and I've spent every day since doing the same damn thing… Fighting to survive.

Every. Fucking. Day.

I live in a permanent state of fight or flight, except I'm not a bird and I *never* run. I've got claws as sharp as the best of them, and a left hook to match. Truth is, this state of living is as unhealthy as the addiction I was born with. I've bounced from one foster home to another, interspersed with a few months in my mum's care when she'd 'got herself clean', only to fall back into bad habits the second shit got hard. Heroin is a dirty drug that strips a human of their ability to function let alone bring up a kid. My mum was the worst kind of addict; weak, selfish and unable to fight for her children, herself even. I've pretty much brought myself up, and along the way have tried to get my younger brothers through this screwed up life we live. I've had to grow up fast.

Now that I'm sixteen going on twenty-six, I've taken life by the proverbial balls and *I'm* deciding how to live it. I'd be a liar if I said I wasn't tempted to pick up a needle and shoot up just to get away from my crappy existence for a few short moments. But I refuse to be a junky like my mum. *I refuse.* She'd forced that on me as a newborn but I sure as fuck won't make the same mistakes she made. I'm grateful that I don't remember those long months being weaned off the drug, no more than a pitiful howling creature full of pain and anger.

Years later, Tracy had told me that I screamed blue bloody murder those first few months of my life. My tiny little fists bunched up, ready to hit anyone who got too close. That was the first time my mum tried to give up heroin. She'd seen how I'd fought from the second I was born, and she did the same. Alongside me she got clean and for three years my mum managed to steer clear of the drug.

But it didn't last.

The day after my third birthday mum left me in the care of Tracy with one goal in mind, to get well and truly off her face. She didn't return for a month. When she did, she was unrecognisable.

That was the first time I was taken into care.

But unlike her, I will not allow myself to be weak. I won't give in to the lingering need that still plagues me even though I don't remember the feeling of being an addict, a state that was forced onto me without any choice or say in the matter.

Growing up hasn't been easy, I can assure you.

These days the only source of joy in an endless line of disappointment and disillusion is my art, because not only is Asia my name now, it's also my *tag*. You can see it spray painted in bright colours across the whole of Hackney. A piece of me brightening the stark and dirty streets of this inner-city London borough where I live.

But like everything else in my life, that too has been taken away from me because some asshats deem it a crime to make something ugly into something beautiful.

Truth be known, there's never going to be a happily ever after for me. I was born during a storm after all, and we all know that storms only ever leave devastation in their wake.

CHAPTER 1

"This is a fucking joke," I mumble, just loud enough for my arsehole of a lawyer to hear.

"Can it, Chen. Sit up, take note and don't say a damn thing," my lawyer hisses at me.

Sitting here now in the magistrates' court with my lawyer, who I'm pretty sure is ready to hang me so he can get back home to his two point five kids and perfect middle class wife, I wait for the verdict.

A clock ticks loudly, the sound of a pen tapping against the table and the constant low hum of my blood pulsing in my ears makes it impossible to concentrate.

"Sit up, Alicia, pay *attention*," my lawyer snaps, repeating the demand under his breath once more.

I huff, feigning boredom and make a point at staring at a spot just beyond the ancient judge as he waffles on about my 'crimes' and my poor choices in life like his shit don't stink. *Dickhead.*

Well he, like all the other adults I've ever come across in

life, can go fuck themselves. I was doing the shopkeeper a favour by brightening his ugly back wall with my graffiti art. I'm pretty sure he gets way more customers now because of it anyway. He should be *thanking* me. Instead, here I am waiting on this fat balding twat of a judge to make a decision about my life, just like all the other bastards I've had to endure these past sixteen years. I wish I was turning eighteen this year instead of next, maybe then I could claw back some of the control I crave. As it is, I've got to wait another fifteen months until that happens. I'm just another kid who's the property of the state right now.

"Breaking and entering, criminal damage, graffitiing, possession of marijuana, anti-social behaviour. The list goes on and on, Alicia..." the judge drones on. His words mingle with the memory of all the other disappointed tirades I've had to listen to over the years from social workers, teachers, lawyers and the endless list of control freaks that seem to want to plague my life with rules and fucking restrictions.

It's not like I need reminding of my petty crimes. I know what I've done and frankly, I'd do it again given half the chance. I didn't hurt anyone. I didn't even break into the store really, given Mr Patel stupidly left the back entrance open. And yeah, so I smoked some weed. What teenager doesn't these days? I'm betting this arsehole next to me drinks himself into a coma most nights on some thousand pound bottle of brandy to blot out some shit or other that he wants to forget. So, what's the difference? I smoke a little weed, big deal. At least I don't shoot up to get a kick.

"You're on a dangerous path, young lady, one that will lead to a life of crime and imprisonment if you continue on as you are. Do you want that for yourself?" the judge asks me, his bushy eyebrows like great big caterpillars kissing as he frowns.

Talk about condescending. I shrug and look away to avoid further eye-contact, making a non-committal sound.

"You *want* this life for yourself?" he accuses, trying to get a reaction.

Folding my arms across my chest, I shift in my seat, refusing to engage.

Yep, that's exactly what I want, arsehole. In fact, being a criminal was the first job of choice on my list of things I wanted to be when I grew up. Actually, being a princess was top of that stupid list my mother had made me write. All because of her crazy stories and my need to please her. I'd have done anything to stop her from picking up a needle and shooting up.

"There's nothing you'd like to say?" he persists.

"No." I manage to bite out.

Both he and my lawyer make a distasteful noise at my lack of understanding or care. Their opinion of me is plain for all to see. I'm just another one of those kids who's a drain on the system. Drug-addict mother, absent father, benefit generation, uneducated, lazy, foolhardy. I'm the shit on their shoe. I'm worthless. *Yeah, I get it.*

"This is your last chance," the judge says, and I'm not sure whether he's now referring to my opportunity to speak or my proverbial last chance in life.

My lawyer, Fitzpatrick or something equally as fucking posh, nudges me in the side. "Alicia, now's the time to get your point across. Don't mess this up."

I turn to face him, sucking on my lip ring and giving him my best *'I don't give a fuck'* stare. I clear my throat, finally making eye-contact with the judge.

"Fuck you," I murmur.

Fitzpatrick stiffens. I can feel the annoyance and judgement rolling off him, battering against me as I resolutely ignore his incredulous look. Once he gets over the shock, I'm betting he's going to love telling his perfect family about the messed-up kid who gave the judge a big fat *"fuck you."* I know what he thinks when he looks at me; I'm the warning to his children. I'm the horror story of a life gone tits-up. You smoke weed, you'll end up like her. You wear those clothes, you're asking to be treated a certain way. You live on a council estate; you're bound to grow up a junky or a fucking criminal. I see it in his eyes, in the eyes of all the adults who make a snap judgement about the person I am based on the way I look.

Fuckwads.

"That's all you have to say?" the judge responds.

But instead of slapping my arse with another punishment, he just sighs heavily as though he's just as jaded with the world as I am. I watch as he clasps his hands together and regards me for a long time before speaking.

"Your crime holds a minimum sentence of eighteen months in juvenile prison, but both your social worker and lawyer have petitioned for a lesser sentence. For some reason they seem to think you're salvageable. Despite your appearance and lack of any remorse for your actions, I'm going to believe them."

I snort, folding my arms across my chest ignoring the pounding beat of my heart and the anger bubbling inside, the hurricane of rage I was born with is never very far away. I know for a fact my lawyer doesn't give a crap about me, and my social worker? Ha! Don't make me laugh. That bitch will be glad to see the back of me. I'm pretty sure she'd rather see me locked up, my case file neatly filed away in some cabinet in her office never to be looked at again.

"You come to my court dressed like that," he says wrinkling his nose at my ripped jeans, Doc Martens and see through mesh top.

"At least I wore a bra," I snarl under my breath, glancing at Fitzpatrick whose jaw tightens in anger.

"You've not even bothered to make an effort to present yourself in a suitable manor..." the judge continues, his words lost behind a growing haze of rage that I can't seem to dampen right now.

What the fuck has my appearance got to do with it? I have blue hair, a nose stud, lip ring and tattoos and that immediately makes me a leper to society, does it? All these thoughts make acid of my blood as he blithers on, but I don't show how I feel. On the outside I'm cold, disinterested, maintaining a sense of aloofness. It's my 'don't give a shit' attitude that I've perfected over the years. Besides, I'm not really worried about me, I can take a stint in juvie. At least I'll get a place to sleep every night and food in my belly. I'm told they even have video games. Sounds like heaven to me. The only thing I don't like about a prison sentence is that I worry for my little brothers and how they'll survive without my visits. They might be living in a different foster care home than me (not that I stay in my own very often), but I still get to visit them regularly. Eighteen months in prison is a long time to go without seeing them both. That thought makes my mouth go dry and my hands turn clammy.

"Despite all of that," he continues, whilst a buzzing fills my ears making it hard for me to actually hear what he's saying, "I'm giving you one final chance to change your ways. You will attend Oceanside Academy in Hastings."

My gaze snaps up to meet his. Oceanside Academy in *Hastings*? How is that any better than a prison sentence? I've heard about that place, a reform school for fucked-up kids just like me, but that's not even the worst part. It's a residential school, miles away from my little brothers. Is this prick insane?

Sitting forward in my chair, my mouth pops open, ready to bombard this shit-stain of a man with my response. But Fitzpatrick grabs my arm and squeezes.

"Don't be foolish," he hisses.

I'm about to tell him to get lost too when my brain finally catches up with the rest of what the judge is saying. His words somehow penetrating the anger I feel.

"You'll be able to return home during the term breaks to ensure you're still able to maintain a relationship with your siblings. I'm told that they're your one saving grace..."

The judge lets that statement hang in the air, and it successfully shuts me up. We make eye contact, and he narrows his eyes at me. But of course, I should've known it comes with a caveat, the motherfucker isn't stupid.

"This is a suspended sentence, Alicia. If you mess up, or you don't meet your obligations at the academy then I can and *will* enforce the full sentence and you'll find yourself in prison as soon as you can whip out your spray can and tag your name on a wall. There will be no visitation rights then. None. Do I make myself clear?"

Clenching my jaw and trying my best not to tell the judge what I really think of him, I simply nod my head. "I understand."

And just like that my life is upended once more.

Outside the courtroom, Fitzpatrick turns to me and rests his hand on my arm. I look at his fingers pressing into my skin, then him with distaste, a scowl drawing my lips up in a sneer. His eyes widen as though he truly thinks I'm about to bite. He releases his hold. Finally, the twat understands me.

"You start the new term in one week. I suggest you spend the time making your goodbyes and thinking about what you want out of life, Alicia. Whether you choose to believe it or not, this is an opportunity, not a sentence. Make the most of it, and whatever you do, *don't run.*"

With that he turns on his heel and walks away from me. I watch him leave with dispassion. "Save your pep talks for someone who actually gives a shit," I call out after him, drawing more snotty glares from the staff milling about.

On the other side of the reception area, someone barks out a laugh. A boy around my age looks at me from beneath his black hoody jumper. I can barely see his features beneath the shade of his hood, but I see enough to get my measure of him. Besides, the attitude he gives off ensures everyone milling around gives him a wide berth. I'm pretty sure he's a misunderstood *'arsehole'* just like me. Or given the shit-eating grin that's rapidly widening across his face, just an arsehole. Folding my arms across my chest defensively and cocking my hip and eyebrow, I wait. He raises his hand, his fingers curled into his palm.

"Wanker," he mouths, moving his fist from side to side imitating a wank. His gaze slides to the retreating back of my lawyer before he smirks at me then pulls back his hood so I can get a better look at his face.

It's a good face. Handsome in a kind of 'lock up your daughters and your family jewels' way. Dark blonde hair falls over his baby blue eyes that are a little too all-knowing to be innocent. I already know from that one glance, as our eyes meet, that he's seen and done shit that would rival any adult in this building. Face of an angel, mind of a sinner, and the type of person I avoid at all costs.

Swiping his hair back off his forehead, he gives me a wink which I resolutely ignore in my calculated perusal of him. He has a light tan, as though he spends a lot of time out in the sun, and he's tall, fit, with wide shoulders and a slim waist.

Honestly, he'd be better served on a beach with a surfboard, than in a magistrates' court in Hackney, but life sucks so here we are.

Two dimples appear in his cheeks as he smiles languidly with a lazy kind of self-assurance. He totally thinks I'm checking him out, and I am, just not in the way he thinks. I'm cataloguing his face and filing it in my memory in case I need to refer to it at a later date. I've learnt to be smart, making sure when I meet a new person, I take my measure of them because you never know when you might need that kind of information.

Here's what I know in the few minutes of checking him out: he's approximately my age, seventeen max because although he's tall, broad, he still has the remnants of youth in the smooth skin of his face. There's not a single facial hair in sight. He's clearly in trouble with the law and given the way his gaze keeps flicking to the Rolex watch sitting on his lawyer's wrist, I'm thinking theft is his crime of choice. He fancies himself as a bit of a ladies' man. Those dimples in his cheek might work wonders on other girls, and probably women, but it won't work on me. Beauty is used to hide a multitude of sins, and I'm not as impressed by it as other chicks my age appear to be. He's scared. That tell is harder to decipher and he's doing a good job at trying to hide it beneath the cockiness, but the way he taps his foot is a big giveaway.

"You here for me, beautiful? Want my number?" he shouts across the room the second my gaze lands on his tap-tapping foot.

Hmm, bravado, another interesting tell. He doesn't like anyone thinking he's weak. Make everyone think you're brave, confident, and they'll believe it even when you aren't. A tool I use often enough myself.

I don't answer him, but I give him a knowing smile as I regard him.

Next to him, the good looking lawyer who has concern written across his face, looks over at me. He gives me an assessing look, his dark eyes narrowing as he regards me. I raise an eyebrow at him as he smooths a hand over his beard. The cocky, dimpled shithead, who's almost as tall as the lawyer, looks between us.

"Bit young for you, Bryce," he says with a smirk.

Bryce? On first names with his lawyer then. Bryce shakes his head and clips the boy lightly around the ear.

"Don't piss me off. You're pushing your luck already, son."

Ah, not a lawyer. Pretty sure they'd get the sack for whacking their clients. So, who is this man? My interest piqued, I watch and wait.

The boy laughs. "*Son?* You might be looking after me, but you ain't my dad, so stop pretending you are. I don't need you here, arsehole. I've been looking after myself long enough before you lot came along."

There we have it, the fit bloke is his foster parent. Pretty sure I've never come across a foster parent dressed in Armani, looking like he's just stepped out of the pages of GQ Magazine. Well, shit just got interesting.

"Wrong, you need me, and Louisa would never forgive me if I let you come here alone today. So suck it up, concentrate on the matter at hand, and stop giving that pretty little thing over there *fuck-me* eyes. I'm pretty sure she'd chew you up and spit you out," the man called Bryce says, turning to give me a wink.

I can't help but smirk, which only seems to piss *Dimples* off even more.

"Pretty sure I'd let her," the boy bites back before giving me a smile that absolutely shows me that he would, and that he'd enjoy it. "Name's Sonny," he says as an afterthought, before being frogmarched into the courtroom on the other side of the hall.

The moment the door slams shut, the world filters back in and I notice that everyone seems to be staring, making a judgement about the boy who was just dragged into the courtroom and the girl with a scowl on her face.

"Should learn some manners. This is a court of law and not some playground for a bunch of delinquents," some snotty-nosed woman says as she walks past me.

"Whatever," I mutter, leaning against the wall, all of the wind knocked out of me suddenly.

What the hell do any of these arseholes know anyway? Apart from that dude Sonny, who's clearly looking for a distraction from his shit day, I'm the dregs of society. I'm a delinquent just like the woman said, and this delinquent is about to join the notorious Oceanside Academy, otherwise known on the streets as the *Academy of Misfits*.

Fuck my life.

Made in United States
North Haven, CT
08 April 2022